The Pharmacy Murders

by

Michael Davies

The Pharmacy Murders

For information address
michaelxdavies@gmail.com

First Printing 2024

ISBN: 978-0-6459672-4-1

Other Works by Michael Davies

The Nightmares of God
The Janus Conspiracy
Accounts of a Killing
A Friendly Killing
Dreamkill
Ready, Steady, KILL!
Helix Dreams
Helix – The Second Renaissance
Helix-Ascension
The Ninth of the Month Murders
The Death Gambit
The Internet Murders
Tales of the Haggis

For the Young Adults (12-18)

The Many Worlds of Mickie Dalton
The Many Galaxies of Mickie Dalton
The Many Universes of Mickie Dalton
The Strange World of Mark and Anna

For the 8-12 age group

The Julie Malloy Gang and the Smugglers
The Quest for the Locket
The Secret of Yuri Kirilenko
The United Nations and the Extra-Terrestrial
The Secret of Charlotte's Cello
The Star of the Yshan Kings
The War of the Yshan Empire
The Star of the New Yshan Empire
The Red Fog of Time
The Mysterious Recorder and The Door to Elsewhere
Prisoners of the Picture
A Step Back in Time
What Can't be Seen Can Exist
How I Spent My Evening

For the Little Ones (3-5)

Mary's World

And in non-fiction

The Business School Approach to Writing Your Novel

Acknowledgements

This is the fourth book written in the Melanie Carter series with the collaboration of Greg Dickson. My thanks for his time, brilliant idea-generation skills and commitment to the process.

Also to MJ Spelliscy who reviewed this and previous works with an eagle eye for typos and factual errors.

Thanks also to Terry Stanton who ran his trained lawyer's eye over the manuscript and found typos and also some legal errors within the story.

Chapter 1

17th July, 2025, Honolulu

"We really deserve this break," said the attractive young redhead in the one-piece swimsuit that outlined a magnificent, trim body.

"Damn right," said the man sitting next her, not even trying to hide his intense scrutiny of the girl's legs and well-displayed breasts. "We worked damn hard all year and the results showed it."

She smiled and waved at the ten other people in the cruising motorboat carving its way along the crystal-clear waters of the sea a few miles off the coast. "We all did well," she said. "It's nice of the boss to treat us to this long weekend here."

It was the last thing she ever said. The explosion tore the boat apart, the fireball engulfing all the passengers and crew in a few seconds, leaving nothing but parts of bodies and very little wreckage to be found by the police boats that arrived soon after.

The Chicago Chronicle, 18th July, 2025

Police remain baffled by the explosion that destroyed a cruising holiday vessel off the coast of Honolulu yesterday. Twelve people, all employed by a company in Chicago and two crew members were killed in the blast which destroyed almost everything of the boat and leaving only a few small body parts to be recovered. The holidaymakers were in

Hawaii at the expense of Maynard Chemicals, a pharmaceutical company that was rewarding the research section of the company for a highly successful year developing several new drugs that were about to enter the market in a few weeks. The president of the company, Alana Green expressed her shock and grief at the tragedy...

* * *

19th July, 2025, Chicago

The reporters' desk, the Chicago Chronicle

"You were too kind in your report about Maynard Chemicals," said the voice in the headphones of Terry Blaine.

"Who is this?" Blaine was facing a deadline, and he was irritated by the interruption.

"You don't need to know. But what you do need to know is that Maynard is a criminal organisation that killed a hell of a lot of people here and around the world."

"Oh yeah?" Despite the irritation, Blaine sensed there was something interesting in this call. "How's that, then?"

"You know that they make pharmaceuticals, eh? Of course you do, you wrote that puff piece in yesterday's edition."

"I do know that, but I wrote it based on the summary from our agent in Hawaii. What about it?"

"What you don't know is that those bastards marketed a drug a few years ago, supposed to cure high blood pressure. They called it Zenaphon, it got approved by the FDA and began selling well. But there was a problem."

"What was that?" Blaine was now fully engaged.

"They had falsified the human trials. They had hidden the fact that many of the people taking the drug had experienced an increase in blood pressure, several of them fatal and most of the others had got no benefit at all. Maynard managed to hide these, the few that were actually conducted and they made up the rest. But after a few deaths here in the USA, they pulled the drug."

"And that was the end of it?"

"No way. What they did was rename it and start selling in a few third-world countries, mostly in Africa with the help of some crooked agencies. They made enough to recover their development costs and then pulled it again."

"And nothing was ever revealed?" Blaine was now fascinated. This was right in the middle of his interest field.

"Not about that, no. But I know that they are doing it again, this time with a drug that is supposed to reduce excess iron in the blood. They say that they are conducting human trials, but they are not. The pill was only partially successful with the very few humans who took it in the initial trials, not enough to get FDA approval, so they are now busy making up fictional results."

"And just what is your involvement?"

"We know of many such crimes. Hell, you can look up the criminal records of all the pharmaceutical companies and see the huge number of court cases where companies have been heavily fined. Mostly it was for defrauding the health insurance companies or their governments, conducting inadequate manufacturing processes and lots more. We are going to make them pay."

"And you caused that explosion off Honolulu?"

"Sure did. And there will be more."

The call was disconnected. Blaine sat back, his mind in a whirl. Was that call genuine? Had he been given advance warning of a war on the pharmaceutical industry? Or was that just some lunatic trying to get his fifteen minutes of fame?

Chapter 2

July 25th, 2025, Mid North Coast, Australia

"Jack, I'm absolutely shat-off with filing papers and writing routine reports. I need to get back to real work."

Melanie rose abruptly from her armchair and strode around the room, radiating irritation and frustration.

"The consensus of most of the specialists is that you're not ready." Jack Savage appeared unmoved, seated in the other armchair of Melanie's apartment. He was a tall, fit man in his sixties, his face lined with the stresses of decades of dealing with the ugliness that infected so much of humanity, but his bright blue eyes reflected a permanent optimism and sense of humour.

"Then you and all the other experts are bloody wrong. Jack, I'm a goddammed Detective Chief Inspector. I'm supposed to be out there finding baddies, not filing the reports of other coppers trying to do what I do better than any of them."

"And I'm a retired Police Profiler, helping you do that as well, not nursing a woman back to operational health after a bad case of post-traumatic stress disorder."

"Okay, Jack, your professional opinion as a psychologist with a national reputation in solving cases of serial killers, some of them working with me, do I have a real case of PTSD? Or would I be better off working as a cop looking for murderers, rather than filing papers and preparing police department budgets?"

"Ah. An interesting question," said Savage, taking a sip of coffee from the mug he had been holding for some minutes. "One that needs real thought."

"Bullshit, Jack. I bet you've been thinking that one out for days now. Come on, out with it, man. We've worked together for some years, you've seen me through the horrors, a near death experience and we've solved some very nasty murders in our time. I need you to be straight with me."

Savage replaced the coffee mug on the side table by his armchair.

"Here's my professional opinion, Melanie. Twice in your life, a man who was critically important to you has been killed, once right in front of you when you were very young, the second just hours after spending a romantic weekend with him, and in that case, he was killed specifically because of his connection to you. That would be enough for any person to be severely hurt emotionally, to the point where they could not function in a high-powered job like yours. A second factor is your appearance. You have been a strikingly beautiful female since early childhood and as a result, all your life, faced difficulties with being seen as a highly intelligent, well-educated and charismatic woman. Only your strength of personality has let you overcome that and become a successful police detective."

"Yes, Jack, I know all that. So what does all that psychobabble lead you to conclude? Am I fit to get back to a proper job?"

For the first time in the two hours they had been talking, Jack grinned cheerfully.

"Yes, Melanie, you are, and that's what I will recommend to the panel reviewing your case. But I know what the counter-argument will be."

"So do I," said Melanie, at last returning to her seat. "They will say that if I am assigned to a case, I will need careful observation to ensure I don't crack up under the pressure, or the sight of a dead body. And they will also say that as a Detective Chief Inspector, I have too high a rank for this location and will need to move elsewhere."

Jack laughed and picked up the coffee mug again, taking a sip.

"Can't get a bloody thing past you, can I? Yes, that's exactly what will be said, and I've already heard similar comments from those on the panel. But I have an excellent idea to rebut both comments. Give me a day or two and I'll see what I can arrange."

"Bless you Jack. Now, fancy a drop of brandy to go in that coffee?"

Jack held out his mug.

27th July, 2025, Mid North Coast, Australia

Melanie's phone rang and the voice of Chief Superintendent Charles Bowden, her boss sounded from the loudspeaker.

"Yes, sir," she said.

"Detective Chief Inspector Carter, will you come to my office?"

That disturbed Melanie. It was an oddly formal communication in a relationship where Bowden normally addressed her as Melanie, at least in private situations.

"Yes, sir," she replied and stood up.

As she entered Bowden's office a few moments later, there was only the large-scale shape of her boss sitting at his desk, but Melanie sensed an additional presence, which probably explained the formality of Bowden's call.

"Detective Chief Inspector Carter has entered the room," said Bowden. He waved her to his side of the desk and to a seat with a view of the pc monitor. She recognized the face of the man on the screen, as much from his face as the air of command of a senior military or police officer.

"Good afternoon, Chief Inspector Carter," said the face. "I am Chief Superintendent Blake Harvey, Australian Federal Police. It's very nice to see you again, I've heard a lot about you since you last worked with us."

"Thank you, sir," she replied. *What the hell is going on*, she thought.

"We have a proposition for you," said Harvey. "While there is a major reorganization about to start in your area of New South Wales, we would like to have you assigned temporarily to the AFP in Canberra to work with a group we have set up to tackle major homicide cases. Two of our most senior agents retired recently and your experience would be immensely valuable."

"And on your return," broke in Bowden, "the new enlarged region would have a slot open appropriate for your rank."

Melanie felt some excitement. She had no doubt that Jack had been the force behind this opening, and she knew it would be perfect for her, with the need to get back to work in a new environment.

"Can I have a day to think about it?" she asked.

"Of course," said Bowden.

"We in Canberra will look forward to working with you," said Harvey.

Melanie got to her feet and left the office to return to her own.

"This was your doing, of course," she said to Jack a few minutes later.

"Bloody obviously," replied Jack's image on the screen. "But I have to say, it didn't take much effort with the rest of the review panel, they were all supportive."

"And the AFP?"

"They knew of your previous involvement and were most impressed."

"And of course, the blokes were all agog to look at

my legs and boobs again, I suppose. What about the women?"

Jack laughed. "The women are all okay with it, they know how effective you were before. But yeah, you're right about the blokes, you'll raise the collective blood pressure alright. But they're professionals to the core. They'll behave as such."

"Okay, I've lived with that situation my whole professional life. I hope we get some good cases to work on."

"I think there are a couple of other factors at play," said Jack.

"You and Allen Miller?"

"Mostly Allen Miller. They sure as hell want the services of the world's greatest computer hacker, but they can't admit it openly or use a wanted killer and multi-million-dollar thief legally. They're well aware that Miller will only work through you and that's the way they want it."

"And you, Jack?"

"The AFP has top class profilers available."

"Maybe. But I'll feel a lot better if I have you available. Would you move to Canberra?"

"No need, Melanie, we can always work together through the wonders of technology. Anyway, I have a new grandson here, and several new additions to the alpaca herd. But I'll always be available to talk, you know that."

"I suppose I'll have to settle for that. Okay, Jack,

I'd better talk to Alex now, see if he'll move to Canberra for a time."

"I'm sure he will. Let me know how that goes."

They smiled at each other as old friends do and the call was terminated.

* * *

"Actually, Ma'am, that could work out well. The sprog is not old enough for school and Belinda has family in the Canberra region. She'd love to move there, even if it's only for six months or a year."

Alex Welland sat across from Melanie, having listened intently as she outlined the proposal. He was dressed in his usual style, a dark suit, crisp white shirt and executive-style tie, with a matched set of tie pin and cuff links. His dark brown hair was cut short with a parting on the left. With his dark good looks, he could have been a newsreader on a television station.

"And if I may say so, Ma'am, I think this would be great for you," Alex continued. "I've really missed working with you. The other detectives are fine, but things always moved faster with you."

"Nice of you to say so, Alex. Okay, I'll tell everybody I'll accept the transfer, but it's conditional on you going along as well."

"That's great, Ma'am. I'll call Belinda immediately."

Melanie didn't even get the chance to contact Allen Miller. As soon as Alex walked out of the office, Miller's face appeared on her screen. Melanie had got used to his sudden, unannounced appearances, but this still surprised her.

"I suppose you've been listening in for a while?" she said.

Miller smiled. "Ever since my name came up when you were talking to Jack. I must say, this is an excellent move for you, it's likely to be a great help to the AFP cops and I'm delighted to help if anything exciting crops up."

"So you approve?"

"Of course. And Jack got it right. They want my help, but I've always made it plain, I deal only with you."

Melanie studied as much of Allen's background as she could and noticed something.

"It's mid-afternoon here, but it looks like nighttime at your place. It would be early morning at your old place in Southern France. You've obviously moved again and you're a good half-world away."

"Agreed. Melanie, much as I was delighted by your visit, I can't take the risk of my location being known to all those security forces around the world that want a bite out of me. I won't make the same mistake again."

"Understood. Alright, you all seem to agree I should do this, so I'll let my boss know. And of course, you'll all know as soon as the move takes place."

"Thank you. And may I say, I'm glad young Alex is going along with you. That kid has a lot of promise."

"Agreed. Talk later."

Melanie disconnected the call and went to see her boss. When she returned and sat at her clear desk with no immediate duties to perform, her mind dropped into a reverie of how she had reached this point.

Chapter 3 - Melanie Carter

Melanie, 2008, aged 16

Her father was irritated. "Melanie, why on earth do you want to go on to senior school? You're sixteen, you're getting offers of modelling assignments already. You could make a fortune, maybe go into movies."

"Dad, I don't want to be just a body and a face. Haven't you seen my grades? I've got a brain, you know. I want to go on to University, get a degree, get a good job."

"What the hell for? You could make more in a month as a model than you could make in two or three years working in some office. And who's going to pay for University?" Melanie's father was becoming increasingly upset by the conversation.

"Dad, I'll be getting scholarship grades in the final grade. University will pay for itself. Anything else, I'll do part time jobs, hell I might do some part time modelling, I've already had offers. It won't cost you anything." Melanie's irritation was beginning to match her father's.

Her father lit a cigarette, opened his newspaper and began to read. The conversation was clearly over.

Melanie went to find her mother.

"Mum, it's supposed to be an advantage in life being pretty. I'm finding it a bloody nightmare."

"Yes, dear, it is, but you're not pretty, Melanie, you're a raving beauty, you have been since you were in your pram. And I can see how it's becoming a problem."

"It really is, Mum. The boys at school won't leave me alone, but they don't want to talk about real stuff, they just want to flirt and try and impress me with how masculine they are. It's giving me the shits."

Her mother laughed, but with sympathy. "I know how it can be. I was quite the class beauty at school, too, not at your level, but enough to get the same sort of treatment. The guys just wanted to wrestle, not talk. I wanted to slap them sometimes."

"So what can I do? I've got another two years of this."

"Let's see if we can reduce the impact. School uniforms are pretty dowdy anyway, let's make them a bit worse. Loosen out the blouses, maybe reduce that bust with some flattening bras, make the skirts down to the knees, hair in something less flattering. It won't stop the crowd, but it might reduce the hysteria a bit."

"Sounds good, Mum."

Melanie, 2010, aged 18

"Mind if I join you?"

The young man sitting reading a book with a mug of coffee in the students' lounge looked up, startled.

"Er... yes... of course. Melanie, this is a surprise."

"It's deliberate, Scott. Any time I join a group when you're there, you always make some excuse and walk away. It bothers me and I'd like to know why. Do I scare you, or something?"

Scott looked embarrassed and stared down at his coffee mug.

"Well actually, yes, you do. And I've never been the sort that hangs around beautiful women to drool all over them and beg for a little attention. When I see the mob around you, I walk away."

"So now you'll have all my attention. Will you please relax?"

Finally, the young man seemed to ease the tension in his body and smiled.

"That's better," she said. "I really would like to talk to an intelligent man without the whole conversation pointing towards getting a date."

He laughed. "I imagine life can be quite complex for a beautiful woman. It could be like being a multi-millionaire, wondering if people like you because of who you are or because of the millions."

"Exactly. I can't talk to a man without him always trying to impress me, leading up to asking me out. There's nothing involving actual friendship."

"Have you been on a date with anyone recently?"

"A couple. But they always end up with me struggling to avoid a slap and tickle session and I have to get away."

"That's horrible. But what about the women? There's usually a bunch of them in the group surrounding you."

"I think they're hoping some of what I've got rubs off on them. And sometimes I sense real hostility under the smiles."

"Christ, I never thought of all that. Being beautiful can be a real curse, eh?"

"That's what my mum told me. I can't help it, I don't know where these genes came from, but they do complicate life. Most people can't accept that I have a brain as well as the other stuff."

"Okay, now we've got that out of the way, I promise I won't drool all over you or ask you out on a date. So why are you studying psychology?"

"Because I want to do something useful. I've got high intelligence, I know that, psychology is really fascinating, maybe if I become a practicing shrink, I might help a few people. How about you?"

"Similar idea, though I think I'd like to specialise in children's psychology. I really like dealing with kids."

"That sounds good, too. Looks like we have a class in ten minutes. Scott, let's talk more. Now, about that date thing."

"I said I wouldn't ask you out."

"Yes, you did. Would you mind reviewing that decision?"

He laughed. "Okay, but only because I like your mind."

"That's the best reason I've heard all term," she said.

"Tell you what," he said. "My dad gave me an amazing car. It's astounding, very rare, super performance, you'll love it and while I'm driving, I have no chance to try for some slap and tickle. Come out with me this Saturday, we can drive to the Blue

17

Mountains, have a pub lunch and I can return you unscathed to your place."

"It's a date," she said.

* * *

Melanie, 2013, aged 21

"Mum, I've got engaged."

"Melanie, that's wonderful! I'm assuming it's Scott?"

"Of course, Mum. We've been together for nearly two years."

"I'm thrilled to bits, lass. We liked him from the start, a truly good young man. When will you get married?"

"Not until we've graduated. We both want to get first class honours and that means a lot of work."

"That sounds good. Make sure you keep us informed."

"Of course, Mum."

* * *

"And the Degree of Bachelor of Science in Psychology with First Class Honours goes to Melanie Carter. Congratulations, Miss Carter."

* * *

"Doctor Phillips, you asked to see me?"

"Melanie, yes! Please sit down. You're familiar with that seat after three years of tutorials in this office."

"Oh yes! I think I've left a deep imprint in that chair."

"Ha! Indeed. Couple of things, Melanie. First, congratulations on the first-class honours. Fully deserved, I must say. It's been a pleasure to teach you. Can I ask one thing though?"

"Of course."

"You once said that you had wanted to study medicine and I'm pretty sure you'd have made a success of that. But why didn't you?"

"I think in the end it was a matter of spending so many years as a student. My parents are not well off, I needed to graduate and start work so that I could help them a bit."

"That's sad. But now that you've graduated, any ideas of what you want to do?"

"Well, that thesis I did for you on the mind of the serial killer really got to me. I think criminal psychology could be the way to go and I wanted to ask you what you thought and how to start."

"Interesting that you should say that. The real reason I wanted to talk to you was the call I got this morning. It was from a Professor Declan Allinson, he's a lecturer in criminal psychology at the police academy in Goulburn."

"The police academy? What could he want?"

"For you to consider a career you almost certainly have never thought of. Become a police detective."

"You're right, I would never have thought of that."

"Like I said." The professor smiled at her. "But while you would have to spend some time as a constable, the fast-track process for graduates would see you entering detective training quite soon and promotion would be rapid, given your educational achievements."

"Actually, that sounds interesting. But there's a problem. Scott and I are planning on getting married this year and if I'm a cop, I could be posted anywhere. That's not a good thing for a marriage."

"That could certainly be an issue. But will you at least talk to Declan and see what he has to say? There may be ways around it."

"That can't hurt."

"Good, I'll set up a meeting with him for you."

* * *

The Sydney Morning Herald, June, 2013

Another senseless killing occurred at the Cross last night when a young man was hit by a single punch outside a restaurant. Scott MacAdam, aged 22 was leaving the restaurant with his fiancée, Melanie Carter when a thug walked up to him and landed a single punch to the head. Mr MacAdam collapsed, hitting his head on the concrete. A bystander called an ambulance, and several others tackled the thug and held him until the police arrived. But the victim was pronounced dead on arrival at St Vincents Hospital. He and his fiancée had graduated recently from Sydney University and were planning to get married later this year.

* * *

Melanie, 23rd August, 2013

"Miss Carter, thank you for coming in to see us."

"I'm puzzled. Why have you asked me here?"

"We're the solicitors acting for the family of Scott MacAdam."

"Scott's family? Oh my goodness..."

Melanie sat back in the seat across from the desk of the young man who had met her at the reception desk of the legal office. Tears rose in her eyes, and she pulled out a tissue to wipe them.

"I'm really sorry to have to distress you like that, Miss Carter. We have acted for Jerome and Cathie MacAdam for some years, and we knew Scott very well. A fine young man and we all feel so sorry for your loss."

"But why am I here?"

"Scott had made a will a few months ago. You may not realise it, but the MacAdams were very wealthy people. They had asked Scott to make a will as soon as he turned twenty-one and had assets of some value. One of those is his trust account."

"I don't want Scott's money. We never married, that would be horrible."

"Indeed, Miss Carter and the family would not have put you to that stress. The trust account is transferred to his younger brother, Geoffrey."

"Good. This whole thing has been horrible for them. I met the family a few times and they were all so nice."

"I said there was another asset. You know it, his Gordon-Keeble car."

"You don't mean...?"

"I do, and the whole family endorses this with great enthusiasm. The car is now yours and with it, $5,000 purely for maintenance purposes to cover your costs until you have secured employment."

This time, Melanie could not stop the tears.

* * *

Melanie Carter, Jack Savage and Allen Miller

2nd December, 2022, aged 30

The explosion shattered a number of windows in the area, set off car alarms up to two kilometres away and precipitated an outburst of dogs barking from further than that.

Two of the shattered windows were in the apartment that Melanie owned, and she woke with a terrified yelp as glass scattered over the floor of her bedroom. Hurriedly, she threw on a dressing gown and slippers and went to the window to look out.

The scene was horrific. Several cars had been blown some distance from their parking spaces in the area reserved for tenants of the building. Many showed a great deal of damage, torn apart by the blast, some still burning.

In the middle of this was a pile of wreckage, the concrete around it burned black, not a single identifiable part of a car. It was where Melanie had parked her Gordon-Keeble the night before.

Struggling for self-control, she slipped into jeans and a sweater, shoes replaced the slippers, and she ran out of the apartment, already sobbing. She barely heard the sirens of approaching emergency vehicles and could only stare at the horror in silence, tears running like rain down her cheeks.

Not fully aware, she walked back to her apartment, through the people standing around in distress and fell onto the bed, tightly curled up.

"Melanie? Melanie, it's Jack."

She drifted back into awareness, realising Jack was sitting on a chair by her bed. The full shock of what had happened enveloped her again.

"It was all I had left of him," she croaked and collapsed back into a tight foetal position.

Jack took out his phone.

A long, confused nightmare kept her in a state of fear, not knowing where she was, only aware that something dreadful had happened. She woke up to realise she was in a hospital bed, alone in a single ward.

"You retreated from the world," said Jack.

She turned her head to see him sitting in an armchair in one corner.

"How long?" she asked.

"Three days."

"Have you been here the whole time?"

"No, just during the day. I went back to my hotel at night, the nurses promised to call me if you came back to the world."

"It really hit me, Jack. It was all I had left of Scott and now it's gone."

"That's what you said when I found you in your apartment."

"Can I go back there now?"

"No reason why not. The windows have been replaced, you suffered no damage but you're pretty weak. You managed to take some food in your occasional waking moments, so when the doctor checks you out, you can probably go home."

"I need to."

"I'll let you get dressed," said Jack and walked out of the ward.

Melanie, 15th January, 2023

Melanie's computer in her apartment's study buzzed, indicating a Skype call.

"I'm glad you had that little chat with Jack," said Allen Miller. "You all made a good decision to leave the book alone."

Melanie said nothing, suppressing the anger.

"Anyway, Melanie, I wanted to tell you how sorry I am that I destroyed that beautiful car. I hadn't realised the emotional connection you had."

Melanie stayed silent.

"It took some searching, but I think you'll like what I've done. This is the last time we'll talk, so I hope you'll remember me more kindly."

He smiled and the image faded.

She heard a truck draw up outside her front door and there was the sound of rattling of metal parts. Curious, she went to the door just as the bell rang.

"Miss Melanie Carter?" A large man holding a clip board almost hid the light.

"Yes."

"Delivery for you. Sign here, please."

"Delivery of what?" She tried to look beyond the man, could only see the front of a large vehicle.

"Would you sign, Miss?"

Irritated but curious, she took the clipboard, signed her name where indicated and the man handed over an envelope containing several sheets of paper and something hard and metallic.

"I think you'll like it," he said and moved away.

Melanie walked out of the door and stared.

The Gordon-Keeble looked perfect. It was in deep blue, the same as her previous one. Breathing hard, she opened the envelope. The registration papers showed her as the owner, the insurance covered her for a full year, a complete maintenance log was included, and the metallic object was the key.

"This I don't believe," she muttered as the delivery truck pulled away. Her policewoman's instincts made her bend down and study the underside of the vehicle. Seeing no obvious bomb, she opened the bonnet and found nothing that shouldn't be there.

She opened the driver's side door and eased herself into the seat. The inside was immaculate. Despite the more than fifty years age of the car, it looked new. She inserted the key in the ignition and started the engine, holding her breath but nothing happened other than the familiar soft purr of the massive engine.

"Allen Miller, who and what the hell are you?" she said aloud and put the car in gear. After a quick test drive round the block, she returned home. She still had to pack her bag for a flight to Melbourne that she had booked the day before.

* * *

Melanie Carter, July, 2025, aged 33

Melanie sat back in her seat, shaking herself out of the memories, some painful, some happy, and began thinking about what the future would hold.

Chapter 4

27th July, 2025, Australian Federal Police HQ, Canberra, Australia

Chief Superintendent Blake Harvey looked round the conference table at the intelligent, curious faces of his team.

"I'm sure you all remember when Acting Detective Chief Inspector Melanie Carter spent some time with us, assisting on a major case of serial killing and international blackmail..."

He was interrupted by an outbreak of subdued whistles and sounds of appreciation from around the table. He looked round the group and saw that these naturally came from the men. The three women in the group were laughing at the display. Harvey waved for silence and got it quickly.

"Alright, kiddies, cool it," he said through his own laughter. "Yes, she's drop dead gorgeous and all that, but as we saw, she's bloody bright, most charismatic, as some of you blokes saw to your cost when you displayed the standard toxic masculinity thing, and she brings with her an incredibly useful asset that we can't access without her."

"Brings with her?" The interruption came from one of the female agents.

"Let me explain," said Harvey. "Without going into detail, Melanie has suffered a severe case of PTSD. She's mostly recovered, but the view of her superiors is that a return to work would be highly therapeutic and in a new environment. The brief of this team is tracking serial killers and Melanie is seriously experienced in that field as you know. So too is her colleague, Professor Jack Savage who has written some much-admired papers on the subject. She is ready to return to work, but her region is undergoing a significant reorganization and there isn't a slot for her now-permanent rank. And the recent loss of Barry and Glenda has left a hole in our staffing. So it's a great opportunity for all of us get some mutual advantage by having her temporarily assigned to this team."

Nods and murmurs of approval ran round the table.

"So Jack is the asset you mentioned?" asked the agent who had spoken before.

"Definitely one of them," said Harvey. "There are two more. The young detective who works with her has agreed to move to Canberra for the duration of Melanie's attachment. He's a bloody good copper with a lot of potential. But we also get the services of Allen Miller."

"Miller?" Shock waves ran round the table.

"Yes, Miller." Harvey waved again to silence the disturbance. "An internationally sought killer and wanted for the theft of millions of dollars from governments and corporations by using what is rated as the world's greatest skill in computer hacking. Nothing seems safe from him. If needed, we will be able to access information rapidly that would take possibly months if not at all if we go through official channels, should we need something like that. We would never be able to use such information in a court of law, but knowing what we need to know would be invaluable in solving any case we might get. But as we know from before, Miller will only deal with Carter and that makes her perhaps even more valuable than her abilities as a detective."

"Well, holy shit, eh?" said one of the male agents.

"Exactly," said Harvey through the laughter. "And now this. Yes, she has film-star looks, but also the dominant personality of an army general. She's coming off a traumatic personal event and would not take kindly to any of you making a move on her. So don't even think of it, guys. This is how it will work. She will be assigned to any crime scene that comes our way. Regardless of rank, one of you will take Scene of Crime Officer position and she will understand that. However, if she offers suggestions and observations, you'd be well-advised to take them. As we already know, she's bloody clever and if you try and fight her, she'll tear you into small, bloody scraps. Okay, back to work, Melanie will join us in a couple of weeks. Let's be ready."

The meeting broke up with quiet conversations taking place between pairs and small groups until the room was empty.

Chapter 5
Hamilton Island, 18th September, 2025

"Welcome all the marketing staff of Royston Pharmaceuticals to the annual meeting. It's been a splendid year and we're here to celebrate."

Charles Mayhew looked happy. His normally red cheeks were even more flushed than usual, indicating some sampling of the liquor supply before he took the podium. His large frame towered over the line of staff behind him.

"As Chief Operating Officer, it is my pleasure to invite you all here to the lovely Hamilton Island resort," he continued.

"This is bullshit," muttered Jenny Cartwright to her friend and fellow sales agent, Jim Peterson. "Two weeks ago, they laid off thirty admin staff to cut costs, this week, we have forty of us at an expensive resort for three days to boast about our immense profits."

"Don't say that loudly," whispered Jim. "It could make you unpopular."

Jenny nodded and turned her attention back to the stage.

"And now I'd like to invite Gerry Landers, our President, to tell you about all the amazing stuff that has happened to the company over the past year. Mayhew turned to the side of the stage and stopped. "Gerry," he called, but received no answer. "Has anyone seen Gerry?" he asked to the line of executives behind him.

"Not since I left the office yesterday," replied one. "But I don't think he was on the flight."

Mayhew looked confused. "That's strange," he said. "He must have been waylaid before the flight. I'm sure he'll turn up soon. Anyway, I can tell you what Gerry would have told you." He began to read from the notes on the lectern.

"Boring," said Jenny.

"Suck it up," said Jim. "It's the price we pay for staying in our jobs."

* * *

19th September, 2025, Port Macquarie, NSW, Australia

"Lots of scratches, cuts, bruises and several broken bones," said the Medical Examiner. "But all resulting post-mortem."

"So what actually killed him?" The young policewoman standing by the examination table looked a little unsteady. The doctor gave her a sympathetic smile and moved the head of the corpse a little.

"This," he said, indicating the shattered area of the skull that was deeply indented. "I'd say a baseball bat, a heavy blow struck from behind at a slightly upward trajectory."

"So by somebody about the same height?"

"Exactly, Officer, good analysis. Is this your first body?"

The young woman gave a smile of gratitude for the understanding. "I imagine I'll get used to this scene."

"Sadly, yes. Anyway, all the indications are that he was killed somewhere else, then thrown out of a vehicle travelling at some speed along the country road where he was found."

The policewoman referred to the documents found with the body.

"Gerry Landers," she said. "Airline ticket for yesterday from Port to Hamilton Island. Wallet, still with over a hundred dollars in cash, two credit cards, an expensive watch still on his wrist, so not a robbery. Business card in his name, job title was President of a company called Royston Pharmaceuticals, offices in Gosford. Okay, I'll get started on contacting the company, finding next of kin and all that terrible stuff."

"A difficult assignment for one so young, Officer. Everybody else was otherwise engaged?"

"Exactly. I think my boss saw it as a test."

"I think you passed. Okay, I'll complete the postmortem, though I doubt we'll find anything more significant, and I'll send you the report as soon as I can."

"Thank you, Doc." The officer returned to her car, but when she closed the door behind her, she burst into tears and took some time before she was ready to drive.

22nd September, Queanbeyan, NSW, Australia

The two women who had found the body were almost calm as they sat in the back seat of the police patrol car. It had taken the young policewoman almost twenty minutes to achieve that state after she and her partner had arrived. The phone call that had summoned them had been difficult. The woman making the triple "0" call had been quite hysterical, and the operator had worked hard to calm her enough to understand what she was being told. Fortunately, the two Welsh Border Collies were perfectly behaved and had merely laid down at the side of the patrol car while their owners were being questioned.

A few metres away, the crime scene was being investigated.

"At first sight, the obvious cause of death would be a heavy blow to the head with a blunt instrument," said the Medical Examiner, kneeling by the face-down body. "There could be more, but you'll have to wait until I've had him on the table. Otherwise, he looks in good condition, maybe sixty, seventy. There's no wallet or any sign of identification."

"We'll get onto Missing Persons," said the police Inspector standing by the body. He nodded at his sergeant who spoke briefly on his radio.

"Can I get a hand turning him over?" asked the doctor and the sergeant moved in to help. As he saw the face, he exclaimed in surprise.

"Hey, I know him," he said. "This bloke was a politician some years ago, dunno what position he held, but it was something fairly big, certainly a cabinet minister."

"That's interesting," said the Inspector. "And it probably means we'll have to hand the case over to the Feds if it could concern national affairs. Are you done down there, Doc?"

"Yep, take him away," said the doctor and stood up. "Talk to you later."

Two men moved over and lifted the body, carrying it to the waiting ambulance. The patrol car with the two women opened the back door and the Border Collies jumped in to be greeted with tearful joy by their owners. The car moved off to take them to their homes. The remaining police officers drove off in an unmarked car, as did the doctor. Within minutes, the dawn scene in the woods was back to its undisturbed state.

AFP HQ, Canberra, 25th September, 2025

The conference room was alive with excitement as the team of AFP investigators took their seats. As they settled down, the door opened, and Chief Superintendent Harvey walked in. But it was the woman following that pulled every eye as they moved to the conference table and remained standing.

"Good morning, everybody," said Harvey. "I think most of you know Detective Chief Inspector Melanie

Carter. She is on assignment from the New South Wales Police, and if our previous experience holds good, she will be immensely valuable to us. Melanie, care to say a few words?"

"Thank you, sir," Melanie said and smiled at the officers around the table. "I'm delighted and grateful to be back with you for a time. The last experience was massively useful to me, and I hope I can provide some help to you as cases arise."

She took a seat next to Harvey. She had dressed in her usual conservative way for work, a dark blue, loose-fitting pantsuit, blouse buttoned up to the neck, minimal makeup, her hair in a ponytail. It had been her style from the beginning in the police force, making the effort to play down her considerable beauty.

"In fact, Chief Inspector Carter's arrival is fortuitous," said Harvey. "Just two days ago, as you know, the body of Avery Sheldon was discovered in the woods near Queanbeyan. Sheldon had been the Minister of Health in the Coalition government of some years ago and because of that, the case was deemed to be the responsibility of the Federal Police. Inspector Howard Spencer, you will be the case officer for this one and Chief Inspector Carter will work with you. Both of you know the terms on which this will be carried out. Most of the rest of you are working on cases, but those of you not yet assigned, you will make yourselves available to Howard as needed. Okay, anything else? No? Then dismissed."

Melanie studied the young Inspector Howard Spencer seated in the front row of the audience. *This may be difficult,* she thought. *Playing second fiddle to somebody of lower rank and far less experience is a bit of a slap in the face, I don't know how I'm going to handle it. But this is why I'm here, maybe I'm not yet up to running a homicide of this national importance and I need to work up slowly. But if that kid tries to boss me around, I'll tear him to bloody shreds.*

"This is an amazing car," said Spencer as they drove to the medical centre and the mortuary. "I've never heard of a Gordon Keeble. How did you get it?"

"It was a gift," replied Melanie, not wishing to indulge in small talk.

Spencer seemed to recognise the cut-off and said nothing. A few minutes passed and then Melanie spoke again.

"This is not easy for either of us. I'm a higher rank than you but I have to take direction from you. I imagine you're not entirely comfortable, either."

"You're right, Ma'am. I've never worked a case in this situation before. I know why this has happened, but it doesn't make it easier."

"Correct. So you will be able to accept that I might suggest something or require something that you haven't thought of. Don't take it to heart."

"I've read your history, Ma'am, I know the experience you've had with serial killers. If you need to take command, I'll try and accept it."

"That should work," said Melanie. "And just for your interest, something nobody else knows. This car was a gift from Allen Miller after he had blown up my previous one. The man showed he had a conscience of sorts."

"Holy shit," said Spencer.

Nothing else was said until they arrived at the medical centre.

"Howard, what do we know?" Melanie asked as she and Spencer walked along the corridor to the mortuary.

"Not a whole lot, Ma'am. There were no wheel tracks anywhere near the body, but there's a tarmac road going past about thirty metres away, so it's likely Sheldon was carried there in a vehicle, then manually moved to where he was found."

"No obvious footprints?"

"There were footprints, but they had been made difficult to gauge, looks like two people, both wearing protective covers on their feet, just like our scene-of-crime officers do. The best estimate is that one of the bearers had a size ten shoe or boot, the other a size eight."

As they reached the door to the mortuary, Spencer opened it for her and she led the way in, with a polite

"Thank you" to the other. *Okay, so he does have a sense of common courtesy,* she thought. *One point to him.*

"G'day," said the medical examiner. He was dressed in hospital scrubs with a large plastic apron covering him almost from neck to knees. A significant amount of blood covered that apron as well as his protective gloves. Behind him, the body of Sheldon lay on the metal table, covered from the neck down with a blue sheet.

Melanie was about to take the lead questioning the doctor, but held back, trying to let Spencer run the case. She was aware of the appreciative stare that the doctor was directing at her, but pretended to ignore it, looking round the mortuary. There were three other examination table, but all seemed sparkling clean, no bodies on them. Two men in similar clothing stood against the wall. Melanie assumed they were technical assistants who had worked with the doctor during the postmortem.

"What do you have, Doctor?" Spencer asked.

"As first suspected, a heavy blow with a blunt instrument caused death," said the doctor, pulling his eyes away from Melanie to answer the detective. "Just one blow on the right parietal bone, crushing it into the brain. No signs of defensive actions on the hands, so I'd conclude the blow was from behind, taking the victim totally by surprise. From the shape of the wound indent, I'd suggest a baseball bat."

"Any thoughts of the physique of the killer?" asked Melanie.

"Definitely," said the doctor. "The position of the impact, slightly to the rear, suggests a right-handed person, several centimetres taller than the victim."

Melanie shot a quick glance at Spencer, but he didn't seem disturbed by her question. At the same time, he didn't look as if he had any more questions. But she did.

"Do you have the victim's clothes?" she asked.

"We do," said the doctor. He seemed surprised by the question.

"Have you examined them for traces of the surface on which he lay while being transported?"

"Er.. no." The doctor looked a little embarrassed. He turned to one of the assistants. "Carl, would you show the Inspector where we have stored the clothing?"

As the two men left the mortuary, the doctor spoke again.

"Don't be too hard on the lad," he said. "I understand you outrank him?"

"It had to be asked," she replied. "And he understands the situation."

The room was silent for a few minutes before Spencer returned, carrying a plastic bag. The doctor pointed at one of the empty examination tables. "That's clean and sterilised," he said. "You'd better handle this, the blood on my front, might mess up the evidence."

Melanie put on thin rubber gloves, opened the bag and laid out the few clothes on the metal table. There was not a lot, just a flannel long-sleeved shirt, a pair of blue jeans, socks and white sneakers and a pair of boxer briefs. Melanie looked closely at the outer wear.

"Do you have a vacuum?"

The doctor nodded and the technician brought a small suction machine. He clicked on a new collection bag and handed it to Melanie. Carefully, she ran the cleaner over the outer garments, resulting in a few tiny specks of material being pulled into the bag.

"Can you get those analysed?" she asked and handed the bag to the doctor. "And the shirt? I see some stains that might be informative."

He nodded and passed it to the technician.

"Any toxicology?" Mel asked. She had obviously taken the lead in the situation.

"Nothing," said the doctor. "Just some aspirin and a standard over-the-counter acid reflux tablet."

"Nothing else that needs attention?"

"Nothing, Chief Inspector. No signs of arthritis, drug use, bruising, physical damage, except for a broken wrist at least thirty years old and a large scar on his left knee, probably from a bad scrape in his childhood. He was in very good condition."

The doctor sounded irritated, as if his medical expertise was being questioned.

"Then we're done," said Melanie. She led the way out, this time opening the door for Spencer who looked expressionless. They didn't speak in the car going back to the office.

The following morning, Melanie got a call.

"Doctor Caruthers at the mortuary, Chief Inspector."

For a few seconds, Melanie felt some shame that she had never asked the Medical Examiner his name.

"Yes, Doctor Caruthers, do you have information for me?"

"I do. The small bits you vacuumed off were particles of a standard lining in the boot of almost all cars. And the stains you saw were similarly specks of oil. The body was obviously carried in the boot of a car, but none of the specimens you obtained can identify the make of the vehicle. The oil is simply stock-standard lubricating oil, nothing unique about it. However, this confirms what the police had already thought, the victim was killed somewhere else, carried in the car boot to the location where it was found and dumped there. I'm sorry I can't be more helpful."

"Thank you, Doctor, that has been most useful."

"One more thing, Chief Inspector."

"Yes, Doctor?"

"Your colleague, Spencer. I think you were a bit hard on him, taking over like you did. He looked pretty upset."

"I'll look into it," said Melanie and hung up. "The good doctor seemed a bit crabby," she said aloud. "I must learn to be a bit more gentle with baby detectives." She sat quietly for a few moments to get her thoughts clear and then picked up the phone again.

"I was thinking I'd hear from you soon," said Jack Savage. "You're back in harness, you've been out on a case and examined a body?"

"Quite right." Melanie almost laughed as she decided she knew what Jack was about to say.

"And the PTSD has vanished like morning mist at sunrise, eh?"

"Dammit, Jack, but sometimes I think you know me too well."

"Melanie, you've been my colleague for a few years now, but all that time, you've also been my patient. Of course I know you. And one thing I've known from the start is the extraordinary internal strength. It's why few people can stand up to you in an interrogation, but also why you recover rapidly from severe stress. So am I right, you feel completely back to normal?"

"I do."

"Then I'll tell everybody concerned that in my professional opinion, you are ready to resume your normal duties."

"Thank you, Doctor Savage," said Melanie and heard Jack's soft laugh.

"No need to be snarky about it," he said. "Now, get back to work."

"Yes, Doctor," she said and replaced the telephone.

Chapter 6 - Jack Savage

12th April, 2006, Sydney, Australia

"Professor Savage, I'm Detective Chief Superintendent Charles Simpson of the State police." The tall, slender man in a well-cut brown suit stood in the open doorway, having just knocked on the door. "Could we have a few words?"

The casually dressed man in jeans, black shirt and a full head of greying hair, looked up from the book he was reading intently.

"Certainly," he said. "But why does a senior police detective want to talk to me? Have I done something that merits official attention?"

The visitor laughed. "Not at all, Professor Savage, quite the reverse. I'm looking for some significant help."

Savage waved to the chair across from his desk. "In that case, please take a seat. How can I help you?"

The detective took the offered seat, took his warrant card out of his breast pocket and passed it to Savage, who took a cursory look at it and passed it back.

"I understand you'll be retiring in a few weeks, Professor. I've asked around the academic world quite a bit and you have a most impressive reputation. Holding the Chair of Psychology at the University would seem to underline that."

Savage said nothing.

"Do you have any plans for after retirement?" continued the detective.

"Obviously you have something to suggest," said Savage. "And I don't think I'll be interested. Yes, I'm retiring, but I do have plans. I've bought a hundred-acre property near Coffs Harbour on the coast, and I've always thought about raising Alpacas. I married quite late and had a couple of kids very late, so I have a daughter who got married last year and is expecting her first child. We'd planned to have her and her husband and little sprog live on the farm. Tom's an experienced farmer, so he can run the place, I'll concentrate on the Alpacas and grandkids."

"We might be able to coordinate plans," said the visitor. "Our police profiler, I believe they're called behavioural psychologists, has just retired suddenly after a stroke. He's over seventy-five and not been in good health for the last three years, so this was not unexpected. He's been bloody great, helped us solve a number of crimes and his loss makes a gap in our armoury. Several people suggested you might like to take on the job on a part time basis."

Savage looked at him thoughtfully. "That's interesting," he said. "Why me, particularly? Psychologists aren't especially scarce."

"But experts in the minds of serial killers are not that common," said Foster. "I've read some of your papers, and they were quite fascinating. This is the problem we have. There have been three murders in the last four months, the modi operandi have been similar, but not conclusive. We have three possible perpetrators in mind, but we can't break them in interrogations. Professor, we badly need your help."

"Hmm," said Savage. "Like I said, interesting. I've handed my teaching load over to my staff, so I have nothing to do except some reviews of doctoral papers by my two students. Okay, Chief Superintendent, how do we go about this?"

"How soon can you come down to the Homicide group in Parramatta? Talk to our team and give us you're your updated opinion on what the classic profile of a serial killer io,s and then interview the suspects we have."

"Give me two days, then I'll come down."

The two men stood up and shook hands, both sensing immediate friendship and respect.

"See you in Parramatta," said Simpson.

*   *   *

"There can be variations according to social influences," said Jack Savage, seated in an armchair in a conference room of the Homicide Group headquarters. Nine detectives, all in plain clothes sat in comfortable chairs in front of him. Six were men, of which two looked over forty years old, the others all under thirty, in Jack's estimate. The three women all looked young, under thirty, he estimated.

"We all know the classic background," said Jack. "More than eighty-five percent of serial killers are white males, the greatest majority under thirty and often quite intelligent. Their IQ is usually between 105 and 120, so at the upper end, most could get a University degree in almost any subject. They almost always come from dysfunctional families, miserable childhoods, they tend to be big day-dreamers and heavy-duty masturbators."

There was a muted chuckle around the room.

"Those last two characteristics represent the escapism that results from the childhoods," continued Jack. "And they are enhanced by the very low self-esteem and emotional difficulties from the same cause. There is also a common factor of being the second or possibly third child and being obviously considered less worthy than the eldest, or possibly another sibling. Rejection is a critical issue."

The discussion continued for another hour, with all the detectives displaying great interest and involvement before Simpson closed the meeting.

"That was great, Jack," he said. "Tomorrow, we'll start reviewing the three cases we have and see if you can begin profiling the suspects."

The meeting broke up.

* * *

"Jack, that was fantastic," said Chief Superintendent Charles Simpson. "You identified some key factors in all three murders and saw which of the suspects most fitted the profile. When young Sergeant David Hunter grilled him, which he does very well, the suspect collapsed and confessed. He's been arrested and is held without bail until his trial starts next month. You sure earned your pay."

"That's great, Charlie. I think I'll head up to my farm now, the first Alpacas are being delivered, the first grandson is due any day as well, so I need to be up there. Call me if you need me again."

"Will do, Jack. Enjoy the rural life."

* * *

10th September, 2022, Mid North Coast, Australia

Jack Savage stood at the doorway to the office of Detective Sergeant Melanie Carter to which he had been directed on his arrival at the police station. He was momentarily shaken by the sight. The young woman sitting at the desk was astonishingly beautiful. He could not recall ever having seen such startling good looks in any woman who was not a top model or actress, and he had met a few of both.

"Jack Savage," he said after tapping on the door. "Your boss asked me to come and talk to you."

"Oh yes," she said and stood up. "Detective Sergeant Melanie Carter."

"Yes, I know that," he said, placing a finger on her nameplate on the office door. "But it took my two doctorates and years of working with you lot for me to deduce it."

The young woman laughed and waved him to the seat across from her desk.

"I'm very glad you were able to come down," she said. "The situation we've got here is getting terrible. We've had eight probable murders this year, but yesterday we had a kidnapping that probably would have been murder if we hadn't got lucky with a witness. Whoever is doing this is expert in hiding their traces and we're at a dead end."

"It took a lot to pull me away from raising alpacas and grandchildren in Coffs Harbour," said Jack. "But this sounds very weird indeed and I couldn't resist it. Let's start reviewing each of the cases."

The next two hours were spent carefully reviewing each of the murders that had been committed in the region and as Jack concentrated on the details, he was able to keep his attention on the psychology of the possible killers and stop being distracted by the almost unreal beauty of the Detective Sergeant. One thing did cause him interest. She had obviously dressed down quite a lot, wearing a loose-fitting trouser suit rather than a skirt and blouse, her hair was done very simply and not at all stylishly, and she wore no make-up. Jack realised that this was deliberate, to try and minimise the effect she had on anyone who saw her.

She must have had problems all her life, being accepted as a real, intelligent woman, he thought. *Such beauty must have been a problem for her. I wonder if she shows the effects of that difficulty. I'll have to be careful and hide my own attraction to her as much as possible. I'm probably forty years older, but how could I not notice a woman like this?*

As she completed running through the details of the multiple murders, she suggested they go and examine one of the murder sites, where a victim had been locked in a sauna and the heat turned up to maximum.

"If we can, that could be useful," he said.

She nodded and picked up her handbag.

"Let's take my car," she said. "I think you'll like it."

They walked out of the building to the parking area and there were three young men staring at her car.

"Happens every time," said the Sergeant. "It's the ultimate macho car of all time."

"What the hell is this?" said Savage, looking at the beautiful machine. It was like nothing he had ever seen before.

"It's a Gordon-Keeble," she said.

"Never heard of it," he said.

"Not surprising. There were only a hundred ever built way back in the sixties in England."

"And how come you have one?"

"A long story. Get in, buckle up and I'll treat you gently for your first time."

He was still laughing as they arrived at the house where the sauna killing had occurred.

Chapter 7

27th September, 2025, Manchester, UK

"Damn, but these mass conferences give me the shits," said the middle-aged, fit man at the end of the row near the back of the concert hall. "They drone on and on about how wonderfully well they have done, the brilliant new drugs they're producing and then they switch to whining about government regulation."

The heavily built man of about the same age sitting next to him smothered a laugh.

"Got to agree," he said. "Funny how they never talk about the difficulties they give us security guys with all their bullshit."

"You're in security?" said the first man. "Me too." He held out his hand. "Jerry Copeland, Consellors in Toronto."

"Tom Fisher, Blackwoods, New York," said the other, taking the hand and gripping it firmly. "Let's get out of here, the bar should be open downstairs."

The two men left their seats and walked out of the hall.

"About the only advantage of these international conferences is that I get to leave the office for a few days and do a bit of tourism in another city," said Fisher. "I was delighted when they chose a British site this year."

"Much the same," said Copeland. "I've been to Manchester once before a few years ago, have to say, I liked it, and British pubs are still the greatest institution in the world."

"I'll drink to that," said Fisher with a laugh, as they entered the lounge with the bar at one end. "Hey," he said, pointing at a woman sitting at a table with another man. "That's Sarah Jensen, I met her at a previous conference. She's the head of security for Fremont in Britain, let's see if we can join her."

As they approached the couple at the table, the woman looked up and smiled.

"Tom, you old bugger, how nice to see you again." She stood up, showing that she was as tall as the two men, well dressed in a smart business suit. Her smile seemed to suit the intelligent face. The man with her also stood up. He was of average height, also dressed in a well-tailored suit with opal cufflinks in his white shirt sleeves.

"Konrad Richter, Fremont, Berlin," he said. There was no identifiable accent in his speech.

Introductions all round completed, seats were resumed, and a waiter approached to be given orders for drinks.

"Not often the heads of security of these companies get together," said Sarah Jensen. "Our jobs don't have high profiles, it seems."

"Not exciting stuff, I suppose, but could cause problems if we didn't catch them," said Copeland. "The worst I've had was some fuckwit taking home the details of a new drug we had under development.

Totally without any safety, documents left on his dining room table overnight. Would have cost us millions if somebody had known about it and got hold of those papers."

"Yes, we had one of those," said Fisher. "Even worse, the silly twat took the papers home, left them on the bloody bus, would you believe."

"Good god, what happened?" asked Sarah.

"Luckily, he'd carried them in his briefcase which he left on the bus, they were picked up by somebody and taken to lost property. The idiot was able to get them back without a problem." Fisher's face showed his contempt.

"It might get worse," said the German, speaking for the first time since his introduction. He had clearly been listening carefully to the others. They looked at him with interest.

"There has been a growing hostility to our industry," said Richter. "I'm sure you are all aware of some of the errors committed by pharmaceutical companies in recent years that we don't like to talk about."

"Hell yes," said Fisher. "I know that all our companies have been fined heavily for failures to follow the manufacturing protocols and for some questionable marketing techniques."

"And some falsification of clinical trials," said Sarah Jensen. She looked around the group. "Just between us, I've heard of some deaths that have resulted from suspect drugs in recent years."

"Oh Christ," said Copeland. "One of our people was murdered here in England recently. No motive has ever been identified. You don't think it was because of these issues, do you?"

"Five years ago, I wouldn't have thought so," said Richter. "But the degree of hostility we are seeing now, it wouldn't surprise me."

"You seriously think this could grow to the stage of active attacks on our companies and people?" Sarah looked distressed.

"Like I said, five years ago, no, but today? It's not out of the bounds of possibility," replied Richter.

"That's right in our court, then," said Fisher. "We'd better be prepared. Okay, Sarah, I know you told me you had been a Detective Chief Inspector in the Manchester police before you moved to this job. I was a detective, a Lieutenant in Chicago. How about you two?"

"The same, in New York," said Copeland.

"Military intelligence," said Richter. "Captain."

"That's what I thought," said Fisher. "So I bet we all had our networks of informants in those days and we could wake them up again if needed."

"Damn right," said Jensen. "Okay, it seems we'd better do just that and get our ears close to the ground to see if we can detect anything potentially dangerous growing. Let's keep in touch."

"Not just us," said Copeland. "How about we all have some informal chats with our counterparts in other pharma companies and set up a communications network to share any information we might come across?"

"Seems like a good idea," said Fisher. "Anyone else?"

Nods of agreement came from the others.

"I think we need another drink," said Copeland, and waved at the waiter.

Chapter 8

Chicago, Illinois, USA, 27th Sept, 2025

The Desk Sergeant picked up the phone on the second ring.

"Sergeant Walters," he said. The response was not like anything he had experienced.

"How come large corporations that kill people never get their comeuppance?" The voice was electronically distorted, quite unable to be identified as even male or female, nor any other indicator of the speaker.

"Listen, buddy," said the Sergeant, his irritation increasing his tones by some decibels. "This is a police station. We don't take kindly to idiots wasting our time." He gestured at his colleague, a young woman sitting at the desk. She understood and began the process of tracing the call, while also recording it.

"And it's not just corporations," continued the voice. "The government does the same, all without facing any retribution."

The Desk Sergeant was a police officer of more than twenty years' experience, and something warned him that there was menace in the voice. He decided to keep the caller on the line to make the trace easier.

"Explain that," he said.

"Do you know how many Americans die each year from bad drugs or poisoned food?" asked the mysterious caller. "You've got two massive bureaucracies supposedly working to prevent that, you've got the FDA and you've got the USDA, their areas of responsibility overlap, and yet hundreds of people die each year because they don't do their jobs right."

"How do they do that?" asked the Sergeant.

"You think you can trace this call?" Even through the distortion, the caller's contempt was audible. "You can't. And recording me is no good either, you'll never identify me."

"Why don't you tell me about all these deaths?" asked the Sergeant, trying to give the woman tracing the call more time, despite the caller's comment.

"Drugs that somehow get through the FDA's review," said the voice. "Food in the supermarkets with poison in them because the USDA doesn't know what it's doing. Do some research, Sergeant."

"And just why are you telling me this?" He looked across to the woman. She shook her head, indicating no success with the trace.

"And here's the point," said the caller. "You people don't do anything about it. The FBI is the same. So now it's my turn. Some of the people responsible are going to pay for their crimes. Be prepared."

The call was disconnected.

"Nothing," said the young woman. "It went from here to Minneapolis, then seemed to go somewhere in Europe before it hit a brick wall. No idea at all where it originated."

"Better talk to the Captain," said the Sergeant. "Allie, hold the fort here till I get back."

"That sound pretty ominous," said the Captain.

"Whoever that bastard was, he's well-armed technically. He diverted his call from somewhere, anywhere, we've no way of finding out and the threat is pretty damned serious. Do you know anything about what he was bitching about?"

The Sergeant shook his head. "Nothing, Sir. But my wife's got a friend, I think her husband works for one of the drug companies. I'll see if I can dig up anything."

"Okay, do that, Andy. But the guy made one mistake."

"What's that, Sir?"

"That electronic voice. Anyone can get that application downloaded through the internet. But what is not well known is that the manufacturers can supply the decoder, though only to the police or security guys. I'll ask the technical whiz kids to look at it."

"Great." The Sergeant got to his feet and returned to the front desk.

"Anything?" he asked as he got behind the counter.

"Quiet as a grave," said the officer.

"Maybe a poor choice of words in this case," said the Sergeant.

* * *

Wilmette, Illinois, USA, 28th September, 2025

"There's a wallet, usual cards and stuff, no money," said the Medical Examiner crouched over the body of an elderly man lying in the sand on Wilmette Beach. Early-morning sun threw long shadows over the scene. He handed the wallet up to the police officer standing on the walkway. The officer opened the wallet and studied the driver's licence.

"Correy Foster," he said. "Lives nearby, in that block of apartments near the bank in Wilmette. Couple of other things here... let's see... no credit card, that was probably taken with the money. It's odd, looks like the killer wanted this man to be identified quickly. Okay, he's retired, member of a couple of societies, we'll need to contact them."

"They'll be upset," said the doctor. "Single bullet through the back of the head, exiting by the throat, fired downwards. First guess is a gangland-style execution, probably he was kneeling, the killer fired from very close, steep angle down. No signs of the bullet, but I'd guess a thirty-eight. I'll know more when I get him on the slab."

"Can't see any traces of a second person in the sand," said the officer. "So he was probably made to go off the walkway himself, kneel down and then shot. He sure as hell doesn't look like a gang member, does he?"

"Not at all," said the doctor, straightening up and brushing sand off his trousers. He stripped off the medical gloves and put them in a plastic bag. "Very expensive clothes, those shoes are probably custom made." He signalled to the two men waiting with a stretcher. "Okay, you can take him now."

Ten minutes later, the area was empty of any movement.

"Not a gang member," said the Captain. The Desk Sergeant sat across from him. "The guys in Wilmette found the two societies that this Foster was in, and they all knew him. Seems he was a wealthy retiree, used to be a pharmacologist, worked for the FDA until a few years ago. Andy, this seems to tie in with that phone call of a few days ago. The man got shot because he used to be with the FDA. How crazy is that?"

"It's getting worse, Captain. I read the circulars this morning, there's a note from the St Louis cops. A woman was shot, same way as Foster here, same condition. Wallet left with the body, just the cash removed. Angela Bladen, still active as a food technologist, worked as an advisor to the USDA."

"Oh shit," said the Captain. "That caller specifically accused the Food and Drug Administration *and* the US Department of Agriculture of negligence, even homicidal negligence that has killed thousands of people. Is this a revenge project?"

"I'd say so, Captain. And it could be happening all over the USA."

"Okay, Andy. Do some research, see if you can find any more like this, anywhere in America. Meanwhile,

I think we need to talk to the FBI. But the only thing that might help, the techies studied the recording and returned it to normal. They say it's an American, probably from the Baltimore region, aged between thirty and fifty, well educated."

"That's all?" The Sergeant looked angry.

"That's all."

"Holy shit," said the Sergeant and left the office. Things got worse when he got back to his station.

"Do you believe me now, Sergeant?" said the ugly, electronically distorted voice on the telephone. "Two members of homicidal government agencies have met their punishments in just two days. And not one of you has the faintest idea of who could be behind it. And it's just starting. Sleep well, Sergeant."

The call was disconnected.

Chapter 9

The Internet
5th March, 2023
Posted by Heraclitus

In mourning today. My favourite Uncle Ron died overnight from liver failure. He'd been suffering for three years and getting the best treatment, but his liver failed abruptly and he died in the ER. The surgeon told me the medical team was taken by surprise as he had been reacting well to the drugs he was getting. It's a stuff called Apethacol, an antioxidant that's been available for a few months and so far, has had good results. I'm really sad, Jack was a great guy, used to take me fishing when I was a kid, encouraged me to read a lot when I was at school and was always a better support than my father. I'm going to miss him badly.

5th March, 2023
Posted by Dallasguy

Hey, Heraclitus, really sorry to hear about your Uncle. Your story echoes one from a friend of mine, Terry, in England. He had liver disease, none of the drugs did any good until his doctor put him on that same stuff, Apethacol. It's a new drug, only came out a few months ago, but the doctor said the clinical trials had been great and it got approval by the authorities very quickly. At first, he responded well, but his wife emailed me a few weeks ago to say Terry had died quite suddenly and the doctors seemed baffled. It sounded fishy to me.

6th March, 2023
Posted by Superjock

Just saw the comments about people dying with liver disease after using Apethacol. I've got a similar story. My cousin in Glasgow...

6th March, 2023
Posted by Oscar White

Can I add to this saga? My dad went through the same thing, couple of years of liver problems, got put on Apethacol...

8th March, 2023
Posted by Charmaine Belle

Hey, these stories about liver disease caught my eye. I've counted over ninety so far in two days. I tell you, that's not the only problem area. My sister was diagnosed with very high cholesterol about a year ago. She was put on the usual Statins and they did help, but the doctor told her about a new drug that had just come out and had incredible results in clinical trials. He put her on this thing called Bravostatin, said its commercial name was Bardamor. It worked very well, reduced her cholesterol within days and he reduced her dose. But then she became very ill, her cholesterol level soared, and she died from heart failure. The doctors were baffled, they said there was absolutely no reason for her death, and there was no way it could have been connected to that drug. I'm not so sure, but I've never trusted the drug companies, they seem more concerned with profits than with patient health.

8th March, 2023
Posted by Jimmy Brown

Charmaine Belle, I read your post. I thought my story was the only one, but suddenly I see another case of somebody who died after taking a new cholesterol drug. Last year, my Auntie Freda....

12th March, 2023
Posted by Lysander

Oh my! Over two hundred posts in a week about pharma problems! I haven't suffered the sort of losses that the previous posters have cited, but I have to say, the pharma companies seem to be the worst criminals on earth. Have you seen the number of times they've been hauled before the courts for defrauding the Medicare organisations of a number of countries? They've had fines of several hundreds of millions of bucks, some of them more than once. They've been found guilty of poor manufacturing practices, illegal marketing practices, kickbacks to doctors and clinics, all sorts of shit.

And their employment practices don't seem any better. My friend Forbes worked for a year for one of the major firms in the USA. He told me once how they had laid off over forty clerical staff one day and then the following week, took their sales team from head office, over twenty people, for a week's stay at a resort in the Bahamas. Talk about tone deaf. He also knew about the kickbacks they offered to doctors to prescribe their drugs, similar vacations in luxury resorts, cash payments under the table, all sorts of stuff that should have had their executives behind bars, but nothing ever seemed to happen to them.

Chapter 10

AFP HQ, Canberra, 13th October, 2025

The tap on her open door switched Melanie away from deep thought about the state of her life. It wasn't particularly pleasant. What most women would regard as an extreme blessing, her looks had been a severe problem for her since childhood. The assumption by friends and family that she would become a movie star or top model had always taken away any recognition of her superior intelligence. Graduating high school with scholarship grades, then taking a first-class honours degree in psychology had done nothing to make men see her as a highly intelligent woman. The death of her fiancé, killed in front of her by a random attack in Kings Cross just days after their graduation had left a huge scar in her mind.

She looked up, relieved to have the dark thread of her thoughts broken.

"Yes Alex?"

The tall, good-looking young detective who came in smiled. She waved him to a seat across from her desk. She had discovered Alex Welland when he was a patrol car officer and had displayed extraordinary skills at researching massive amounts of data and extracting invaluable information. He had transferred to Criminal Investigation at her request, and he had been a major part of her success as a detective.

"I've been digging into this victim's past as you asked, Ma'am. It got interesting."

"Oh yes?" Melanie's interest perked up.

"As we already knew, Sheldon had been the Minister for Health in the Government of some years ago. He had that portfolio for three years without any great distinction and lost his seat at the next election. He had attracted some unpleasant attention for his overt support of the pharmacy industry in general and one company in particular, Blackwood-Harding, a major corporation based in Switzerland and with operations worldwide. Here's the interesting thing. After leaving politics, he became a lobbyist for Blackwood-Harding."

"A fairly common path for retiring politicians," said Melanie. "Hardly a motive for murder."

"Quite agree, Ma'am. But in the research, I found something that made my nose twitch, though I can't claim it's even remotely connected."

"Yes?" Melanie stayed expressionless but something stirred her interest. Several times in the last few years, Alex's sense of something wrong had led to major cases being opened and then resolved.

"Probably not connected at all." Alex looked a little embarrassed.

"Let's have it, Alex."

"Two years ago, there was a murder in Byron Bay, that's up the northern edge of the NSW-Queensland border..."

"Alex, I bloody well know where Byron Bay is! Get on with it, man."

Alex showed no reaction. "The victim was Felix Honneger, a research scientist with a pharmaceutical firm in Melbourne..."

"Blackwood-Harding?" Melanie sat up straight.

"No Ma'am, another similar corporation, Consellers, a Canadian firm based in Toronto but again, with global operations, including here in Australia. He was found in a similar state to Sheldon, fully dressed, killed by a single blow to the head by a blunt instrument, probably a baseball bat. No killer or killers were ever identified."

"It's interesting, but a bit thin, Alex. Nothing else to connect the two?"

Alex looked up from his folder. "Yes, there is, Ma'am." He sat back in his seat and grinned cheerfully. "Actually, Ma'am, it gets bloody interesting, if you have an evil, suspicious mind like I do."

Melanie had to laugh.

"Spill it, Alex. You have my full attention."

"Several years ago, Consellers developed a drug after nearly eight years of research that was successful in countering liver disease. After the usual approval process by the Canadian authorities, it was released for sale and became an immediate hit. Several hundred patients were prescribed it, and many found it beneficial. But three of them died and distribution was halted. After intensive investigation, it was found that Consellers had falsified the human trials results. They were heavily fined, and the drug was killed. It cost them millions, but the company was so successful, it went almost unnoticed and after a heavy drop in the share price, they were back to normal within a year."

"Okay, an interesting story, but still nothing we could build a case on. Anything else?"

"Several years ago, Blackwood-Harding had a similar episode with their US operations. They developed a cholesterol drug that appeared to be supremely effective. In fact, it was, but again, several deaths resulted, the trials data were found to be falsified and again, massive fines, withdrawal of the drug, a temporary share price drop. But just as with Consellers, the company spent a shit-load on public relations and suppressing news reports and within a year, they were back to normal operations."

"This is ugly, Alex, but I believe the pharmaceutical industry has a bad name generally. Remember the Thalidomide horror?"

"All too well. When my wife got pregnant, we irritated the hospital by having frequent scans to make sure nothing like that was happening with our kid. And you're right about the industry having a bad name. A simple Google provided a long list of nearly all the major manufacturers being heavily fined by the courts, mostly for fraudulent marketing techniques, kickbacks, Medicare fraud and stuff like that, but a few cases of bad manufacturing practices. And I have one more case for your consideration."

"Go ahead." Melanie was becoming intrigued by Alex's work.

"An American company called Fremont-Sims, based in Chicago but like all the others, with global operations. They began marketing a drug to counter bone density loss. They fiddled the trials data, submitted data that showed significant improvement in bone density in cases of weak bones, it showed huge success and sold very well. But the test data had been created with the object of proving that success, it was mostly fictional and after a massive attack by the health authorities in several countries, it was withdrawn, and the company fined half a billion dollars."

"That's nasty." Melanie could not hide her shock. "Are they still operating?"

"That's another story," said Alex. "I tried to find news reports of these events and I couldn't. It looks like the companies applied a hell of a lot of effort and money to suppress the reporting of their crimes. Believe it or not, Consellors, the mob that sold the dangerous liver drug received an award for their research into liver disease a few years later."

"So are you suggesting that there's a war of revenge against the industry?"

"I think it's possible."

"Great work, Alex, but I'd never get support from the authorities for such a charge."

"Agreed, Ma'am, but if okay with you, I'll keep digging."

"Dig on, Alex. You never know."

Alex didn't move but remained staring down at his notes. Melanie could sense his discomfort.

"Something else, Alex?"

"Yes, Ma'am. This worries me."

"Go ahead."

"I talked with Belinda, my wife about this last night, because I knew she had some history with this stuff. She's told me about this soon after we met a few years ago. She had a cousin, Amy, they'd been very close, the same age, since they were in infant school. Amy got liver disease when she was eighteen, she was prescribed a new drug that had good trial results."

"Oh no, Alex, she died?"

"Yes, Ma'am, she died after three months of treatment."

"And it was the Consellors drug?"

Alex nodded.

"That's not enough to disqualify you from the case, Alex. It makes it more critical, though. It will possibly make you dig even harder."

Alex nodded again, stood up and left the office.

* * *

"Melanie, something interesting for you."

Miller's face appeared on the monitor on Melanie's desk as she sat quietly, lost in thoughts about where her career was going and the ups and downs of the previous cases over the years involving serial killers. Her first case had been bizarre, a series of murders with no apparent motives and no discernible clues. Only after intensive digging had the pointers appeared, indicating a group of writers, run by a woman called Nona Markham. It was Jack, realising that Markham was one of the most extreme cases of dominant personality he had ever encountered, who had influenced a group of writers, all with severely damaged personalities that had made them totally subservient to her. Somehow, she had convinced all of them but one, commit a murder as the basis of a short story.

As Melanie's team identified Markham as the suspect, Melanie had interviewed her. She would never forget that interview, a massive clashing of dominant personalities that only ended with Markham making an error and finally falling before Melanie's dominance. Only then did Melanie realise the power of her personality, when Jack told her, after observing the battle with Nona Markham.

The one exception to Markham's power had been Allen Miller, who turned out to be a long-hunted criminal from the USA, believed to be the best computer hacker in the world, who had escaped capture in the USA by forging a detailed and false history and identification for himself and emigrating to Australia. In his final act before facing capture after Melanie's team had identified him, he escaped, but not before killing Nona Markham. Much later, he broke into Melanie's computer to talk to her, but always hiding his location. For many reasons, Jack suspected guilt over his previous life, Miller had remained in contact and had been an invaluable help in solving subsequent cases of serial killings.

The sudden sound woke her from the slight trance.

"Yes, Allen," she said. "What do you have?"

"I did my usual brilliant thing and broke into the tight security files of one of those nasty pharma companies we've been thinking about."

Something tickled Melanie's awareness. Outside her office, a bright sunshine lit up the urban landscape of Canberra.

"Your lights are on, Allen," she said. "You're a long way from Australia, I see."

Miller grinned cheerfully. "Far more places to hide from you," he said. "But I'm not going to reveal my location again. Much as I enjoyed your visit, that was the one and only occasion."

Melanie had to laugh. "Okay, Allen, what have you got?"

"It took a couple of days, but I got into a heavily guarded file in the computers of the firm, Blackwood Harding. Some years ago, they released a cholesterol drug in the Bravostatin category, their trade name was Bardacom."

"And?" Melanie sensed that something interesting was to be revealed.

"I found the minutes of a fascinating board meeting. It's not surprising that they kept it away from prying eyes."

"But they never anticipated an Allen Miller poking around, eh?"

"Exactly. I have to tell you, I have never read minutes like these before. The secretary was obviously highly involved and put in the odd comments that were quite extraneous. I think he or she knew they would never see the light of day and they were secured by additional security locks. In fact, I don't think these are the actual minutes, they read more like the personal record of somebody who thought they might be needed one day. The events almost leap out of the pages."

"Send them over, Allen."

"Read them and weep, Melanie."

Miller's face was replaced by the image of a document. Melanie printed out the pages and began reading.

January 15th, 2008

Minutes of Meeting of Blackwood Harding Board of Directors.

Meeting called to order at 2:15pm by Chairman Jeffrey Stewart.

Present – Jeffrey Stewart, Chairman; Kyle Fleming, Chief Executive Officer...

Melanie skipped over the other twelve names, all would be unknown to her. But almost immediately, a sentence leapt out of the page:

"All directors seemed tense as the meeting began."

This was surely not a regular type of statement in a formal record of a business meeting? As she read on, she understood what Allen had said. This meeting was war by other means and the events came alive in front of her as she read on. She could almost see the scene as it unfolded.

The atmosphere in the boardroom was like a thunderstorm about to break. Chairman Jeffrey Stewart rarely raised his voice, but the seemingly normal tones were like a sword about to strike somewhere. Coming from such a huge man, a full two metres tall and heavily built, the impact was frightening to even the most courageous.

"How much did we spend on development?" asked Stewart. His eyes rivetted on the Chief Executive Officer, Kyle Fleming. If anyone could stand up to Stewart, it was Fleming. Though of only medium height, he was exceptionally fit, the result of many regular hours in the gym with a personal trainer. But even Fleming looked uncertain.

"Fifty-three million dollars over eight years and we tested over seventy possible compounds," he said. His voice was not the usual confident baritone.

"That's about average for a new product when it goes to market."

"And yet, having done the normal processes to bring Bardacom to market, we end up with a disaster like we have." Stewart seemed calm but was obviously furious.

"The problems arose during human clinical trials," said Fleming, clearly under stress from the harshness in the tones. "Although all the animal tests showed great promise in reducing cholesterol, the human tests just didn't work. There was not the faintest, identifiable reduction in cholesterol in any of the human subjects. In fact, in our own internal trials that we continued, a number of the subjects experienced small increases in cholesterol."

"And how well known is this now?" Stewart seemed to be a little calmer and the tension in the room faded a little.

"I doubt it's been identified yet," said Fleming. "We were able to create a whole series of false trial reports that got it through the approval process and onto the market just six months ago. Our usual marketing efforts with doctors finally had prescriptions being issued for it almost immediately, but patients with high cholesterol normally are only tested every six months or even longer. We have probably got three months before this starts to be revealed."

"And what do you plan to do about it?" Stewart's face was still apparently calm, but the underlying storm was evident to those in the room.

"We have a few choices," said Fleming. "One, we could withdraw Bardacom immediately, saying we have identified a manufacturing fault that must be rectified before distribution starts up again. We'd have to contact all the doctors who had prescribed it and advise them to return their patients to whatever they were using before."

"And can you find out what the fault is in the drug?"

"We've had the best pharmacologists on that for some weeks," said Fleming. "We'll find the answer soon, I'm certain."

"How much will that cost us," asked Stewart.

"Millions in lost revenue. Similar amounts to find and correct the problem. And then a couple of years of sharply reduced revenues as we rebuild the brand name and the public's confidence. That doesn't include the money we must spend on public relations efforts."

"I bet that went down like a train smash," said Melanie aloud. "And look at that statement from the secretary. Since when do meeting minutes describe indications of somebody's anger? What's with that pen?"

"And your second option?" Stewart was tapping his notepad with his gold pen, a well-known sign to

the board members that his anger was boiling just under the surface.

"As for the first, withdraw the drug permanently from all the first world regions and while we look for the fault, rebrand it and sell to those primitive places with lax controls. We have always known the less ethical distributors in those regions, and they will support us, given how much of our other products they sell. We can almost equal revenues in those regions that we will lose in first-world areas."

"And if some nosy medic realizes that Bardacom does nothing, or even makes the problem worse, then what?" The gold pen was tapping a little faster.

"Then we'll lose sales unless we find the fault soon." Fleming had resumed his full self-composure and seemed almost defiant. "But the public relations damage will be minor in primitive countries, and we can fight any efforts to broadcast the story by spreading a few bucks around."

"Any other ideas?" asked Stewart.

"Only to own up completely, accept the decisions of the licencing authorities, pay a massive fine and take the shit the markets will throw at us." Fleming's defiance was fully on show.

"And we must consider the possibility of removing you and finding a replacement without the black mark that will be on your record as you take the blame for the whole mess." Stewart's smile was not friendly.

"Oh my, the sword has been unsheathed," said Melanie. "This is not a meeting, it's bloody combat."

"You can do that, of course," replied Fleming. "But my record will speak against your efforts to throw shit at me. I've increased revenues by thirty percent since I took over the top job five years ago, added five highly successful products to our range in prescription drugs and eighteen in our over-the-counter products. The industry knows me, and I could be in another organization working against you within a month."

The gold pen was silent. Stewart's smile had gone. For the first time any of the board members could recall, he looked defeated.

"Go with the second option," the Chairman said. "But bloody well find the answer." He stood up, followed by the three executives who had come with him and walked out of the boardroom.

Melanie closed the document and Miller's face returned to the monitor.

"Holy shit, what a scene that must have been," said Melanie. "The words on the page don't fully describe the reactions in that room, but I bet it was a real firefight. What happened?"

"Fleming did as instructed, withdrew Bardacom, renamed it, repackaged it and began marketing in some central African regions and a few Eastern Asian countries. They never found the flaw in the compound and when a number of deaths resulted from heart failures from excess cholesterol, it was killed off and never appeared again. Fleming was right, they were able to suppress the bad news from spreading and the company continues as a successful pharmaceuticals manufacturer to this day."

"Good grief, Allen, is this common in that industry?"

"Not to this degree, no. But if you look up the legal woes of almost all of them, fraudulent use of marketing or misuse of the national insurance schemes in many countries are almost commonplace. It's no surprise to find a generally negative view of the industry."

"Not surprising. Okay, I'll store these pages in the safe, they're obviously not for public distribution."

"Stay with it, Melanie."

"Have a nice evening, Allen."

Chapter 11

Who is Allen Miller?

September, 1970, Wilmette, Illinois, USA

"Auntie Gloria, it's fun conning these rich men out of money. I liked pretending to be your son."

"I got sixty thousand from that one, Danny. You played that role beautifully, the guy never suspected. For a ten-year-old, you're one hell of an actor."

"It was a bit difficult, living in that awful apartment for a few days, but it was a lot of fun watching that fool just melt when he saw you. He really believed that tale about being broke and me needing an operation. When could we do it again?"

"Like I said, I have this advantage that men find me attractive in a slutty sort of way, and I play on that. Now, what do you want to do next?"

"I've been reading up on business in the library, Aunt Gloria. This whole computer thing is becoming an essential part of commerce and I reckon we should look into this. The big corporations, that's where the real money is. I wonder if somebody could use computers to get into it?"

"That's interesting, Danny, a couple of these rich suckers I've been conning have said the same. Tell you what, one of my genuine partners, not a potential sucker, I know he works for one of the computer companies. Let me see if he can suggest something."

June, 1976, Wilmette, Illinois, USA

"It seems I have a real aptitude for this stuff, Gloria. I've learned everything there is to know about operating systems in computers. Your friend says I'm a better programmer than anyone working at his company. He lets me work in his office when he's not scheduled to be out at all, and he's put in a computer terminal just for me to use."

"Pretty cool, young man. Have you found a way yet to make money from it?"

"It's coming. I was able to use the terminal in your friend's office and I got into the company's bank account. I pulled out again quickly, so nobody will see the access, I didn't take any money, because that would have been obvious."

"That's amazing, kid. Now what?"

"I need to find some way of hiding the transaction and then some way of moving money to another account. That's going to take work."

"Keep at it, Danny, this has potential."

May, 1984, Wilmette, Illinois, USA

"Gloria, it's time we moved away from this nickel and dime stuff we've been doing, conning rich guys out of a few thousand and move into the big time."

"Better explain yourself there, sonny. We've both got goddammed rich on this nickel and dime stuff over the last few years." Gloria didn't seem offended.

"It's the internet, Gloria. It's finally given me a way to access computers all over the world and I've spent the last five years working out how to get into the files of even the most secure systems and change the data."

"Holy crap, Danny, what can you do?"

"Well, for a start, I opened a bank account for you in England. It's under the name of Margaret Webber. I've created a rental history in that name for an apartment in Birmingham and now the best bit, I transferred fifty thousand in pounds sterling to it, all taken from a couple of big corporations."

"Good grief, Danny, won't they notice that money missing?"

"No chance! I set them as valid payments for various stuff, even updated the inventory records to show the receipt. They won't spot it until they do a stock-take and then they'll just write it off as a book-keeping error."

"I always knew you were a genius, Danny. This may be just in time."

"How's that, Gloria?"

"One of those guys we conned. Remember the Finnish business guy we got to lend me $75,000 to buy him discounted equipment for his firm here? He's reported it to the cops, given them a description. We may be in difficulties."

"Okay, Gloria, we need to move fast. Get your passport, pack a bag and get a plane to London right away before the cops put a travel block on you. Once you get there, go to that address in Birmingham. It's been rented in the name of Margaret Webber and there's that money I transferred in a bank account in that name also. In a few days, I'll have the bank send you a credit card so you can draw cash out for daily needs. I'll ensure all the utilities are on and set up a payment system."

"I'm going to have to write off this house and my Mercedes, then."

"They're chicken-shit, Gloria, compared to what we're going to do. Now, the next thing is a new identity. I'll get all the documents prepared and submitted, you'll have a new passport in another name in a few weeks, and you'll also be getting immigration to Australia."

"Good god, Danny, you can do all that?"

"Like I said, I seem to have an aptitude and I've spent the last few years working on it."

"What about you? What are you going to do?"

"Me? Well, say goodbye to Danny Harper, say hello to Allan Miller. I've got a complete history as an entrepreneur, very rich, I've already been approved as a business immigrant to Australia."

"I'd better go and pack then."

"Damn right, Gloria. See you in Australia."

Chapter 12

AFP HQ, Canberra, 15th October, 2025

"Chief Inspector Carter, there's a Doctor Ramesh Sengupta here, asking to see you."

The puzzlement in the front desk sergeant's voice was obvious, even through the phone line. Melanie echoed it in her own response.

"Does he say what he wants?"

"Just that he has information on a major crime."

"That's bound to get my interest. Have him brought up."

A few minutes later, there was a tap on her open door. Two men stood there. One was a very large sergeant that Melanie had got to know fairly well over her initial weeks with the Federal Police. She knew his devotion to sushi and single malt scotch and that he had a degree in maths from Melbourne University.

"Thank you, Sergeant," she said and looked at the other man. He seemed tiny next to his escort, very thin and frail. His features matched his name, Indian, Melanie judged.

"I'll leave him with you, Ma'am," said the sergeant and gestured slightly with one hand to indicate he would stand outside the door.

Melanie nodded and moved from her desk to sit at the small round table in the office, taking a small notepad with her. "Come in, Doctor," she said and waved at the small man to take a seat across from her. The sergeant closed the door, but Melanie knew he would stand close and listen intently for any sound of alarm.

"Can I have your name so I can get it right," she said with a smile to remove any possible offence from the words. She wrote the name down as the man spelled it out. "Thank you," she said. "Now, Doctor Sengupta, why have you come to see me?"

"I wish to report a large number of deaths caused by corporate corruption," said the doctor. His accent was that of a well-educated Englishman, not a trace of any foreign tones.

Melanie took a deep breath. "Okay, that's as good a reason as I have ever heard for reporting to the police. Before you give me the details, why have you come to me specifically? You asked for me by name."

"I used to live on the mid-north coast of New South Wales. The Medical Examiner in one of the regions was a good friend of my uncle and he had worked with you on a case of a series of murders carried out by a group of writers. He said you were the best detective he had ever met, and most able to solve this."

"That's quite a recommendation. Okay, now tell me what this is all about."

"First, my background. It will help understand what I'm about to tell you."

Melanie nodded.

"I graduated in Medicine at Sydney University," said Sengupta. "My family moved to Britain when I was a baby, I went to school in Birmingham then we moved to Australia nineteen years ago. After I completed my medical degree, I spent three years specialising in internal medicine. Four years ago, I decided to try and repay everything I had been given. I could also tell you that I found Christ, but that's not really relevant."

"Understood," said Melanie. "So what did you do?"

"I went to Botswana and began practicing among the small villages in the region who never saw a doctor."

"I'm impressed. But where is this taking us?"

"We're getting there, Chief Inspector. One of the worst problems I had to deal with was liver disease. It was rife. Drugs were available, some fairly effective, some less so. But soon after I started, I heard from the main pharmaceutical distributer in the country that there was a new super-drug released by a company called Consellers, based in Toronto, Canada and it had proved really successful in treating liver disease. Trouble was, Consellors had been found to have falsified much of the trial protocol results and the drug was killing people around the world."

"That's appalling, Doctor. What happened?"

Sengupta smiled a cold, brief smile. "It's not as uncommon as you might imagine. Just about every pharmaceutical firm in the world has been found guilty of one sort or another serious crime, usually fraudulent marketing. Consellors was tried, found guilty, fined a humungous amount, close to half a billion dollars and the drug was removed."

"That must have nearly killed them, surely?"

This time, Sengupta laughed. "Not a chance! They paid the fine out of petty cash and applied massive pressure on the Canadian and American media to hush up the whole thing and carried on."

"So what happened next? This must surely be the point at which you needed to talk to me?"

"Exactly, Chief Inspector. Not long after that ugly episode, Consellors released a new drug, claiming it was an enhanced version of the original and equally as effective. It had a new name, but the interesting thing is, it was only released in a small number of third-world countries, those with very lax controls over medical products. My distributor urged me to get it and use it. I did and applied it to a number of patients. What struck me immediately was that the percentage of deaths among the patients was the same as with the original. I asked the distributor for a detailed analysis and to compare it to the first version. I received a report stating that it was a much-enhanced version and the clinical trials had been excellent."

Melanie sat back. "I think I see where this is going," she said.

"I have no doubts," said the doctor. "I sent samples of both to a laboratory I knew in South Africa and they told me the drugs were identical."

Melanie was silent for a few moments. "Doctor, you did the right thing coming to us. Who else have you told this?"

"Nobody, but of course the laboratory in South Africa knows of the fraud and the distributor in Botswana is aware that I am suspicious of something."

"Is that drug still marketed in the countries you nominated?"

"It sure is. Consellors have millions to make up from the first episode and there's nobody going to raise the questions."

"Except you, Doctor Sengupta."

"Correct, except me. It may prove costly."

"And what are you going to do now?"

"I have met the embassy of Zimbabwe here in Canberra and have been granted a work permit there. I plan on leaving Australia next month. I know that there is nothing I can do about this crime without risking my life, so I am leaving it with you. I pray that you can bring the right forces to bear on the company and anyone else that has done the same thing."

The doctor stood up and walked to the door, he opened it and looked back at Melanie with a smile. "This very large officer will see me to the front door, I assume?"

"Doctor Sengupta, you have displayed great courage and great commitment to your profession," said Melanie. "I wish you huge success in Zimbabwe."

She waited while the two men had moved away and sat back at her desk.

"Allen, did you hear all that?"

"Of course," said the image of Allen Miller in her monitor. "What a bloody horrible story."

"What can we do about it?"

"I'll have to think about that," said Miller. "First thing, though, is to verify the doctor's story. Leave that with me. Did you record his meeting?"

"Standard Operating Procedure," said Melanie.

"Ah, those good old SOPs," said Miller. "Play it for Alex, will you?"

"Of course. Keep me informed."

"Don't I always?" Miller waved and his image vanished.

Chapter 13
Canberra, Australia, AFP HQ, 20th October, 2025

"Yes, Alex?" Melanie looked up with some relief from one of the jobs she hated, the expenses reports and budget comparisons that she was faced with at regular intervals.

"Some more interesting stuff, Ma'am, I'd like you to see it, even if we can't do anything formal about it," said Alex as he sat down across from Melanie's desk.

"Understood," Melanie replied. "Officially, I'm not interested, unofficially, I suspect you may have a tiger by the tail and one day it may turn on us. Tell me what you've got."

"Can I say first, I've been doing this in my own time? I don't want the wrath of the Feds turning on us for wasting Federally funded time."

"Very wise, Detective Senior Constable Welland." Melanie's smile took all offence from the words. "What have you found in your own time?"

"I got the idea that maybe there's been some public discussion about these horror stories about Big Pharma. There should have been, given the multitude of crimes they've committed, mostly fraud, but a few even worse."

"And?"

"I started to look at public chat boards. There are plenty of them and some vary from downright hilarious to painfully sad. It's also amazing how people open up their hearts and souls when they can post anonymously to a huge audience."

"I've avoided that cesspit, Alex. What have you found?"

"I had to register a membership with a lot of these things in order to access them, and then go back some years, not a lot of interest, but then I struck gold. Go back six years and there's a huge amount of sad, angry, despairing and ugly discussions. Let me show you."

He passed a wad of stapled papers across the desk and Melanie took it, began reading and was silent for several minutes. Finally, after reading only the first few sheets, she put the papers down and stared at Alex.

"Holy clucking duckshit, Alex, this is terrible."

"Indeed, Ma'am. So far, those posts indict two major companies, Blackwood Harding and Consellers. And if it seems to prove the point, both those drugs named were withdrawn from the market within weeks of those posts and less than six months after their product launches. But I found another chatboard, similar stories, but this one was only about another company, Fremont-Sims, a US operation with headquarters in Chicago but major manufacturing and research facilities in Manchester, England. Same story, a drug developed, this time for osteo-arthritis, supposed to counter poor bone density. It was developed, supposedly went through intensive clinical testing, voluminous reports submitted to the approvals board in the UK, licenced and began sales.

Highly successful, but when a few people fell over and cracked bones that should not have cracked, followed by some deaths that post-mortems did link to the drug, it was pulled, and Fremont-Sims fined half a billion pounds, over a billion Australian dollars."

"But no doubt they're still operating?"

"Of course. And I can find no reference in the media to that horror story."

"Are you thinking what I'm thinking, Alex?"

"I believe so. We've got the first hand on the tiger's tail, it's one huge bloody tiger, one that can cover its tracks very well and we need specialist help from this point."

"Exactly," said Melanie. "Allen, are you there?"

"Of course," said the voice of Allen Miller as his face appeared on her computer monitor. "That is one godawful story young Alex has uncovered. Well done, young man."

"Thank you, sir," said Alex with a cheerful smile.

"And I imagine you want me to break into the secure files of those companies and see what else I can find?"

"And when you do, I think you will find a serious set of international crimes," said Melanie.

"As you already know, I've done some that digging already," said Miller. "Even then, I could see that there was some seriously nasty stuff to be found."

"So you'll do it?" said Melanie.

"Leave it with me." Miller's face disappeared from the screen.

"I hope we've got good tiger-defence equipment," said Alex, gathering up the papers.

"We're going to need it. Keep digging, Alex and maybe you'll find if any form of coordination takes place. And you can do it at work. If anyone queries you, I'll exert my well-known super-dominant personality, outline what you've found and give them the smile that no man can resist."

Alex suppressed a laugh. "A terrifying prospect, Ma'am," he said and left the office.

Chapter 14

18th May, 2023, The Internet

Posted by Kansas Kid

Hey, all, remember a few weeks ago, we were chatting about the evil shit that Big Pharma gets up to? I'd like to go back to that tale because I've just experienced a new horror.

My younger sister, she was forty-three, had suffered from excess iron in the blood for years since her early twenties. It had caused her a lot of difficulties and ill health, starting with belly pain, troublesome periods and a lot of joint pain like arthritis. Then it got worse, jaundice and liver problems that were starting to show cancer.

She was getting some hi-tech treatment, including having blood removed every couple of weeks to try and reduce the amount of iron in her blood, but it just got worse. Then about five years ago, this American pharmaceutical company announced a new drug that would do wonders by reducing the iron content. I won't name them, because they'll probably try and have me killed – yes, I'm serious. These people don't mess around. Linda's doctors said the clinical trials had been going on for two years or more and the results had been excellent, so the drug was approved for general human use. She prescribed it for Linda, and she started taking it a year ago.

Linda died last month. I know she'd been getting worse all the time. The problem is that I can't see any results of a postmortem. The doctor won't say anything, but the expression on her face said volumes. She was frightened. But she did say the drug had been pulled.

I think this stinks. Something is not right. Frankly, I'd like to shoot everybody connected with this sort of evil.

19th May, 2023

Posted by Harry Smith

Kansas Kid, I'm so sad to hear about Linda, my sincerest condolences for your loss. I empathise, because I've had the same experience. Not my relative, but the brother of my old army buddy, Jim. His kid brother, Gerry, died three years ago in much the same way as you have told us about Linda. He'd been diagnosed with what they call Haemochromatosis, high iron in the blood when he was a teenager and he'd had all the horrible conditions that result. No point in describing them, but they're pretty ugly.

Jim told me about three years ago that a new wonder drug had been approved for general use for this condition and Gerry had been prescribed it. But it had got worse, and he died two years ago.

The odd thing is that Jim said he'd got the same stone wall reaction from the doctor, he refused to tell Jim anything other than Gerry's condition had been too severe. But Jim hadn't got to be an Intelligence Officer in the army without knowing how to read people. He said the doctor was scared of saying anything.

So I agree with you, this whole thing stinks like week-old cod.

19th May, 2023

Posted by Caroline

Kansas Kid, I'll also cry for you, this is tragic, and it sounds like another criminal blunder by Big Pharma. God knows, we've had enough of them. I'm sure we all remember Thalidomide. I can throw a tiny light on the picture.

My best friend from University days became a journalist and established a good reputation as an investigator. She did a few stories for British television, then worked in Australia for a couple of years and a few times she caused a stir with what she produced. There's a company that produced hair shampoo that went out of business when she broadcast a story on them and their shitty product. The point is that she has some contacts in the journalism world and got the sniff at a couple of rumours floating around.

First, it seems your story and that of Jim are only two of quite a number. She has no idea how many deaths resulted from this drug, but the real story is that some people believe the company falsified the clinical trials. They even covered up the fact that a few deaths had resulted in those trials and somehow, they got the drug approved. Again, no real evidence, but the suggestions are that the company was massively fined, the drug pulled from use, but all of that was covered up to protect the big money interests in the industry and political heavyweights.

I don't know if we ordinary mortals could ever do anything about this, those bastards just have too much power, but like you, I'd cheerfully shoot any of them I could.

19th May, 2023

Posted by DownUnderBill

Kansas Kid, Harry Smith, Caroline, and all of you who have reported the crimes of drug companies, I do feel for you and echo your grief. I had two losses like this in recent years. My favourite Uncle David, a doctor himself, contracted liver disease and after talking with some colleagues, prescribed himself a new drug for this problem. It didn't work and he died within weeks. The drug was pulled from the market and somehow the story never got out. I heard from one of David's colleagues that the company had suppressed the news, got it hidden and it never became the scandal it should have done. The friend said he'd heard that the clinical trials had been falsified to get approval. Then my mother was diagnosed with brittle bones, she'd broken a couple in minor impacts. Another drug company had done the same as the first one, sold a drug that was supposed to strengthen brittle bones. Apparently, it had gone through clinical trials with great success and got approved by the authorities around the world. But it didn't work, people got worse, as my mother did, and she died after a fall that caused a rib to break and puncture her heart. The company must have changed the drug, because it's been successful since then, but I can't forgive them. They never faced any retribution for the crime. I'd cheerfully kill the lot of them.

20th May, 2023

Posted by Avenger

I count more than twenty-two posts on this subject, all of them filled with helpless fury directed at the pharmaceutical industry. I support your anger, it is well-deserved. I believe I can help you.

Kansas Kid, Harry Smith, DownUnderBill, if you would like to discuss this, please email me at Avenger@Retribution.com.

* * *

20th May, 2023

Email from Avenger

DownUnderBill,

Actually, I know your name is Donald Hayes, you are 39 and you live in Australia, on the mid-north coast of New South Wales. I must tell you, I have already researched your background and found your years in the military. You would be an invaluable member of my organisation.

Thank you for contacting me. I should tell you right off, as soon as you emailed me, this email address was deleted without trace. Future contacts will be only at my initiative, and I will have unusually secure safeguards in place to make certain nobody can track either of us. Just to tell you, your email went from your home in Australia to Berlin, then Cairo, Tashkent, Warsaw and then to me, each time deleting the trail. So here's the point.

I am setting up an international operation that will focus on punishing the pharmaceutical industry for the crimes it has committed. Actually, I've already had a couple of people killed for their part in the crimes. The one you talked about on the chatboard, the faked blood-treatment drug is only one of many such criminal activities. While financial fraud is all too common, deaths by drugs that have not been properly tested are also more common than you would believe.

Here's my invitation. If you would like to be part of my operation, post a message to the same chatboard you were on before and somehow work in the word "Laphroaig" to indicate your acceptance. We plan to initially operate in Australia, North America and the UK.

* * *

22nd May, 2023

Posted by DownUnderBill

I hope everybody is enjoying this glorious summer weather in the UK. I certainly am, I'm following an old bucket-list item I've had since my teenage years, I'm visiting Britain and spending the week touring Islay, an island off the west coast of Scotland devoted almost entirely to making single-malt scotch. It feels like Heaven to me! We've toured several distilleries so far, and today we visited (and sampled the products of) Bowmore, Laphroaig and Kilchoman. Three more tomorrow. Life is very good.

26th May, 2023

Avenger

DownUnderBill

Welcome to the Avenger program! We will be causing the Pharmaceutical Industry a great deal of pain in the future. I shall be sending you a few emails, all secured against intrusion and access by anyone other than yourself, giving you instructions and contacts. Good luck.

Chapter 15

Donald Hayes

Port Macquarie, August, 2004

"What do you mean by it, eh? What do you mean by it?"

Another heavy slap on ten-year-old Donald's face rocked him backwards. He couldn't say anything and just stared down at his feet, tears rising to his eyes. His father continued to glare at him from just a hand's width from the boy's face.

"You're stupid, that's what you are, stupid." Yet another blow landed on Donald's face. "You'll never amount to anything, you're just a failure. Now get upstairs and stay in your room until I say you can come down again."

Donald ran for the door and raced upstairs to his room, falling onto his bed, weeping. He had no idea what had precipitated this latest assault by his father, but then, he never did. The man's temper could just erupt without warning and the violence would be directed at Donald. Eventually he fell asleep, and it was morning before he was able to venture down again, by which time his father had left for work. His mother said nothing about the previous evening, she was only interested in lighting up another cigarette, one of the many she consumed every day.

* * *

Port Macquarie, June, 2010, Donald Hayes

"I'm not spending money keeping you here, you've failed all your exams, you're going to have to get out and go to work, earn some money and pay something for your keep."

Donald's father didn't bother looking at his son as he spoke but kept reading the newspaper as if the conversation was unimportant. Dona's mother sat across from him, reading a woman's magazine and smoking another cigarette which she had lit from the end of the previous one. The room stank of cigarette smoke.

Donald already knew what he could do, he had visited the army recruiting centre two days before, when he turned seventeen. He went up to his room, packed a bag and quietly left the house for the last time. He felt no loss, just a massive sense of escape.

An Army Base in Australia, April, 2020, Donald Hayes

"Sir, I've been a Corporal for three years, I'm not going to make it to Sergeant. I need to start something new."

The young Captain looked thoughtfully at him for a few seconds.

"Okay, Corporal, sit down."

Donald relaxed from his "at ease" stance and took the seat in front of the officer's desk.

"That's very perceptive of you, Corporal, and I

have to agree with you. It's the conclusion the review panel reached a few days ago. You will have no difficulties with the release and an honourable discharge. Any ideas what you will do?"

"I talked to a work advisory office a few weeks ago, Sir. I'll have no difficulties in finding work. The army has taught me motor mechanics well and I've had a couple of offers from engineering companies around Sydney. I got enough computer training to make me quite useful, too."

"Okay, that seems the best route for you," said the officer. He took a form from his desk drawer and slid it across to Donald. "That's the discharge application. Fill that out, bring it back to me and we'll get the process started."

Recognising the signal, Donald stood up, gave the Captain a formal, snappy salute, and left the office. A month later, he found a well-paid position with an engineering company near his old home town of Port Macquarie. The small bed-sitter he took was the other side of town from his parents' place and he avoided that area like the plague. Despite the new-found comfort and easier routines, he still felt a general dissatisfaction and anger that his father had been right, he couldn't help but feel he had been a failure, having achieved nothing notable all his life. His general low level of self-confidence that had haunted him since childhood had made his social contacts with women difficult, having nothing but brief relationships that had ended unhappily. His alcohol consumption began to climb.

* * *

December, 2022, Donald Hayes

A great deal of his time was spent at the computer screen. With his limited social life, he took refuge in pornographic websites which only exaggerated his sense of loneliness and inadequacy. He hadn't made many friends at work, none that he spent much time with, and the women avoided him. But an accidental reference by one of the men at the pub sent him searching for a website and he found the chat board that the man had mentioned.

Immediately, he was hooked. He had created an email address for himself as "Downunderbill" and that assisted him in registering on the chat board, but it was weeks before he could rouse the courage to make a post. And then he saw the discussion about the crimes of the pharmaceutical companies, and he saw an opportunity to make some friends. He thought at length and made up the fictional story of an Uncle David who had died as a result of malfeasance by a drug company. For additional force, he made up a wild story about his mother dying of brittle bones after a failed pharmaceutical course. It worked, and soon he had engaged in several sympathetic discussions with people who had suffered losses of loved ones.

And then came the exciting breakthrough from somebody who seemed to consider him important enough to discuss some action.

* * *

30th May, 2023

Email to Donald Hayes

G'day Donald.

First let me assure you that this email is quite secure. My organisation has possibly the greatest set of computer skills of anyone in the world and that includes the people at Microsoft, Google, or the computer manufacturers. Nobody, not even the CIA and the other Five Eyes spy group can break into this system and read this, so we are quite safe from intrusion.

You have shown considerable interest in making the pharmaceutical companies pay for their many crimes. I am in a position to start making them pay for these crimes and it sounds like you would like to be part of the operation. This is how it could work.

I can identify hundreds of people who have been part of this criminal network. All of them deserve to die. Many of them worked for the companies making the drugs, more of them were part of the marketing and distribution operations and some of them worked for the regulatory bodies that approved the drugs for public sale.

Here's how I will help you.

First, I have already got assurances of support from people who can do the work of elimination of the criminals. I can put you in contact with those in your country, using the same secure communications methods we are using now.

Second, I will provide the list of people in your country who merit elimination.

Third, I will send you a monthly schedule of recommended eliminations.

And finally, I will give you all the details of how to avoid leaving any clues for the police as to the identities of those who do this essential and valuable work. One of those features will be a software routine that distorts the human voice beyond recognition and that is valuable because part of what we do will be to talk to the police in the area and to the management of the companies we damage. This way, it will be broadcast to the world and damage the companies even further.

If you decide to continue with us, just type "YES" and hit send. Then we can start work.

Donald read the email with mounting excitement. It seemed to be offering a role that would require management skills, assigning critical tasks to subordinates, similar to the role of an officer in the army.

He typed the three letters and pressed the despatch key. His new life was about to start.

Chapter 16

14th December, 2025, Canberra, Australia

"Melanie, I have some more interesting stuff for you."

Allen Miller's face appeared on Melanie's computer monitor as she was trying to study the details of some of the department's early criminal investigations.

"I'm listening, Allen. Is it useful?"

Miller laughed. "Of course it is. It took me a while, but I repeated my brilliant hack into pharmacy company systems, and I got another set of minutes, this time of one called Fremont-Sims. It's very similar to the previous one I found and I'm certain this will grab your attention. I think whoever wrote this did not intend for the document to be available to the general public. Again, like the previous document, it's more like something written for future use for some unknown purpose. It had a specific security lock on it, which took me a while to break. Better get Alex in."

A few moments later, Alex appeared in the doorway and took a seat at Melanie's gesture.

"Here it is," said Miller.

Melanie printed two copies of the document from her computer and handed one to Alex. Just as with the previous minutes she had received from Miller, the details came alive in her mind as she read through.

July 8th, 2008

Minutes of Meeting of Fremont Sims Pharmaceuticals Board of Directors.

Meeting called to order at 11:15pm by Chairman Connor gates.

Present – Connor Gates, Chairman; Floyd Morris, Chief Executive Officer...

As with the minutes she had received of the Blackwood Harding company, Melanie didn't bother reading through the list of names, as he knew none of them. But the minutes jumped out of the document in a way that no standard minutes should do.

"How the hell did you let this happen?" The Chairman of Fremont-Sims Pharmaceuticals was almost spitting, so furious was he. "Half a billion dollars handed over to the government and the court cases haven't been started in the other countries. We could be facing four or five billion in fines. We may not survive."

"We'll survive." Floyd Morris, the Chief Executive Officer seemed calm under the onslaught, though the other ten members of the board showed serious discomfort. Connor Gates was notorious for his temper and a tendency to look for scapegoats when problems arose. "You might remember, Connor," continued Morris, "you had no objections to our submission of test data to the FDA, knowing full well that much of it was fictional."

Gates's fury did not subside.

"I assumed that you had prepared the data in a more professional manner," he said, anger making his voice harsh. "We'd spent two hundred million developing a compound that had showed a lot of promise and we needed to get it out to market to start recouping that money."

"And the tests we conducted had showed great promise," said Morris. "There seemed little risk in adding a lot more results based on those, even though we hadn't actually conducted them. We're not the first to do this and the FDA could sometimes turn a blind eye to the data if it seemed that the product would work as shown. At least we didn't have a Thalidomide situation."

"No, we didn't have deformed babies, thank god." *Gates appeared to be cooling down. "But we did have a lot of deaths and the postmortems showed a direct cause-effect with our drug. So what are you going to do about this?"*

"We've had a disaster plan in place for years in case something like this happened," said Morris. "We've been building an emergency fund over the years, and we have enough to cover these fines and those we'll get around the world. Third, we've already started negotiations with the media to play down the whole event. We've promised significant expenditure on advertising, and in return, we'll ask them to play down the reporting. They like money just as much as

anyone else and I have no doubts they'll agree, just as they have on the occasions when we've been accused of kickbacks to doctors and hospitals and off-label promotions. And then the big one."

"Which is?" Gates had calmed down completely.

"We'll rebrand the stuff and begin marketing in countries that don't have the controls we have in the west. We have a number of distributors who have questionable ethics, and they know doctors with the same attitude. We'll run campaigns in those countries showing the success of the drug and suppress any reports of deaths. We may not make the same profits we do in Europe and North America, but we'll make enough, and we'll avoid the bad reputation that could hurt us."

"And where will all this take place?" asked the Chairman.

"The usual." Morris relaxed as he saw the Chairman's obvious approval. "Mostly Africa, the Middle East, some of those old Soviet-era satellite countries like Uzbekistan, Azerbaijan, Kazakhstan, Kirghizia and similar. These all lack good government controls and we'll have no problems."

Gates nodded. "Okay, get on with it."

"Everybody okay with this?" asked Morris and saw nothing but nods round the conference table. "Then the meeting is closed." He waited until Gates stood up and then everybody followed suit and the room was cleared in minutes.

Melanie took a deep breath and looked across at Alex who had finished reading just a few seconds before her.

"Holy crap, Ma'am," said Alex. "Another one, just as evil as the previous one. These are like no minutes I have ever read before. I wonder how the secretary got away with it. No wonder somebody hates these people. To be honest, Ma'am, I could almost have some sympathy with the killers, after what happened to Belinda's cousin."

"Almost," agreed Melanie. "But not. Our job is to find them."

"Yes, Ma'am. I'll get back to work." He stood up and left the office.

* * *

The Offices of Fremont Sims, Chicago, Illinois, 8th July, 2008

"You gave me a good blast there, it was a hell of a performance." Chief Executive Officer Floyd Morris sat in the Chairman's office, looking a lot more comfortable than he had during the official meeting of the company two hours earlier.

"It was necessary," said Connor Gates. "If it ever does become public, I want the world to think it was just something we cooked up between us and not the fault of anyone else. This whole schemozzle has cost us millions. We've had problems before that cost us, but not like this."

"All of us have had problems," said Morris. "They go with the business, and we spend a fortune with our attorneys fighting in court. But this one was serious."

"And goddammed costly," said Gates.

Morris nodded. "Agreed. Paying fines for imperfect manufacturing protocols or somewhat questionable marketing practices, that's just the cost of doing business. But we got caught in a trap with Trimecal. Clinical trials had been going fairly well, but we weren't ready to submit to the FDA, and then that mob in Los Angeles started making noises about their clinical trial for the competition drug being completed. We had to get out there or we'd have lost that market for ever. God knows it costs us enough to get a drug to market after trying dozens of compounds that result in nothing. We had to try something."

"And we'll no doubt have to do it again," said Gates. "It's a shitty business these days. The research to develop a new drug is getting faster and faster, we're all in a race the whole time."

"And the pirates can break down a new drug quicker, modify the recipe just enough to avoid the patent and they've got a competitor on the market at a fraction of the cost we faced. You're right, it's a shitty business. Maybe we're in the wrong one."

"Can't see what else we can do," said Gates. "And our products are still essential. Imagine a world without them?"

"Hell on earth," agreed Morris. "But I can see one possible solution."

Gates bent down to the small cupboard beneath his desk and brought up a bottle of scotch and two glasses. He carefully poured two helpings and passed one across to Morris. "Tell me," he said.

Morris picked up his glass as Gates did the same and they briefly touched the rims before taking a small sip.

"I once thought about moving into this business," said Morris. "Sampling the product would have been fun. But making whiskey has become a global business. It's not just the Scots, everybody and his uncle is doing it these days. Australia, Japan, God knows who'll be next."

"I think we'll stick to what we know," said Gates with a grin. "So, what's your idea?"

"We set up an arrangement with a couple of our competitors. Let's say we get caught this way again, we cut some corners bringing a drug to market and the regulators jump on us. Okay, we pay the fine, withdraw the drug, repair the recipe and remake it."

"But that way, we've lost our name, nobody will buy it again after a noisy scandal like that."

"Agreed," said Morris. "But what we do is hand the revised product to one of our competitors, let them market it under a new name, everybody flocks to it, and we pay them a commission, while taking the money. Let the finance wizards hide the details from the taxman, I've no doubt they can. Everybody wins, especially if we have a few such arrangements going."

"Hmmm," said Gates thoughtfully, and took another sip of scotch. "Let me think about that, it might work. I'll have a chat with my opposite numbers at a couple of manufacturers, I'm sure they'll be interested."

Chapter 17

Skegness, Lincolnshire, UK, 14th December, 2025

The four men in the expensive motor launch were having a great time. For mid-winter, the day was beautiful, the sea was calm, and the fishing had been good since dawn when they first put the boat into the water. But as the sun rose, the fish were hardly biting at all, and the attention of the friends was increasingly diverted to the cooler of beer cans.

"Definitely the way to spend a weekend," said Trevor, the owner of the boat, sitting relaxed behind the steering wheel.

"Damn right," said Gordon, his brother-in-law. "I reckon this is the best investment you ever made."

Sounds of agreement came from the other two, punctuated by the hiss of beer cans being opened.

"Reckon the fish have stopped biting?" said Andrew.

"They usually do once the sun is up," said Trevor. "But it's worth leaving a couple of rods in the racks and something sparkly on the line if we just trundle along. You never know, might just snag a monster tuna or something."

Conversation faded as the four relaxed in the sun as the boat motored at barely walking pace. In the distance, faint sounds of music and the loudspeaker broadcasting announcements of the day's activities drifted out to them from the huge holiday camp on the shore.

"Holy shit!" exclaimed Trevor, as the line suddenly whirred furiously and the rod on one side of the boat bent sharply. "What the hell is that?"

"I'll take it," said Gordon, stood up and took hold of the rod. He stopped the line unwinding from the reel and began carefully winding it in. "This is bloody weird," he said. "Whatever it's caught, it's not fighting. But it's big."

All four men watched as he wound in the catch to the boat. The shock hit them all at the same moment.

"Oh god, it's a body," said Trevor. The hooked object reached the side of the boat. "It's a bloke," he said. "And it's naked."

"Jesus Harold Christ," said Andrew. "What the hell do we do now?"

Trevor took charge.

"Gordie, there's a tarpaulin in the storage cabinet. Get that, the rest of us haul the body in and wrap it up."

It proved extraordinarily difficult to do as he said, but after ten or fifteen minutes, they had the body on board, wrapped in the tarpaulin and unhooked from the fishing line. Trevor got on the phone for a short, terse conversation with the police.

"We're heading in," he said.

Twenty minutes later, they docked at the jetty from which they had left at dawn to be met by two uniformed police officers and a man in civilian clothing. An ambulance was parked to one side of the jetty. Trevor expertly moored the boat and assisted one of the officers and the civilian onto the boat. The three stars on the officer's shoulders indicated a Chief Inspector, immediately confirmed when he introduced himself.

"Chief Inspector Rowlands," he said. "This is Doctor Fanning, the police surgeon. Let's see the body."

The unpleasant task of uncovering the corpse took a few moments and the doctor busied himself with his examination.

"White male, between fifty and sixty, in excellent physical condition. Looks like a heavy blow to the head with a blunt instrument, possibly a cricket bat from the type of indentation. Well-manicured hands, not a labourer, good facial skin suggests the same. He hasn't been in the water long, probably just overnight, judging by the limited fish bites on the body. Can't tell if he was dead when he hit the water, I'll have to check his lungs when I get him on the slab. Okay, can we get him onto the jetty?"

Between all of them, it was not difficult to rewrap the corpse and lift it out of boat. There was an ambulance waiting and within a few minutes, it had departed with the medical examiner.

"I have to ask you some questions," said the police officer. "Is there any chance you can give me some idea of where you found the body?"

"I can do better than that," said Trevor. "My navigation system records every yard we move. I can tell you exactly longitude and latitude and the time to the second we hooked it."

"That could be helpful," said Rowlands. "We might be able to check the tidal patterns for the last twenty-four hours and work out where the body was put in the sea." He folded away his notebook and the two officers left in their patrol car.

By silent agreement, the four fishermen helped the boat get placed on its trailer and then departed for their homes. The shock was evident in all of them.

Back at the police station, both officers had work to do. Rowlands began typing the report on the computer terminal in his office, the other also went to a terminal to look for missing persons in the system. It didn't take long.

"Just three possibles, sir," he said, entering Rowlands' office.

"Tell me," said the senior officer, waving his colleague to a seat.

"The first is unlikely," said the younger man. "Peter Henderson, aged fifty from nearby, missing since last week, reported by his wife."

"Why unlikely?"

"First, completely bald, second, he was a labourer working for the council. His hands would not be like the corpse, the doctor said they were nicely maintained."

"Okay, next?"

"Even less likely, sir. Jong Hee Yang, Korean, missing for two weeks, vanished while on a tour of England. Aged fifty, but quite short, well below the victim's height."

"Is there any hope with the last one, Brad?"

"Very much so. Kyle Fleming, aged forty-eight, Chief Executive Officer of a pharmaceutical company in the US, on vacation here, reported missing by his wife and by his company just four days ago. They were in Wolverhampton, visiting his son and daughter-in-law."

"Sounds probable," said Rowlands. "There's something deeply suspicious about it, as well. He vanished for days ago, but his body has only been in the water for a day. Where the hell was he for the three days? This is going to be difficult. Brad, call the Wolverhampton nick, email them the details and a picture of the man's face, ask them to send the most gentle, empathic officer to his address and break it to the family while asking them to confirm it's him. See if the wife or one of the family will come up here for the formal identification."

The constable nodded and left.

Chapter 18

Skegness Police Station, 14th December, 2025

Two hours later, Rowlands' computer warbled as he worked on the report of the body's discovery. He looked up and was astonished to see a circus clown's face looking at him. It was an image, not a live face. The voice coming from the speaker was electronic, distorted and could not be identified as male or female or what age it could be.

"So you found the body, eh, Chief Inspector? That was quicker than expected. Lucky those blokes were out in their boat."

"Who the hell are you?" Rowlands touched the switch to record the proceedings. He sensed that this was critical, not a fraudulent claim to have committed a crime as so often happened after every murder.

"Ah well, that's going to be a long and difficult problem for you, Chief Inspector Rowlands and it's going to be fun watching you struggling with it."

"Bollocks," said Rowlands, knowing that the caller was deadly serious, but trying to goad a response that might be informative. "You're just another dimwit trying to get your five minutes of fame. Get off the line."

"Here are some facts, Chief Inspector," said the ugly voice. "The dead man is Kyle Fleming, he was the Chief Executive Officer of a pharmaceutical company called Blackwood Harding, with the international head office in the US and offices and factories and laboratories all over the world. We found him visiting the UK and dealt with him here."

Rowlands was convinced. Whoever was hidden by that clown's face knew all about the killing of the body in the sea. He said nothing.

"So let me tell you why Fleming died," continued the distorted voice. "It was his punishment for driving the corruption that is prevalent in that industry. People died because his company told lies to get a faulty drug approved and marketed all over the world. And when the lie was discovered, he changed the name, rebranded it and continued to sell it in third-world countries that didn't have the safety regulations that other countries do. More people died."

"And you are judge, jury and executioner, are you?" said Rowlands.

"Nobody else was going to make him pay. And we sure made him pay. We gave him a nasty time in a cellar before we finished him off and dumped him in the sea. And more people are going to join him in paying for this crime."

"Why not just publicise it?" said Rowlands. "Give all the details to the newspapers, to the television companies, let them shame the company and get the product stopped?"

There was a laugh from the monitor. With the distortion, it was a weird, frightening sound. "They all knew about it when it happened. But Blackwood spread millions around and bought the silence about the company and the people responsible. No, Chief Inspector, a lot of people are going to die for this crime. And I will be calling a lot of people to tell them and challenge them to stop it. I tell you now, they won't be able to, just as you won't be able to trace this call. Eventually, companies around the world are going to fail, which is what they deserve."

"You've got delusions of grandeur," said Rowlands. "We'll find you eventually."

"Why don't you call Chief Inspector Melanie Carter in the Australian Federal Police?" said the voice. "She's already facing up to this problem and you might want to compare notes."

The clown's face vanished as the connection was broken. Rowlands picked up the phone and called his technical support team.

"I just got a video call," he said. "Track it, find out where it came from."

At the end of the day, having heard nothing from the technical group, Rowlands went to see them. The look of disappointment on the young woman's face told him the worst.

"Nothing, sir," she said. "I've been wrestling with this since you asked, but I got nowhere. I tracked the call to a public phone booth in Leicester, then to Guernsey, then Madrid and then I lost it, hit a brick wall. Whoever this was is a bloody expert. I'm really sorry, sir."

"The fact that he or she could get through our firewalls to my computer should have told me that," said Rowlands. "Don't apologise, Dianna, we're obviously up against somebody fearsome. And we're not the first, it seems to have met it."

"Yes, he said it, he's already boasted to the Australians. Will you contact this Chief Inspector Carter that he mentioned?"

"I sure will. Okay, go home, Dianna. I'll locate this Carter and check on time zones in Australia, then I can call her. I wonder what the hell this person has done."

He returned to his office and looked up time zones in Australia. Six o'clock in England, the computer told him it was five in the morning in Sydney where it was on summertime and eleven hours ahead. The clown caller had said Carter was in the Australian Federal Police, that probably meant she was in Canberra. If not, then the Canberra office would know where she was. He closed down his system and went home for the evening and a disturbed night.

Chapter 19

Pyong Yang, North Korea, 5th January, 2026

The meeting room was small, sparsely furnished with just a table that could fit six people around it and four chairs. All were occupied by men in military uniform, all officers. One of them, a *Daechwa,* Senior Colonel with four stars within two red lines on his shoulder was clearly in charge.

"We have received a new direction," he said. "The great leader has seen that many commercial organisations in the west, notably the United States, Britain and Australia have had some of their senior staff murdered. It seems that some unknown groups are committing these murders as a war of revenge against some pharmaceutical firms and probably the industry itself, as several other people have been killed who are not employed by the companies but are associated with the industry, such as researchers, distributors and the like."

The other three officers held the rank of *Chungjwa,* Lieutenant Colonel, with two stars within the red lines. One of them smiled. "So people in the west are doing our work of attacking capitalism," he said. "But just why are they hitting the pharmaceutical industry?"

"We have learned that somebody calls the local police stations after each murder and boasts that it is in response for the many crimes of those companies," replied the Senior Colonel. "They say that drugs are being sold that have not been properly trialled, sometimes even sold after evidence has shown the drugs to be faulty, even fatal." The officer's face showed contempt.

"Exactly the greedy capitalists that our great leader has so often spoken of," said a second two-starred *Chungjwa*. "Profits over lives, the guiding principle of capitalism."

"Exactly," said the Senior Colonel. "So our instructions are to use this development and cause even further problems for the criminals. We are ordered to kidnap several people with the same high profile as the victims so far, senior executives of pharmaceutical companies, people on the drug approval panels, distributors, and so on. I shall give each of you details as far as we have them of those people killed so far in the three countries, keep close to those. Now, I want you to contact your primary staff in those countries and have them plan to kidnap at least three people in each."

"And do we kill them?" asked the last officer. "Or just hold them and perhaps demand a ransom?"

"Our instructions are just to hold them for now. We might as well make some money from this venture, and you can instruct your people to demand at least twenty million American dollars or equivalent for the return of the personnel."

Nods of approval ran round the table.

"But I must warn you," continued the Senior Colonel. "This must be done with the greatest of care. The police will naturally assume it is the other groups that are doing this, and it must be made to look that way. When you call the companies for the demands, use the electronic voice distortion software. Do not let the captives see your face or hear your voices. Many of our staff in the west have received British or American educations and speak with near-perfect accents, but even those must not be heard. But if the police start to get near to the captives, instruct the staff to kill them and leave the country at once. This must not reflect back on our leader. Now, do your research very carefully, identify people who are critical to the success of the companies you pick. I suggest top executives, science personnel, maybe heads of marketing. And plan the operations very carefully. Your people must not be found out."

All four men stood up, exchanged salutes and left the room.

Chapter 20

AFP HQ, Canberra, 20th January, 2026

Melanie's pc monitor issued a musical warble to indicate an incoming call. She closed the file of crime scene notes she had been reviewing, searching for any small clue to indicate some path of further investigation into the death of the retired Health Minister.

"Yes," she said. "Chief Inspector Carter. How can I help you?"

"Can't think of a damn thing," said an electronically distorted voice from the monitor. There was no face on the screen. "And there's sure as hell no way I'm going to help you."

Melanie restrained her irritation. "So why are you calling me? And who is this?" Despite the irritation, professional habits made her lightly touch the key that initiated the conversation being recorded.

"Nobody you know," said the ugly, electronic voice. "But I just wanted to tell you that I know you're investigating the murder of that old fart Sheldon, but you'll get nowhere."

"You know what?" she said. "After every murder, the police get several calls from fuckwits claiming they did it. Of course, the real killer never makes such a claim. So may I suggest, you get back to the basement of your Mommie's house, open up your comic book and carry on with your infantile fantasies?"

There was a pause from the caller. And then... "That was stupid, Melanie. And it justifies what my group is doing world-wide."

"Oh, so now it's a world-wide conspiracy is it?" Melanie's irritation was growing. "Look, fuckwit, get off my line, stop wasting my time and go and masturbate or something. That will be far more useful for you."

"Do you know, that guy in Byron Bay, Felix Honneger, we did him as well. Same way, baseball bat to the head, beat his brains out."

Melanie's irritation faded. She realized that something severe was occurring. Linking the two murders, two years apart, was nothing a prankster would have thought of. And the electronically distorted voice – that had happened before in a terrible case of serial murders for blackmail.[1]

"Did you really?" she said, trying to make the contempt highly obvious.

"We did," said the anonymous caller. "Have you realized yet, that both those two dead 'uns were associated with the pharmaceutical industry?"

Oops! Melanie went to high alert. This had been the topic of conversations with Alex and Allen Miller very recently. She said nothing but kept her face expressionless. She might not be able to see this mysterious caller, but she was certain that the caller, male or female, could see her.

---

[1] "The Internet Murders" by Michael Davies

"It wasn't a coincidence," continued the ugly voice. "Maybe you don't know it, Chief Inspector Carter, but the pharmaceutical industry is probably the most hated industry in the world."

"Oh, I see. And you and your funny little friends are going to punish them all over the world, are you?" Melanie deliberately laughed to see if the caller could be affected by her cynicism.

"That's exactly what we are going to do. They've committed fraud, failure to maintain safe manufacturing processes, they've lied about clinical trials and they've committed murder."

"And this is world-wide, eh?" said Melanie. "If it's such a global crime, why are you calling a detective in Canberra? What can I do about it? And while we're on that subject, just why have you called me?"

"We're ramping up operations in several countries," said the unknown caller. "We'll expand as we get more agents. And I know you very well. I heard about you some years ago when you tracked down a group of killers who were committing murders as stories for their books. They were quite mad, of course, but so was the woman influencing them."

Nona Markham![2] The extraordinary, dominating woman was always a presence in Melanie's mind. She was the key figure in Melanie's first serial killer case, back when she was a Detective Sergeant and had first

---

[2] "The Ninth of the Month Murders" by Michael Davies

met Alex Welland, then a patrol car officer, and Jack Savage, a retired police profiler.

"I knew a couple of the people involved," continued the caller. "You were impressive. And I've followed your career ever since."

Several thoughts ran through Melanie's mind. The first was that this was a serious development in the possible connection to the pharmaceutical industry. Up till now, the detailed digging by Alex had indicated a link with the two murders in Australia, but now, unless this was a massive hoax, it pointed to a possible large-scale war of attrition against the world-wide industry. The second thought was that the caller had made a serious mistake. He or she had no knowledge of the fact that the electronic distortion could be reversed, and the true voice revealed.

"So I'll ask you again, fuckwit. Why are you calling me? I'm just a cop in Canberra. If, as you claim, you're conducting a global war of revenge, you should be talking to our government, or at least our security services."

"Oh, I know they'll get involved, Inspector. But I just wanted to laugh at the infantile way you lot will tackle the problem and assure you the bodies are going to mount up and you'll be able to do nothing at all about it."

The call was disconnected.

Melanie left her office to go and talk with her boss.

Within minutes of her return, the computer warbled at her again. The indication on the screen was a call from a police station in Skegness, England. Puzzled, she hit the "Accept" key.

"Detective Chief Inspector Carter," she said, being as formal as possible, not knowing who was at the other end. A man's face appeared and displayed the usual small indications of surprise she was accustomed to when men saw her face.

"Er.. Detective Chief Inspector Rowlands, Skegness. Good morning, Detective Chief Inspector Carter."

Melanie decided he was a half-decent-looking man with a pleasing speaking voice, so she smiled in an attempt to disarm him and put him at his ease.

"This is an unexpected call, Chief Inspector Rowlands. What is it, late evening there?"

"Actually, past midnight."

"Then this must be urgent."

"It is, and very ugly. Two days ago, we fished a body out of the sea. His name was Kyle Fleming and he was a senior executive with a pharmaceutical company in the UK."

Melanie hid the shock that this caused her. "Then you're right, this is ugly and now I know why you're calling me with this. You got a distorted voice boasting to you?"

"Exactly. Not only boasting but telling us there's a war on against the industry and I should tell you about it, because for some reason, you're the focus of all this."

"We're having the same problem. Before we go on, I should warn you that the people behind this have some high skills in computer hacking and it's almost certain that somebody is listening in to this conversation. So, just two things. Did you record the call?"

"We did."

"Then please transmit that recording to me. Second, I'll have another high expert in data security call you on a secure line, giving you a phone number at a secure location where you can call me and give me a number where I can call you, somewhere without any computers that can be hacked."

"This is an international war, then?"

"It is. Thank you for calling, Chief Inspector Rowlands, we'll talk more when it's safe." She smiled her best man-killing smile and waved in a friendly manner before disconnecting the call.

Chapter 21

Denver, Colorado, 31st January, 2026

Cheryl Fraser drove up the hundred metres of rough driveway to her large, sprawling old house, as always feeling the wave of pleasure at the experience. It had been a lifelong dream of hers to own a country home like this, not the manicured lawns and paved driveway of the very rich, but the charmingly rustic home away from the city.

Upon the promotion to Chief Executive Officer of Wynyard Pharmaceuticals two years ago and the receipt of the first breath-taking bonus six months later, she had bought this house and never had failed to be delighted by the drive home every evening.

She stopped the Cadillac under the carport at the side of the house, reached for her purse and began to walk up the steps to the side door, then stopped in shock.

From behind the bushes at the side of the house appeared a black van. It had no windows beyond the windshield and front doors and no markings. It stopped next to the Cadillac, the back door flew open, and four men jumped out, one seized the driver's door and two hauled Cheryl out of her seat. The fourth joined in and pulled a black bag over her head and she felt herself dragged to the black vehicle pushed inside onto a hard metallic floor and the door slammed behind her. She had barely felt the tiny prick in her arm during this, but within a few seconds, she blacked out. Not one of the captors had spoken a word.

"Wynyard Pharmaceuticals, how may I direct your call?" The attractive young woman at the reception desk expected a standard request to be put through to any one of the people in the building, but what she heard frightened her badly.

"Tell your directors that we have your CEO in captivity. If you want to see her again, you will pay twenty million dollars. Do not call the police or she will die. We will call again later to tell you how to get her back." The voice was horrible, ugly, distorted by some electronic means and the call was disconnected immediately.

The receptionist found she was breathing hard and her throat was dry, but she was still aware enough to check the source of the call. But nothing registered. Gathering herself, she called the first director she could think of.

* * *

Windsor, NSW, Australia 3rd February, 2026

William Goddard found the late evening stroll along the riverside the best time to think about his work, which he loved. His genius with pharmacology had shown during his degree course at Sydney University and even more during his doctorate work when he had gained his PhD with the development of a drug that dramatically improved the symptoms of the common cold. He hadn't minded that the University made a huge amount of money by licencing the compound to a manufacturer, he knew there was a brilliant future ahead. He was quite correct. Several companies had competed for his services on graduation and offered mouth-watering salaries, and over the last three years, he had completed the development of three new drugs that were still under clinical trials and would soon burst upon the market with forecast sales of massive levels. He knew that he had dramatically raised the reputation of the Australian research laboratory within the international pharmaceutical industry and this thought was always a comfortable companion within his mind.

This evening, his mind was full of the newest project, a pill that would reduce the disfiguring effects of acne. William was pleasingly certain that in time, he would reduce the pain and embarrassment of life for millions of teenagers around the world. The huge bonus he knew he would receive was secondary to that.

The workings of his mind were abruptly cut short as two men advanced on him, seized his arms and held him motionless as a needle was placed against his neck. He was unconscious almost immediately.

The call that came to the receptionist the following morning shocked the woman into near catatonia. The voice was harsh, inhuman, quite unidentifiable and the message it gave was frightening. It was a while before she could calm herself down enough to call the company head.

Sydney, NSW, Australia, 8th February, 2026

Jamie Ward was pleased with life. Only five years after joining the growing pharmaceutical company's sales force, his rapid rise had resulted from an almost magical ability to sell the company's products and even more, to energise and guide the sales personnel to do the same. Shares of the company had climbed the charts and his bonuses had climbed with them. His recent promotion to sales director after the tragic drowning of his boss in a boating accident had completed the almost fairy-tale story and finally let him buy the penthouse apartment in a classy, fashionable block in the inner city he had always fancied. Every time he pressed the device on his dashboard to open the secure gate into the block's parking lot, he smiled to himself.

This was a late return home. The official gathering of the company's directors at a dinner in the Harbourside hotel had ended late, much later than such events normally closed, but there was so much satisfaction with the company's profits and the recognition of his major contribution, that people seemed unwilling to leave. It was after eleven when he opened the entrance to the basement parking level and drove to his allocated spot.

As he opened his driver-side door, a figure appeared at the back of the car.

"What the..." was as much as he was able to say before the wet pad was placed over his mouth and nose and the world faded into blackness.

The phone call to the company's reception desk the next morning caused the young woman who answered such a shock that she was unable to say anything. Her distress was noted by her colleague who retained enough composure to call the Chief Executive Director.

Global Zoom Call, 15th February, 2026, New York, Toronto, Manchester, Berlin

Jerry Copeland checked all three faces on his pc monitor.

"We're all here? Good," he said. "Thanks for responding to my call so quickly, but the situation keeps changing."

"The kidnapping?" asked Sarah Jensen. "We've had one in our Australian development labs in Windsor and we've already received the ransom demand. William Goddard was not actually on our payroll, he worked for an independent lab and was contracted to us after licencing a major new drug to us."

"And our friend at Wynyard Chemicals in Denver got one too," said Copeland. "Their Chief Executive

Officer was grabbed and a ransom note sent."

"Oh God, Cheryl Fraser?" burst out Sarah. "I knew her quite well, we were on an executive training program together in Chicago some years ago and we kept in touch."

"And one more in Australia," said Tom Fisher in Toronto. "The news came through a couple of days ago. A guy called Jamie Ward, brilliant marketing man with an Australian subsidiary of ours, taken from his car as he arrived home after an evening reception."

"The modus operandi is changing," said Konrad Richter in Berlin. "Up till now, whoever is doing this has made a call the local police station where the killing took place, and a couple of times to newspapers to boast about it and claim that they are punishing the pharma industry. But this is so different, I have to think it's a different group conducting it."

"Some things are the same," said Sarah. "The companies have received a phone call with the same electronic distortion that the killers have used, and then they have sent the threats of a ransom demand note on paper."

"On paper?" Richter spoke loudly as the surprise hit him. "Has anything been found to indicate who's behind it?"

"Well. Not exactly ransom demands," said Sarah. "They sent the usual proof of having their captives, a picture of them holding that day's edition of a local newspaper. But they haven't as yet demanded money.

The printing was by a standard laser-jet printer, impossible to identify either the brand or the owner."

"How do you know all this?" asked Copeland.

"I still have contacts in the police force. I've talked to a couple of them and the details have been circulated around the various forces. That's standard, even though the kidnappers have made the usual demand for no police to be informed."

"If Interpol has the recordings of the kidnapper's voices, then I'm sure my contacts in Military Intelligence can get them," said Richter. "And then they can do the same restoration of the original voices and analyse them as they did before."

"As quickly as possible," said Copeland, echoed by agreement from the other two.

* * *

"I have the results of the analyses by the MI technicians," said Richter two days later. "I'm afraid it's rather disappointing."

"Best tell us," said Fisher.

"They couldn't restore the voices," said Richter. "The system used was one the technicians had not met before. They said it had been created for a specific group or purpose, possibly the security operation of a country outside of our regular cooperation. They'll keep trying, but it will be very difficult."

"So we're no further along?" said Sarah, disappointment obvious in her tones.

"Well, there's one thing," said Richter. "Even with the distortion, a few indicators could be identified. The analysts said there were definite pointers to an accent, almost certainly Asian tones. They said not any of the Chinese dialects like Mandarin or Cantonese, but a harder tone. They think it could be Japanese, but far more likely Korean, whether North or South impossible to tell."

"Now that is certainly interesting," said Copeland. "Is there anything that can help us further?"

"There certainly is," said Richter. "From some events some years ago, my department experienced the work of Allen Miller, considered the best computer hacker in the world. At one point, we even spoke with Miller when he offered his skills in locating a mass murderer in Hannover and we managed to reveal his phone number."

"I've heard of this guy," said Copeland. "He stole millions from various organisations before he disappeared and left the USA."

"That's the one," said Richter.

"Is there any way Allen Miller could help?"

"Possibly," said Richter. "I'll try the number I was given, but there's no guarantee he'll want to be involved."

"Oh, I'd like to be involved, alright," said the voice of Allen Miller from all their computers.

"What?" exploded Copeland. "You've been listening all this time?"

"Stop panicking," said Miller. "I located your computes a week ago, though I haven't tuned in at all. But my system tells me as soon as my name is mentioned, and I came on quickly. It's obvious what you've been talking about, and I'd like to help if I can. This is not my usual practice but this is a major problem and I can probably assist."

"What do you think you could do?" asked Sarah.

"Don't know yet," said Miller. "I'll try and trace the calls to the pharma companies, but they've been lost already. And judging by the unique distortion systems, they have some very clever people working for them. Leave it with me, I'll get back to you when I have something."

The meeting ended with the usual round of farewells and the screens all went blank.

Chapter 22

AFP HQ, Canberra, 16th February, 2026

Melanie's heart sank as the computer monitor came alive. No face appeared, just a blank fuzziness, but she knew what was coming. She was having a brief review of ongoing AFP cases with Alex Welland who seemed to be enjoying his assignment in Canberra. She had disconnected the computer from power and internet connections during the meeting and had just reconnected it, intending to have just a final, informal discussion with Alex, and the interruption was unwelcome.

"Good morning, Detective Chief Inspector Melanie Carter," said the distorted, electronic voice. She could hear the mockery in the voice, despite the distortion. The caller was emphasizing his control over her. "And how are you enjoying this lovely city of yours?"

Alex was sitting out of the line of sight of the screen and a quick look between them was a clear understanding that he would remain silent and not reveal his presence.

"What the hell do you want, fuckwit?" she replied.

"Oh dear, Melanie, is that any way to treat the opposition that is so obviously beating you like a rug? I might have to make things even worse for you if you don't show some respect."

Melanie said nothing.

"And now you've learned that this operation is not only happening in Australia but also in the UK. And let me give you advance warning, you'll soon hear about our American performances."

"Tell me again, just why is this going on? What do you hope to get from it?"

"Revenge, Melanie, nothing but revenge and maybe give the drugmakers a reason to change their habits."

"By killing people at random?" A quick look at Alex showed his face was expressionless but was clearly concentrating deeply.

"No, by killing people who have been responsible for the criminality of the drugmakers and the deaths they have caused and causing them the same grief that they caused innocent people."

"And how long will this go on? Until everybody who has ever worked or is still working in the drug industry is dead?" Melanie tried to add some sarcasm into her tones. The unknown caller didn't seem to notice.

"Don't be silly, Melanie, the world still needs the stuff they produce. But this goes on until there is some recognition of their guilt and a clear message that they will change."

Melanie remained silent.

"And so, for this episode, let me tell you what will happen and why. A few years ago, a family in Gosford was struck by tragedy when their teenage son died from the effects of a drug that was supposed to clear the disease of his liver. Instead, he died, one of several people who died before the company withdrew the pill and was found to have forged the clinical trials that allowed it to be approved for sale. The parents and the little sister were traumatised by the death and all of them have needed psychological help since then. Of course, they were not the only family affected, but they're the ones providing the example. In a few days, you will find the body of a teenage boy, the son of a couple who also have a younger daughter. The father is a senior pharmacologist and researcher with a major drug company. That family will now experience the grief and pain that they have contributed to in others."

"For god's sake," burst out Melanie, "you can't make an innocent family pay that way for a mistake made by others, years ago."

"Yes I can, Melanie. Now you can spend a little time waiting to hear about this boy's death. Maybe you can tell the family just why their son was killed."

The screen went dead.

"Jesus," whispered Alex, "that is one sick bastard. Where the hell does this go?"

"Everywhere, it seems," said Mclanie. "We've had three in Australia, maybe just one in the UK, and it seems there have been events in the US we haven't heard of. Can you see if you can find out about those, Alex?"

Alex nodded, his face tight and left the office.

North Canberra, ACT, 18th February, 2026

"I won't know what killed him until I get him on the table," said the Medical Examiner. "But rigor has passed, it's been a warm night, so an initial estimate is that he's been dead about eighteen hours. No sign of violence, no blunt force object."

"Any identification?" Melanie and Alex stood a few paces away, wearing full protective covering to avoid damaging the crime scene.

"Nothing," said the doctor. "Good quality clothes, no sign of any force having been applied. No sign of defence wounds on the hands, this is going to be difficult." He nodded at the two men standing near with the stretcher and they picked up the body and carried it the few metres to the waiting ambulance.

"Can't find anything, Ma'am," said one of the investigating officers, also clad in full protective clothing. "No footprints, no bits of anything, no tyre tracks. I'd say the kid was killed elsewhere, driven here to somewhere on the pathway.." he pointed at the sealed road running through the small wood where they were all standing.. "and carried to where he was left. Nothing on the road to indicate the vehicle, not even the tyre size."

Melanie nodded and indicated to Alex that they should leave and return to the office.

"He did this deliberately in our patch, so I'd be the copper called in," said Melanie as she drove back to the AFP headquarters. "Get onto missing persons when we get back, but we know damn well the victim is from an affluent family that has at some stage, maybe still is involved with the pharmaceutical industry. There will be a young daughter as well."

"Can't get much more vindictive and merciless," said Alex. His voice was subdued.

Neither of them spoke again until they reached the office.

The answer was waiting for them when they returned. The middle-aged couple had already been shown into an interview room, having arrived just minutes before Melanie returned. The woman was in tears, clinging to her husband's hand while he was clearly struggling for self-control.

"Ivan often stays out overnight," said Carl Smith. "He's always been very self-disciplined, and he stays with several friends when they go out in the evening."

"Where did he go last night?" asked Melanie.

"He didn't tell us. He's free to run his own life."

"I need some details, Mr Smith. What is your occupation?"

"I'm the head of research for the Australian unit of Consellors Pharmaceuticals in Canada."

"Any other family?"

"We have a twelve-year-old daughter, Janice. She's going to be shattered by this, she's always hero-worshipped Ivan."

Melanie exchanged a rapid glance with Alex.

"How did it happen?" Emily Smith found her voice, strangled by tears but able to function a little.

"We don't know, Mrs Smith," said Melanie. "A postmortem is scheduled for this afternoon, but so far, we have no idea of how your son died. There are no signs of violence on him."

"Can we see him?" The grief in the mother's voice was almost overwhelming.

"Of course. We need a formal identification, so if you can handle this, we'll take you to see him now."

Proceedings stopped for a few minutes as the woman collapsed in a storm of helpless weeping again. Her husband tried to help her, but Melanie could see tears running down his cheeks and frequent swallowing as he tried to retain his own control. Finally, the bereaved couple were taken to the morgue. Melanie tried not to think about what they were feeling as they stared down at the face of their dead son on the medical table. Once they had gone to continue their own private hell, Melanie returned to her office.

"Christ alive," she muttered as she took her seat, "if I do anything else, I'm going to find you, you bastard. Nobody has the right to do that to innocent people, I don't care what crimes a drug company has committed."

* * *

AFP HQ, Canberra, Australia, 19th February, 2026

Melanie sighed in irritation as the all-too-familiar electronic voice sounded from her pc.

"Going to boast about your latest triumph in killing innocent people, are you?" she said, hoping that by irritating the caller, he might make some revealing error. The fact that none of the cops anywhere had been able to identify a single clue was beginning to get her down.

"You'll hear all about it when the news comes out," said the ugly voice. "But let me give you an advance tip. It will be in Gloucester, and the victim will be the retired head of research for regulatory body and had recently moved to a new home."

Melanie swallowed her rage. Nothing had been heard yet about any such killing and while she hoped it was just fiction to goad her, she doubted it was and she'd hear about the latest murder within hours.

"And have you added kidnapping to your crimes also? What's happening, do you need money to continue this horrible game of yours?"

There was a short silence at the other end.

"You what?" said the caller.

"You heard me. Have you decided to kidnap some innocents and get money out of their companies to finance murder?"

"What the hell are you talking about? We haven't kidnapped anyone."

"I don't expect serial killers to tell the truth," she said, putting as much contempt into her voice as she could. "But it seems you've expanded your range of operations. You're demanding a hell of a lot of money for each one. I have to tell you, kidnapping is a bloody horrible crime but it's also the one most likely to make you stumble when you try and collect the money."

"But we haven't." Even through the distortion, she could hear the panic in the man's voice. Somehow, she believed him. A whole new dimension had been added to this case. She made a note to get her boss to ask the Americans and British if they knew of any kidnappings of people involved in the pharmaceutical industry. She heard a click as the call was disconnected.

"I think I believe him," said Jack.

They sat in a coffee shop in the suburb of Curtin, several kilometres from the police HQ. She had called Jack two days before to discuss the developing war on the pharma industry and he had decided immediately to drive down from the mid-north coast. Thirty minutes earlier, she has asked Jack and Alex to join her in a remote site, free of any risk of being hacked.

"So do I, but that's not based on any professional analysis," said Melanie. "Just why do you believe him?"

"Murder and kidnapping are two totally different crimes," said Jack. "From the start, the justification for the killings has been revenge for the crimes believed to have been committed by the pharma industry. The victims have been chosen with care to inflict the maximum message to the world. The killings have been carefully done, with some knowledge of how to avoid leaving clues and they haven't required a large organisation beyond that."

"But kidnapping?" Melanie was engrossed in this.

"Kidnapping requires considerable organisation, several people to be involved in the process and critically, a place to keep the captive. And as we all know, the process of collecting the money and releasing the captive is where the exercise tends to fail. Managing a successful kidnapping and collecting the money is fraught with massive difficulties. There are two different organisations here. The revenge killers are new to this, the kidnappers are professionals with a lot of resources at their disposal."

"Why have they entered the game?" asked Alex. "Have they seen the opportunity to make money and use the killings by somebody else as a smokescreen?"

"Very likely," said Jack. "But there may be more to it."

The other two looked at him.

"If there are more kidnappings than the two we've heard about here in Australia, perhaps several in the UK and America, the reason may be to cause embarrassment to our countries. If we hear about more over the next week or two, then it may be a deliberate political act, in which case we have to think about the spooks from Russia, China, perhaps even North Korea."

"Oh shit," said Melanie.

*　*　*

Manchester, UK 19th February, 2026

"Floyd, we're all delighted when the Chief Executive Officer comes over to visit us, but these are dangerous times right now. I don't think this is a good idea."

Floyd Morris smiled. This was his third meeting in two years with the British subsidiary's security director and they had always got on well. There were times when Morris admitted to himself that he found Sarah Jenner most attractive, but as the corporate boss, he could not allow himself to reveal it. There was definitely a spark between them, but both seemed to be committed to business rules and tried not to let it show.

"Sarah, we have to maintain this excellent relationship with our subsidiary and our distributers. I think it's been a key factor in our success over the years."

"I have to agree with you, Floyd, but somebody is conducting a war against our industry. We've lost people, people are being killed, some have been kidnapped. Dammit, Floyd, I don't want to see your name among the losses."

"Hell, Sarah, I don't want that either, but I'm

dammed if I'm going to let them know we're running scared. That wouldn't do our share price any good."

"Okay, but can you cancel this trip to Reading, perhaps? It puts you well away from our offices and makes you badly exposed."

"No chance. I've been promising myself this trip ever since the last one when all I saw was Manchester. Nothing wrong with Manchester, I agree, it was a great trip, but all I've seen of England in my life has been London and Manchester. This time, I'm going to rent a car and drive down to Reading. Those people are our biggest distributors, they deserve a visit and this way I'll see something of the countryside."

"You're okay with our amazing style of driving on the left?"

"I think so, I rented a car briefly in Australia last visit, it took a little time, but I caught on after a while. But I'll make sure they give me an automatic. I'm ashamed to say I have never driven a manual shift in my life."

"Okay then, but I'm going to insist you have one of my people with you. He could share the driving and he goes with you all the time you are out. I'll assign one of my people, Jim Burroughs, he's large, expert unarmed combat practitioner and about the best I can think of."

"That's fine, Sarah, but he'd better share my taste in music when we're in the car."

"Oh Lordy, what hideous racket will you inflict on him?"

"I brought my best mix of Chicago, Blood Sweat and Tears, Pink Floyd and Led Zepplin."

"A weird mix for a fifty-year old Chief Executive Officer."

"That's what my kids say."

Leaving at dawn the following day, the drive down from the northwest of England to Reading in Berkshire was easier than Morris had expected. He and his security expert, Jim Burroughs found they got on well and in fact shared the same taste in music. Morris insisted on doing most of the several hours of driving to ensure that he got used to it and after the first hour of hesitancy, Burroughs admitted he felt quite safe. With a coffee break every two hours, they arrived in the town of Reading, and the satellite navigation system put them at the front of the distribution company. The opening to the underground car park allowed them to drive in and park in a line of several vehicles, then take the elevator up to the reception area. Burroughs stayed with Morris during the three hours of talks with all the employees, the private lunch and the demonstration of the sophisticated forecasting and control system. Soon after five, they said their farewells and descended down to the parking area.

That's when things went wrong.

As Burroughs opened the car door, two men jumped out from behind a large van. Morris felt hands grab him by one arm and his neck, automatically lashed out with the free hand and felt a hard contact with the captor, but then had barely time to feel the prick of a needle in his neck and lost consciousness within seconds.

Chapter 23

Gloucester, NSW, Australia 21st February, 2026

Terry Sully was enjoying his retirement after forty-five years as a scientist, the last ten with the Therapeutic Goods Administration, the regulatory body that checked applications for new drugs being developed by the pharmaceutical companies. He had taken great satisfaction in his work. In the first phase of his career with a pharmaceutical company, he had developed several new products in teams of research scientists and in the second phase with the TGA, it gave him immense work experience checking through the compounds and the clinical trials of new products, most of which improved the conditions of a good-sized proportion of the human race.

His favourite part of the new phase of life was getting up soon after dawn and taking a slow, easy stroll in the small park across the road from his new house near Gloucester. He had made it a routine – twice round the park and then relax on a park bench and absorb the peace and calm of the start of the day, usually with nobody else around to disturb it.

This morning was perfect. Total calm soon after the sun had risen, warmth from the early rays and no sounds beyond the bird calls. He grinned cheerfully as the insane cackles of a flock of Kookaburras broke out from the woods across the lake.

But then a small sound that didn't fit the day came to his ears. Puzzled he looked around, could see nothing as the buzz came closer, and finally he saw it. It was a tiny drone moving slowly towards him at about a man's head height. Too intrigued to be irritated at the disturbance, he watched it as it grew closer and hovered a few metres away, directly in front of him. Never having seen one before, he didn't notice the metal object attached to the drone's belly.

The drone moved closer and Terry began to feel irritation at this invasion of his space and interruption to his morning routine. He didn't hear the explosion as the handgun attached to the drone spat out the bullet, because he was dead before the sound reached him and the bullet hit him perfectly between the eyes.

"A nine-millimetre," said the medical examiner bent over the corpse of Terry Sully. "Fired from a hand-held automatic by what I estimate was a very tall shooter, possibly approaching two metres tall."

The green gazebo erected over the park bench hid the ugly scene from the curious onlookers standing nearby.

"The bullet hit him between the eyes on a downward trajectory and exited the lower skull, so there's a good likelihood that it ended up in the ground about..." The examiner stood up, positioned himself in front of the corpse and pointed along the likely trajectory. "...About there."

The plain-clothes detective standing alongside the doctor walked behind the park bench and examined the ground. He grunted slightly as he saw a small disturbance in the short, well-maintained grass, took a penknife from his pocket and carefully dug into the ground. A moment later, he extracted a bullet with his gloved hand and examined it.

"Well done, Doc," he said. "Nine millimetre it is." He dropped the bullet into a small plastic evidence bag. "Anything else you can tell me?"

"I can estimate time of death fairly accurately. It's been a warm night and I doubt he was walking in the dark. So most likely some time after six, not later than eight when somebody called the police. He's in his late sixties, his wallet is still here, so not a robbery, and he lives locally."

"Terence Sully," said the detective, opening the victim's wallet. "You're right, aged sixty-seven, local address. Okay, can we move him?"

"Sure," said the examiner. "I'll call you when I've had him on the slab, but the results are unlikely to be different. You've got a homicide on your hands, Callum."

Half an hour later, there was no sign that a murder had taken place, just a few people standing around discussing what they had seen.

Detective Sergeant Callum Mackay picked up the phone on his desk on the second ring.

"Callum, there's somebody here wants to talk to you," said the desk sergeant at the front desk of the police station. "She says she has information on the shooting this morning. I've put her in Interview Room six with her young son."

"Right there," said Mackay and rose to his feet. His main feeling was interest. The bullet he had recovered was critical as a technical examination would indicate the gun and possibly lead to the shooter's identity. Handguns were rare in Australia, usually only held by criminals, apart from police. Could somebody have actually witnessed the shooting?

He entered the interview room and saw a young woman sitting with a boy aged perhaps ten or eleven.

"Good morning," he said. "I'm Detective Sergeant Callum Mackay. I believe you may have some information on this shooting?"

"I'm Jessica Jackson," the woman replied. "This is my son, Walter."

Walter looked frightened. Callum tried to ease the situation.

"Hi, Walter. I'm really glad you came to talk to us. Can you tell me what you saw?"

The boy still looked frightened.

"Come on, Wally," said the woman. "You're not in any trouble, is he, officer?"

"Absolutely not," said Mackay. "When we're done, I'll show you round the station and if you like, we'll let you get into a police car and see what brilliant stuff we have in there."

That seemed to do the trick. The boy's face eased and he smiled.

"Me and my friend Harry were in the woods across from the lake," he said. "We often come to the park very early, we like to stick some cricket stumps in the ground and play cricket together before people start coming in."

"Hah, I did that when I was your age," said Callum. "It's amazing how it can improve your game."

Wally lightened up even more. "We saw that old bloke sitting on the park bench while we were still in the trees, he'd sat down just a minute or two before, we've seen him a few times, he does that walk often."

Callum said nothing. He could see the boy was talking freely now and just let him say what he wanted.

"It was a drone," said Wally. "But not one of those little drones anyone can buy, this was a big one, maybe this big." He held his hands about half a metre apart. "It took off from the other side of the park just about as that guy sat down. It flew towards him, then it hovered just a bit away and then we heard the shot. It must have been a gun in the drone."

Holy shit! thought Callum. *We never thought of that one.* "Could you see who was controlling the drone?" he asked.

The boy shook his head. "He must have been behind a bush or something."

"Wally, you've been a huge help," Callum said. "Look, I'll get somebody to show you round the station and then a patrol car while I type up what you just told me, then when that's done, you can sign it and your mum can also sign it because you're a minor. Is that okay?"

The boy nodded enthusiastically as Callum picked up the phone and asked the desk sergeant to assign somebody do the tour and when a young policewoman led the boy and his mother out, he returned to his desk and quickly entered the report to the computer before calling his supervisor.

* * *

"That's got to be a first," said Detective Superintendent Robert Hunter. "Hard to know what the motive would be. What do we know about the victim?"

Callum consulted his notes. "Terence Sully, aged 67, wife and three adult children living in the UK, Canada and in Melbourne, all graduates of good universities. He has a PhD in pharmacology, spent thirty years with Consellors, a Canadian pharmaceuticals firm, working in the laboratories in the Australian company as a research scientist, very well regarded, transferred ten years ago to the TGA, the regulating body here in Australia, retired just a few months ago."

"Ah!" Hunter sat back in his seat. "That's the critical part. Callum, we've had a circular sent around all the cops in Australia and probably in other countries, also. Somebody is conducting a war of revenge against the pharma industry. There have been murders in the UK, the USA and here, all of people who have been involved in the industry. Now for some reason, the hunt is being coordinated here by a Chief Inspector Melanie Carter in the Feds..."

"Melanie Carter?" Callum sat up. "I've heard of her. I thought she was in the NSW force, wasn't she based up near Coffs Harbour? Apparently, she's drop dead gorgeous, quite brilliant but keeps herself to herself."

"That's the one. She's had more experience in serial killings than most, and she's on temporary loan to the Feds. Anyway, what this circular said was that if we have another case like this, talk to her and give her the details. We keep the case, so don't ease up on the investigations. When you get the results of the inspection of the bullet, let me know and I'll talk to Carter."

"Okay, boss, will do."

"And see if you can find the owners of drones in the region. They must be registered somewhere."

"Being done as we speak, Guv. I'll arrange to interview all of them."

"Good man."

"Hey, I did it! Damn, that was a thrill and the bastard deserved it!"

"Good. You got the right man and the cops are baffled, as they should be. You followed all the instructions, made sure there were no clues, got him well out of sight of any possible witnesses?"

"Well, not exactly. I reckon I improved on the process. You're going to love this."

"Explain."

"I'm an aircraft engineer and I've been playing with a drone for a while, taking fabulous pictures of the local scenery. And I had a nine-millimetre pistol I'd been able to get a few years ago. So I rigged up the drone, put the pistol underneath it with a firing mechanism, the camera was still there, so I found him as you said, crack of dawn, nobody around and I shot him with the drone as he sat on the park bench."

"You did WHAT?"

"Like I said, I shot him with the drone. Brilliant, eh?"

"You damn fool. How do you know nobody heard the shot and looked at the scene from the road or a local house? Did you recover the bullet?"

"Well, no, I just thought..."

"Thinking was the last thing you did. You were given clear instructions and you disobeyed them."

The call was cut off.

* * *

"Detective-Sergeant Callum Mackay, how can I help you?"

"Hey, g'day. My name's Gordie Hammond, I run a car service place in town. Look, I'm not sure if this is important and I feel a bit silly calling the cops, but I'm a bit worried."

"You shouldn't feel silly, Mr Hammond. If more people called us when they think something's wrong, our jobs would be a lot easier. So what is it?"

"It's my lead engineer, Neal Butcher. He hasn't shown up for three days, he doesn't answer my calls. I've been round to his house, I can't raise him."

"He wouldn't have just taken a break?"

"No chance. He's never taken a day off before, except when he got Covid a few years ago. He has no family that I know of."

"Okay, give me the address, I'll have somebody go and look around."

"Thanks, Sergeant, I hope everything's okay with him."

"I'll call you when we know something."

"Sarge, Constable Fletcher, I'm at that address."

"Yes, Fletcher, what can you see?"

"Not a lot. No sign of anything moving, but there's one indicator. There's a dinner table with a plate of something, a wine glass half full. Somebody started a meal and didn't finish it."

"Okay, stay there. I'll call a locksmith and we'll be there as soon as possible."

"Right-o, Sarge."

"Shit," said Callum Mackay, staring down at the body on the bed. Half the skull had been shattered by a ferocious blow and blood drenched the pillow and the sheet underneath it as far down as the corpse's chest.

"Doesn't need a detailed report from me, I suggest," said the medical examiner. "That's one king-size blow from a blunt instrument."

"He must have been interrupted in his dinner," said Callum. "Then forced into the bedroom and shot there."

"Looks like it," agreed the doctor.

"Sarge," came a call from the garage. "You need to see this."

Mackay left the hideous scene and walked down the stairs and found the entrance to the garage. Most of the space was taken up by the Subaru Forester, one door open. The uniformed cop pointed at the back seat and Mackay peered in. Leaning up against the seat back was a drone. Even at first glance, Callum could see this was no normal, small drone. It looked almost twice the size. Obviously attached to it was an automatic pistol.

"Well, fuck me sideways," said Mackay.

Canberra, Australia, 22nd February, 2026

"It's interesting," said Melanie. She sat in the coffee shop they had used before, seated round a table a little separated from the others in the shop. "The cops say it was definitely the gun that killed Sully. They checked back through Butcher's life, it seems he lost a younger sister when a drug supposed to help with liver problems failed and she died. That drug was withdrawn but the company wasn't penalized in any way."

"My guess is that this is much like any other gangland killing," said Jack. "None of the murders so far have left any clues, the killers, or whoever is running this, knows how to take precautions, protective coverings, gloves, face masks, etc. But this Butcher guy wanted to use his technical expertise and didn't follow instructions. He was killed as punishment and also to warn the others, if there are any others."

"I didn't think a drone could carry the weight of a loaded pistol with whatever it needed to pull the trigger," said Jack.

"I looked at the details the Gloucester cop sent," said Alex. "This was the top end, more an industrial drone and they can carry up to about four kilos. They'd had their experts examine it and it had also been modified quite a bit. Butcher was an aircraft engineer before he got fired for drunkenness, so he had the skills to modify it."

"But this tale reflects badly on the intelligence of whoever is behind this," said Alex.

"Explain." Melanie looked curiously at him.

"I had a chat with the desk sergeant at Gloucester," said Alex. "They had already done the obvious thing and checked the drones registered within a fifty-kilometre area. They found seven, and one of them had the same registration as this one. Even if Butcher's employer hadn't called the local cops, they'd have gone and checked him out soon after. Then they'd have found the drone, the gun, Butcher's body and checked the gun against the bullet that had found at the crime scene."

Melanie laughed, joined by Jack.

"Agreed, not bright," said Melanie.

"But I'm not surprised that Butcher wanted to use his prize toy," said Jack. "Technical types love creating things and then they just have to play with them. It must have been irresistible to him to ignore whatever instructions he was given."

"What we don't know is how he received instructions and reported to the leader," said Alex. "I would think they've been using the dark web, somehow. Could we get Allen Miller's help?"

"Good thinking," said Melanie. "I'll call him."

Chapter 24

Somewhere in NSW

William Goddard slowly returned to full consciousness. His scientific training made his careful self-analysis of the symptoms almost automatic and, despite the awful sickness and dryness in his mouth, he decided he'd been dosed with a drug commonly used by anaesthetists to put a patient into a general coma before surgery.

As he opened his eyes, he saw that he was in a small, bare room with only a table and a single chair against one wall in addition to the camp bed on which he was lying. What took his full attention was the jug of water and a glass on the table. He dragged himself into a seated position, struggling to ignore the dizziness and reached for the jug. Not bothering to use the glass, he drank greedily, nearly emptying the jug before he felt better.

Only then did he start to think about how he had got here and where this was. The memory of being taken by faceless men returned rapidly, bringing a powerful sense of fear.

"Good god, I've been kidnapped," he muttered. Despair washed over him. The research company for which he worked was not a massively rich organisation and he could not imagine they would have the sort of funds to pay out a ransom. Nor could he see that he would be worth any large amount. His current project was already documented to the stage where another pharmacologist could complete the development and he had been looking forward to beginning retirement in the next few months. His professionally scientific analysis of the situation was not encouraging. If his employers simply could not afford a large ransom, the only conclusion he could see was his death at the hands of the kidnappers.

His black thoughts were interrupted by the door opening and a man entered. He was wearing simple jeans and a roll-top shirt with long sleeves. But he wore a mask that covered his face from forehead to chin. He took the chair next to the table and turned it, sitting down to face William who remained sitting on the camp bed.

"So, Mr Goddard, how are you feeling?" asked the newcomer.

William said nothing. He decided to try and identify the man as much as he could. Instead, he pointed at the almost empty water jug.

"More water? That can be arranged, but I require some cooperation from you."

William stayed silent but listened intently. The newcomer spoke with a perfect English accent, no trace of any regional dialect. That in itself raised William's interest.

"Ah, saying nothing. Well, that can't last if you want to get out of here and even if you want more water. You have obviously gathered that you have been kidnapped. We have contacted your employers and we have demanded ten million pounds paid in Bitcoin."

"I can't talk with this dry mouth," said William, slightly exaggerating the croak in his voice.

"Very well," said the other man, stood up and opened the door, spoke briefly to somebody outside and resumed his seat. He said nothing and silence reigned until the door opened and another man entered, carrying a jug of water, which he placed on the table. He was similarly dressed to the first one, face mask covering the entire features, but William noticed the hair. It was jet black and stood up like a brush. Jug deposited, he left. William studied his gait carefully, then took another drink of water.

"Better?" said the first man. "Good. Now, as I said, we have demanded the sum of ten million pounds for your release. I am sure they will pay it, knowing your reputation and skills."

"Not a chance," said William.

"And why is that? Your company has made huge sums from developing new products, many of them developed by you, and licencing them to pharmaceutical manufacturers. Why should they not be able to afford to rescue you?"

Keep him talking, thought William. *There's something in that speech...* "Yes, they've made a lot of money," he said. "But you've made a mess of your research and you've screwed up."

The other man showed some reaction. "What do

you mean, screwed up? We identified a successful company and a brilliant researcher. How is that making an error?"

Some ego there. Keep him talking. Now for some creative licence. It's almost there... "What you totally failed to realise is that the owner of the company is a fool with money. Have you seen his house? A bloody mansion. Did you see his car? Who can afford a Rolls-Royce? Do you know that he loses thousands at the race track almost every week? He can't afford to buy me out of here."

Again, there was some reaction. The man sat up straight and his whole body showed tension.

Study the eyes. They may tell me something. Ah, the mask has slipped a little, one whole eye is showing. Guess what? Another tell-tale... "So yes, you silly bastards have screwed up. There's no way you could get even a million for me, never mind ten million."

There was silence from the other man.

"Now let me tell you a little about me," said William. "This will underline why you've fucked up badly and the only way to get away cleanly is to let me out of this house, or whatever it is, then pack up and leave as fast as you can, First thing for you to know is that I'm a high-class amateur musician as well as a pharmacologist. I learned the clarinet when I was ten, played in several orchestras, even played the Mozart Concerto when I was fifteen. But I've also learnt the oboe, the violin, the viola and the piano. I have perfect pitch, but that can be a pain in the arse, I must admit."

"Why are you telling me this?"

Ah, that did it. Now I know exactly where this bastard comes from. "Another thing you failed to learn about me, was that I've travelled a hell of a lot. I've lived and worked around the world, North America, Europe, Africa and a lot of the travels were in South-east Asia."

"Mr Goddard, you are wasting my time. I have no idea why you are telling me all this, it does you no good. I am quite unimpressed by your talents as a musician or your extensive travels."

"One of the side-effects of the musical ear that I have is an ability to identify accents," said William. "And my scientific training makes me study the way people move, walk, even the way they use their hands when they speak. I spent quite a large part of my travels in the Asia-Pacific regions, studying the music of those parts. And that's why I can tell that you are Korean, you must have studied at a classy English school, probably also University, Cambridge I suspect. And because of this game you are playing, I would say North Korean, conducting some sort of hostile act against the west. Am I right?"

The other man looked rigid in his pose. After a few moments, he got to his feet and left the room.

"Maybe not the wisest way to do this," muttered William. "If they're sensible, they'll just run and leave me here. But I may have banged some egos there, they may take it badly."

It was fifteen minutes before the door opened again and the interrogator returned.

"You were right, Mr Goddard," said the man. "I have consulted with my superior and we have decided that this project cannot continue."

"Good," said William. "I don't know how many others you have kidnapped, but the best thing would be simply to release us and then get the hell out of England."

"That is one option. However, we have decided to follow a second one."

He pulled a handgun from his jacket.

William had just a second or two to realise that his planned retirement, composing a symphony for his local orchestra would never happen. Then the bullet struck him between the eyes, and he collapsed back onto the camp bed.

AFP HQ, Canberra

"Something has gone terribly wrong," said Melanie as her group met in her office a few days later. "We've had reports of two men found shot in an unoccupied house in Bankstown, in the Western suburbs of Sydney. One was Jamie Ward, the newly appointed marketing director for a pharmaceuticals firm, the other was William Goddard, a well-respected pharmacologist who worked for a research firm in

Windsor. Both had been reported missing within two days of each other, and their companies had received ransom demands, one by distorted voice, one by print."

"This is not part of the pharma war," said Jack. "As we discussed, murder for revenge and kidnapping for ransom are two quite different processes. The kidnappings are most likely a different organisation."

"But why kill them before the companies have even had a chance to pay the ransom?" asked Alex. "Had those two companies said they would pay or not?"

"Local police talked to them," said Melanie. "Neither of them had indicated one way or another, they were still trying to work out a course of action."

"Something must have spooked the kidnappers," said Alex. "Maybe one of the victims had sussed out who they were?"

"As good an explanation as any," said Jack.

Chapter 25

AFP HQ, Canberra

Melanie sat at her desk, deep in thought. The conversation with Robert Hunter had angered her, not directed at the detective, but because another murder had taken place. She felt quite helpless. The only positive factor had been the discovery of the fatal bullet, which meant the gun could be some sort of clue. But as Hunter had said, no gun with that distinctive marking on the bullet had been identified and would prove difficult to identify. Legal ownership of handguns was very rare, almost all such weapons were owned by criminals and gangsters and there was no database of them. The use of a drone was a far better clue and she looked forward to the results of finding all registered drone owners in the region. She resolved to ask Hunter if she could sit in on the interviews that would follow. She knew her particular expertise in interviewing suspects would be invaluable.

The signal that there was a caller on her computer was almost a relief and it was quite without surprise that the voice came from the man behind the war on the pharmaceutical industry.

"Hi there, Melanie," said the voice, as always distorted by the computer software. "And how are you on this lovely day?"

Ignoring the obvious mockery, Melanie said nothing, but switched on the recording system.

"Not talking to me, Melanie? Well, not a surprise, we're really making you cops look like fools, aren't we?"

The caller paused, perhaps waiting for some response. Melanie didn't satisfy him.

"Well then, so we removed another criminal from the drug trade. The bodies are piling up, Melanie and maybe you've noticed, we don't leave clues. You'll never get us, I promise."

Don't leave clues? Does he not know that a bullet can be a signed indicator? Does he not know that a drone was used and that somebody had seen it? Melanie noted the slip. Together with the obvious ignorance that distorted voices could be unscrambled, the man organizing this was showing some weaknesses. Melanie knew she'd call Jack on the subject soon.

"You have heard about the death of Terry Sully in Gloucester, haven't you?"

Even through the distortion, Melanie heard the irritation in the caller. Feeling that might provide more information, she decided to reply.

"Yes, I heard about it," she said. "But the cops there know rather more than you think. Keep going, idiot, you'll fall flat on your face eventually."

The conversation was cut off.

Chapter 26

AFP HQ, Canberra, 26th February, 2026

"Jack, there's no way I'm entering the dating game again. It's pretty damn clear, any man I get drawn to, he dies. I'm not going to risk another man's life."

"Melanie, that's exaggerating the case. Yes, two men have died when they became close to you, but the first was nearly twenty years ago and just a random thug, nothing to do with your work. The second, yeah, okay, he was killed by forces out to punish you for threatening them, but there's no reason to expect that to happen again. Melanie, you need some warmth and closeness in your life."

"Maybe, but I can't do it. I think I'm emotionally frozen, I can't let myself get close to a man without panicking that he's going to get killed and it will be my fault."

Jack sighed. "I understand. So what are you going to do?"

"What I did before. It worked perfectly well for some years, going well away from home, pretty well taking my choice of the men who approached me, using them just as they used me and then come home well satisfied."

"It seems an awful waste of a wonderful woman, Melanie. You deserve more than that shallow life."

"Jack, I quite like this shallow life. These sex-goddess looks have been a curse for me for most of my life, but they have one advantage. When I need a sexy weekend, I can guarantee I'll have one. I put on my glad rags, short skirt, show some skin and I'm approached immediately. I pick the one most likely to do it for me and I can stop thinking. Two nights of that and I come home, my head is clear and I'm ready to get to work."

"And are you preparing to resume that? It's been a while since Rob was killed."

"Next weekend. I've booked a flight to Perth, a nice hotel and picked out my sexiest dress."

"I hope it works for you, Melanie."

"It's guaranteed, Jack."

*   *   *

Melanie sat before the mirror in her hotel room, carefully applying the makeup. On finishing, she studied the image.

"Still pretty good, Melanie," she said aloud. "That will pull them out of the woodwork, for sure. And there's always at least one who looks like he can perform satisfactorily. If I take care, I can probably do this for another fifteen years and then maybe I'll be tired of it."

She checked her purse and called the front desk to summon a taxi. Twenty minutes later, she was at the club that had been recommended to her.

The next hour was very familiar to her. Seated at the bar, nursing a glass of white wine, a series of men approached her. With each, she ran through her standard process, first glance to check for a reasonably masculine body, check his breath and the first two were quickly dismissed with that problem. The process was resumed with the next group, smile, see his teeth, then engage in light conversation. A nice, educated voice was essential, some signs of a sense of humour and if those hurdles were passed, she tested how self-absorbed he was. Any man who tried boasting about his wealth, his accomplishments, his status and so on was dismissed. She wanted his attention on her, with the self confidence that he didn't need to try and impress her.

The barman was clearly amused at the skilled way she ran through the suitors and the disappointed looks of the failed prospects.

"You're good at this," he said as he refilled her glass. "And I can see you've had a lot of practice."

"More frogs than princes," she said with a smile. "A girl needs to be careful if she wants a good time."

He laughed at that. "I know almost all these guys. And those I don't know, I can usually tell who's worth it. Twenty years behind a bar teaches you that skill. Tell you what, look at me at some point with each bloke, I'll give you a nod if I think he might suit. But I have to say, a girl like you sets a pretty high bar."

She nodded at the compliment, just as another man moved next to her. At first sight, he seemed suitable, tall, good body, nice teeth, but the voice doomed him. Uneducated, self-absorbed and just a bit too eager. She didn't need the barman's slight shake of the head to tell the prospect he wasn't up to the mark.

"Bitch," he said as he left the bar.

And then...

"Daryll," said the newcomer. "Can I buy you the next drink?"

"Melanie," she said. "Why not?"

As the barman came over and refilled her glass, she studied the arrival. All seemed well so far, she decided and glanced at the barman. He gave her a minute nod as he finished pouring the man's whiskey.

"Are you local?" asked Daryll, taking a sip.

"Brisbane," she said. "I'm here on business."

"And what is that? Can I assume you're a model?"

"I was. Now I manage modelling assignments for other girls. And you?"

"From Melbourne, also on business. I'm a consultant, looking at a shipping company's use of containers at Fremantle."

Melanie decided this was about right. He came from somewhere far enough away that they'd not likely meet accidently, and physically he met the required standards. She gulped down her drink and took the man's hand. "Your place," she said.

He grinned in delight and did the same with his drink. "Let's go," he said.

The following morning, Melanie woke early, dressed quietly and slipped out the door before the man woke up. The night had been perfectly satisfactory, Daryll was an experienced lover and had tended to her needs with great care. But one night was enough, she decided.

Back at her hotel, she undressed, showered and dressed in jeans and t-shirt for spending a day of touring the city. That night, she repeated the process at another club, joined another man similar to Daryll at his house and left early. Checking out of the hotel, she caught the afternoon flight and was back in Canberra by the evening.

It had been a successful return to her old habit, she decided. It would be three or four months before she felt the need to do it again.

Chapter 27

Manchester, UK, 3rd March, 2026

Sarah Jensen was at her desk in Manchester, the UK offices of Fremont Sims, when her phone rang, not an unusual event for the head of security for the British subsidiary.

"Sarah, this Conrad Richter in Berlin."

"Conrad! We haven't spoken for a while."

"It's on that subject that we need to talk. But I have been advised that conversations anywhere near a computer are subject to hacking by some very talented people. Can you find a location that is without any computer nearby and make a call from there?"

Sarah held her composure. This indicated something very serious.

"Yes," she said. "I have a friend with an apartment not too far from here."

"Good. Please go there now, if you can. When you get there, call this number." Richter read out a telephone number. "Advise the man who answers what your number is. He has no computers in his house, so he will then advise me in person of how to contact you, and I will then call you from another location which is just as secure."

"Good grief, Conrad, this sounds terrible."

"It is, we all know of people who have been murdered in this insane war against our industry, so we must take no chances."

"It will take me half an hour." Without further words, Sarah hung up her telephone and left the office. She had the keys to her friend's apartment from a time when she had played nursemaid following heart surgery, and within half an hour, she was calling the number Conrad had given her. A man answered, said nothing but "Yes" and she read out the telephone number of the apartment. The call was disconnected.

Ten minutes later, the phone rang.

"This is Sarah," she said.

"Let me tell you what I have done," said Richter. "As I told you, I was previously in Military Intelligence, and I have excellent contacts. I have been given some invaluable information. The first was a contact to Allen Miller."

"Yes, you told us. He's reputed to be the world's greatest hacker."

"That one. I talked to him yesterday. He knows all about this situation and works closely with a detective in Australia, a Chief Inspector Melanie Carter. He has agreed to help our little operation. The first thing he is doing is downloading his own personal security firewall to the computers of our equivalent officers in Toronto, New York and ourselves. After today, we will be able to liaise without fear of being hacked."

"If Miller developed it, I can believe that," said Sarah.

"And now the other information. First, what we already knew, is that the electronic voice distraction can be reversed, once we can identify the software used. The voices used in the kidnappings have so far proved impossible, but I wonder if those used in the murders were done with more standard software. So can you contact the police stations in the UK and the USA that have received such calls and have the recordings sent to you?"

"I can get the UK ones, I'm sure Tom Fisher in New York can get one or more of the American calls."

"Good. My one-time colleagues then tell me they have some of finest voice analysis experts in the world, just as all operations like MI6, CIA, and ASIO have. They will analyse the voices and find some invaluable information."

"Conrad, this is amazing. When does Miller expect to have his firewall downloaded to us?"

"He said two days. I'll contact you when he tells me it's done. Now I think we both have to get back to our offices."

Sarah disconnected the call and did just that.

10th March, 2026, a Global Zoom call

A week later, Fisher in Blackwood's New York office, Copeland in Counsellors' Toronto office, Sarah Jensen in Manchester and Richter in Berlin, all at their desks with their office doors locked, looked at each other's faces in a Zoom call.

Another outline of a face appeared on their screens, the features blanked out.

"Good evening," said a pleasant, male voice. "My name is Dieter, you don't need any more, and I'm the analyst who examined the recordings you sent me. Let me tell you about each."

The four security officers answered the greetings with minimal words.

"Before I tell you about these men, and they are all men, it's interesting to note that they have a prepared script. The wordings of their calls are similar. Now let me show you.

"First, the two American recordings. One came from Detroit, though there were traces of influences from Buffalo, St Louis and Chicago. However, he was certainly a long-time resident of Detroit and still lives there. He's Caucasian, between thirty and forty-five, average education and sounds like he spent some time in the military, judging by his mannerisms. Let me play his restored voice for a few moments."

The sound of the recording came though the speakers in all their offices and lasted just a minute or two. None of the listeners showed any reaction.

"The second has had a much wider geographical exposure, though was originally in San Francisco. He has lived around the USA, nowhere long enough to have much impact on his accent, but I can say he spent some time, probably between two and four years in prison. He's about the same age as the previous candidate, but he's definitely African-American."

Again, a man's voice was played, again no reaction from the listeners.

"The third is younger, late twenties, obviously a Canadian accent but he's an immigrant, probably at a young age, estimated early teens and his origin is Pakistan. I haven't yet placed exactly where, that will take a little longer. However, he is well-educated, the data indicates British Columbia, with university experience from Ontario, probably Southern Ontario, so perhaps university in Hamilton, London, Waterloo, unlikely to be further east, so not Toronto."

Another man's voice sounded for a minute. All the listeners could hear the mix of Canadian accent with overlays of a distinctive Pakistani tone.

"The next is British, originally from the West Country, probably Cornwall, though that accent is overlaid with Midlands, Black Country to be exact. Estimated age much like the others, thirties, early forties. Education no higher than High School. The interesting thing about this man is that he suffered severe trauma in childhood. It's obvious from the graphs of his voice, it's a common indication."

As the new voice came from the speakers, Sarah Jensen began to show a reaction.

"Dieter, keep it going," she called, and the voice continued for a further five minutes before Sarah called for it to stop.

"I know that man," she said. "His name is Derek Wilson, known as Mumbles. I arrested him in

Manchester about ten years ago for causing Grievous Bodily Harm to his girlfriend."

"Why Mumbles?" asked Copeland.

"In serious stress, like when he was arrested, he tended to mumble an old nursery rhyme and switch off from what was happening, to the point of becoming catatonic."

"That's exactly the reaction we could expect from a sufferer of severe trauma as a child," said Dieter. "It's quite common."

"This is a major breakthrough," said Sarah. "We now know one of the killers. We have to find him."

"Could you contact your old department in the Greater Manchester Police?" asked Fisher. "Would they help? After all, it's been ten years since you left."

"Probably," said Sarah. "When I was an Inspector, I dated a fellow officer, also an Inspector for a very nice two years. We're still in touch and he's a Superintendent now. I'm sure he'll help, especially as he'll get the credit for an arrest of a serial killer. I'll call him."

"In that case, I'll say goodbye," said Dieter and the shadow face vanished from their screens before any of them could say anything.

14th March, 2026, A House in Old Trafford, Manchester

"He's a killer, so it's a safe bet he's armed," said Sarah.

"That's why I've loaned you half a dozen Fire-Arms Officers and why you and I are wearing flak jackets," said the Superintendent standing next to her. They were round the corner from the house, out of sight of any of the windows. The black van that had carried them there was parked a few metres further away. Six officers in black protective gear, full helmets and shields, carrying automatic rifles stood in line, waiting for orders. A few curious faces peered out of nearby windows, but the armed police had encouraged everybody away from the street.

"I'll never be able to thank you enough," said Sarah.

"No need," said the Superintendent. "If you're right, this is a serial killer, part of a global operation and we need to get him. So remember what we agreed. If we get him, you can interrogate him first. But from what it said in his file, this Mumbles bloke may not be able to say anything. If that's the case, we take him back to the nick, get him sedated and then we'll try again. Have you still got that sexy blue and white dress I liked so much? Good, wear that, hair down, perfume, all that seductive stuff to try and make him feel safe and keep him sane. Okay?"

Sarah nodded and the police officer gave a short gesture to the line of armed officers. They ran round the corner, two of them advanced to the door of the house and banged hard.

"Police! Open up!" called one. Nothing happened. The first man nodded and the second swung a heavy ram at the door lock, crashing it open. The armed officers entered the house, shouting loudly, "Armed Police. Get down on the floor."

Two of them raced up the stairs, continuing the shout, then changed it to "Clear," as each room was checked.

Down on the ground floor, the same procedure was in operation, then stopped as one of them called, "Sir! In the living room."

Sarah and the Superintendent walked into the back of the house to see a tall, heavily-built man sitting in an armchair, his legs pulled up to his chest and his arms folded round his knees in a classic foetal position. His eyes were closed and he seemed to be whispering to himself. Sarah moved closer to him until she could just make out the words.

"Little Bo-Peep has lost her sheep and doesn't know where to find them," she heard, and the words continued the rest of the ancient nursery rhyme, repeating when the speaker reached the end.

"We'll get nothing from this one today," said Sarah. "Let's bring him in."

The Superintendent nodded and two of the FAOs hauled the man from his armchair and lifted him bodily out of the house and to the black van.

"He's had twenty-four hours of gentle care, good food and I've fed him a fair quantity of sedatives," said the doctor as Sarah returned the next afternoon, after getting a call from the police station. She had followed the advice, let her hair down, wore a feminine blue and white dress, put on make-up and used a quality perfume on her neck and arms, all in an attempt to provide a calming environment.

"In there," said the Superintendent, pointing at a door. "He'll be alone for you, but there'll be two big blokes by the door outside. There's a hidden microphone and camera in the ceiling, any sound from you, they'll be in there like a rat up a drainpipe. And we'll be watching on the video next door. Good luck."

Sarah took a deep breath and entered the interview room. Derek Wilson was sitting in an armchair, looking relaxed. This was not the usual interview scene, but Sarah understood why this was so. She had read Wilson's file the night before and knew his dreadful history. At nine, his father had died in a road accident and a year later, his mother married again. Wilson's stepfather had been a violent man, subjecting the child to regular beatings and within weeks, Wilson had been forced to watch as his step-father killed his mother with a vicious punch to the head which had knocked her down, banging her head on the corner of the coffee table, which had caused her instant death. The boy had not spoken again for two years, and only intensive psychiatric treatment had restored him to any degree of normalcy.

"Hello, Derek," she said and took the second armchair in the room.

Wilson looked at her, showing no reaction. Sarah was relieved that he didn't seem to recognise her as the officer who had arrested him ten years before.

"My name is Sarah and I'd like to talk to you. Do you know where you are?"

"Police station in Manchester," said Wilson. His voice was indistinct, almost sleepy.

"And do you know why?"

"I've killed a few people."

Oh my, thought Sarah. *That was unexpected.* "And why did you do that?"

"Because they killed my sister."

"Your sister? How did they do that?"

"She was just a toddler and she got ill. The doctors gave her drugs, but she died."

That wasn't in the file, thought Sarah. "Can you tell me more?"

"My mother said they gave her a pill that didn't work."

"And what happened?" Sarah felt unsure about this line of questioning. It might send him off into the fugue state again.

"She began screaming in pain. I tried to help her, she was my baby sister, but I couldn't. My bastard stepfather didn't do anything, so I called an ambulance, but she died before..."

Wilson stopped, drew his knees up to his chest again and began mumbling.

"Little Bo Peep..."

The rest faded into an incoherent murmur and Wilson began rocking back and forth in his armchair.

"Oh shit," said Sarah and looked up at the camera. Within seconds, the door flung open, and the doctor rushed in. He looked over Wilson, opened his bag and filled a syringe, carefully injecting it into Wilson's arm. Within seconds, Wilson had calmed down, stopped mumbling, and lowered his feet to the floor again.

"Get close to him," said the doctor. "Maybe touch his cheek, let him smell your perfume, be the supportive female." He stood up and backed away into a corner of the room, watching closely.

Sarah did as suggested, knelt down by the side of Wilson's seat, stroked his cheek and leaned closer to him.

"It's okay, Derek, everything is fine, you're doing very well." She continued talking gently to him and after a few minutes, the tension in Wilson seemed to fade and he looked across to her face just inches from his.

"You're nice," he said.

"Thank you," Sarah replied and smiled. She stayed where she was, hoping that the closeness would keep him relaxed and communicative. "That must have been terrible, losing your baby sister like that. Is that why you hate the drug companies?"

He nodded, and tears began to run down his cheek. "They deserve to be punished."

"And did somebody tell you how to punish them?"

"Yes."

Holy shit, thought Sarah. *Is it going to be this easy?* "Who was it, Derek?"

"Dunno his name. He called me after I'd talked about it on a chat board with some other people. He said he knew who made that pill and that they lied to say it was safe. He told me who they were, and I killed them."

"How did he contact you, Derek?"

"On the internet. He gave me a special address that he said nobody would ever find."

"Do you still have that computer?"

"Yes."

Sarah could see that Wilson was almost asleep. But she had everything she could use. She stood up and walked out of the room. She was met by the Superintendent.

"I've sent people to the house to confiscate that computer. We'll see what it can tell us."

"Great." Sarah was feeling exhausted from the tension she had felt through the last few minutes. She needed to get home and go to sleep. "You'll call me when you have something?"

"Indeed," said the officer. "Go home, Sarah, while you can still drive."

Chapter 28

14th March, 2026, AFP HQ, Canberra

Two weeks after her return from Perth, after continual grinding work looking for clues to the series of killings, Melanie received a call.

"Melanie, you do understand that I care greatly for you and need to protect you as much as possible?"

Allen Miller's face had appeared in her monitor without her having to call for him. Things were fairly quiet in the office, little evidence had been found to point to the killer of the one-time Health Minister and the unit was engaged in mostly routine work.

Allen's comment surprised her and caused a small ripple of concern.

"Of course I do, Allen. What brought this on?"

"Please don't be offended," said Allen. "But after the last episode with Rob in Adelaide, I wanted to make sure."

The words sent a small shiver down her back. The last time she had done one of her sexual adventure weekends, she had met Rob and for a change, found him very appealing, enough that they had stayed together and become very close. Then he had been killed by a hired gun to try and scare her off further investigations of a criminal gang.

"Oh god, Allen, what have you done?"

"Please remember that you consented to my tracking your phone as a security in case of kidnap, as had happened before."

"Yes, Allen, I did."

"So I saw that you had flown to Perth, I saw the hotel you stayed at and the club you visited that first night."

"Yes, I understand. It's all a bit too close to home, but I recognise that I have been targeted by the bad guys before. But I can't see why this was really necessary."

"Bear with me, Melanie. This is critical. I went through the files of the taxi companies and found the hotel you had gone to. I also saw the name on the credit card of the man you went with."

"Allen, this is getting dangerously close to intrusion of my privacy. I am no longer comfortable with this."

"Be grateful that I did, Melanie. When I did, I checked the guest list, found the booking in the name of Daryll Hoskins and checked him out. There's a problem. It's a false identity."

"Not a huge shock, Allen. He was probably looking for the same as I was, a casual night of steamy sex without risking a wife finding out."

"Probably. But I want you to do something for me. I have the recordings of the distorted voice that has called you a couple of times to mock your efforts to find the Minister's killer and as you know, I have the software to return the voice to its normal one. I'm going to play one of them. Tell me what you think."

"If you must, Allen, but I think you're being a bit paranoid."

"Quite likely, but bear with me."

From the computer's loudspeaker, came a man's voice.

Melanie turned cold.

"That's the man in Perth, Daryll," she said, her throat tight with tension.

"That's what I was worried about," said Allen. "It was not a casual pickup. He had found your travel schedule and was watching you. And either he or the people running him have got serious computer hacking skills. Things have got nasty, Melanie."

Thee's two

Chapter 29

16th March, 2026, AFP HQ, Canberra

Melanie carefully switched off her PC and disconnected it from the power source.

"Just being careful," she said. "Whoever is behind all this appears to have some of the hacking skills of Allen Miller. We don't want him or her or them listening in to this. Allen says he's downloading his own software firewall to this computer, but until he confirms he's done it, we'll play safe."

"Agreed," said Jack Savage. He sat comfortably in the armchair in Melanie's office, cradling a mug of coffee. He was dressed informally, like a man who hadn't worn a suit or a tie in some years. Seated more formally in the chair that normally sat across from Melanie's desk but had been moved to make communications with Jack simpler, was Alex Welland.

"Jack," continued Melanie. "This is becoming bigger than Ben Hur, certainly bigger than anything we have tackled in the past."

"Better fill me in, then," said Jack.

Melanie nodded and consulted the sheaf of notes on her desk.

"So far, whoever is behind all this, at least in Australia, we know that he has boasted to me about the murders of one-time Health Minister, Avery Sheldon, the killing of Kyle Fleming, the CEO of Blackwood

Harding, a major pharmaceuticals company, and Felix Honneger in Byron Bay, a research chemist with another pharmaceuticals company. In the call to me to announce the events, he said the killings were for revenge against the entire industry for causing the deaths of hundreds of people through failings in quality control of their products and then the cover-ups of their responsibility."

"It's curious that he's called you about all these events," said Savage. "He's said that he had some knowledge about our first case of a serial killer. But boasting to the cop that solved that case, knowing the risk he must take, that's a bit psychotic."

"He was happy to tell me," said Melanie. "And not just happy, he was positively eager to tell me."

"So he's keen to publicise this," said Jack. "That's some ego in play. That's three countries involved in this war of revenge. Presumably there are more?"

"That's why I'm glad you're involved, Jack," said Melanie. "We've had reports of three similar events in the USA. One of those was a mass killing of several people employed by one company who died when their boat was blown up off Honolulu. There were three other people who had some connection with the pharma industry, directly as employees or indirectly in distribution agencies or regulatory bodies."

"Have you had calls about those?"

Melanie shook her head. "No, but the information was passed to us from MI6 who themselves had been informed by the FBI when the police in those locations informed them, as they felt there was a national conspiracy in the making."

"Very intelligent of them," said Jack. "Are all the agencies sure that these are the total killings?"

"No, they're not," broke in Alex. "The problem is that there are many murders committed in the last year or so and we don't know how many, if any are connected to this revenge war. I've spent some midnight oil researching every killing in the UK in the last few years to see if any of the victims were in any way connected to the pharma industry, so far without luck. So, it's possible that this is a recent development."

"Nothing in any other country?" asked Jack.

"Can't say," said Alex. "I'm limited by language, can't work in anything but English. I did have a look at New Zealand but found nothing there."

"Good work," said Jack with an approving nod. "Presumably the voices have been recovered to the original state. Have they been identified for nationality, region, etc, and has there been only one in the UK?"

"The cops in Britain have a good contact, one of the security officers in Fremont Sims who used to be in German security. He had the recorded voices from the UK killings analysed," said Melanie. "So far, it's just one voice. But it gave a major breakthrough. The security officer of the UK company who used to be a police detective, recognised him as somebody she arrested ten years earlier. She still had contacts with the local cops and they were able to arrest and interrogate this man, somebody called Derek "Mumbles" Wilson for some reason. They took his computer and Allen is trying to break through into the Dark Web to identify his contacts."

"And in the US?"

Melanie shook her head. "Allen tells me that their German officer, the ex-Military Intelligence man had his old department examine the US recordings as well. Initially, they were blocked, just as Allen was, but they eventually found the key and reported on several American profiles, but not detailed enough to identify them."

"Can you ask your department to request those recordings? It might help us."

Melanie nodded. "Let me tell you about something that happened to me quite recently," she continued. "It supports the claim of criminal activities by the industry."

She quickly related the story told to her by Doctor Ramesh Sengupta. "It's not just selling of untested products, or the falsification of testing data in order to get approval to market, what the doctor said was that even after being found out, these companies have renamed the product and continued to sell in less-controlled regions, usually in third-world countries."

The expression of disgust was obvious on Alex's face. "Sounds like a case of negligent homicide," he said. "Could even be manslaughter."

"A good description." Jack looked equally dismayed. "But I doubt if such a charge could be brought against those massive organisations, without starting a global war that the companies would spend many millions defending. I hate to say it, but I could almost feel sympathy with whoever is conducting this war."

"Jack, I need to tell you," said Alex. "I've told my boss this, but I do have some genuine reasons to feel sympathy."

Quickly, he related the history of his wife's cousin and her death from a drug supposed to cure her.

Melanie nodded. "Yes, Alex told me and I do have sympathy."

"Yes, that's a horrible story. It could provide mixed feeling," said Jack.

"Almost, but not quite," said Melanie. "Just as well the pc is disconnected and switched off. It wouldn't help to have those comments released to the world."

"Probably," said Jack. "So where do we go from here?"

"We do our jobs. We look for whoever is doing this in Australia, and we coordinate with the cops in other countries where this is happening. Jack, any thoughts on what's driving these people?"

"Could be a variety of impulses," said Jack. "The one who called you said he was focussing on you because he knew somebody involved in one of our past cases. Whether he's the one driving the global process is unlikely, so I suspect whoever that one is, it could be somebody with a straight-forward desire to punish criminal behaviour. Or it could be somebody with a tendency to multiple murder and has found a way to justify it. So if you can get the recordings from the police organisations in the US and Britain, I can try and determine the psychologies of the speakers."

"I'll get that in motion," said Melanie.

"Then I'll get back to work," said Alex and stood up.

"I'll start reviewing any similar events and the results of examining the guilty parties." Jack also rose to his feet and gathered up his notes.

"Let's do lunch at one," said Melanie and bent down to plug in her pc and connect to the network. She gave a small wave as the two men left the office.

"Back in the world again, eh?" said the familiar voice from the pc. "That must have been an important meeting if you disconnected the computer. Anyone I know?"

Melanie said nothing and suppressed the cold disgust she felt at knowing who this man was.

"Ah, the silent treatment, eh, Melanie? Well, I can understand that. So let me tell you what faces you from here on. We're going to punish the pharma bastards a hell of a lot more. The killings will increase in the coming weeks and we're going to tell the newspapers and the tv stations why they're happening and just how useless the cops have been at finding out who the culprits are. Your life is going to be intolerable, I can assure you."

"You said you've been following the previous cases of serial killers I've had," said Melanie. "So you'll know that I solved those and we got the killers. We already know more about you than you realise. So I assure you, we'll get you eventually."

"No chance. You think my people can't evade you dumb plods?"

Even with the distortion, Melanie heard the irritation in the other speaker.

"This is wasting my time," she said and broke off the conversation. She switched off the pc and hand-wrote a request to her boss to speed up the acquisition of the American recordings and any analysis the police had conducted of those voices. She shook off the feeling of needing a shower after talking to the man she knew as Daryll Hoskyns.

Chapter 30

30th March, 2026, Port Macquarie, NSW, Australia

"Most likely a baseball bat," said the Medical Examiner. "Hit from behind, judging by the angle of the blow, just behind the right ear. It's a female, about forty to fifty, very healthy, expensive clothing and this happened between four and six hours ago, so perhaps midnight to four this morning. It's been a warm night, so I can't be more accurate."

He stood up and handed a woman's handbag to the police officer standing next to the body in the large gazebo that had been erected over the scene. Detective Sergeant Alana Trent opened it and looked inside.

"So robbery was not the motive, it seems," she said and pulled out a purse. "Over a hundred dollars in there." She passed the notes to her colleague. "Bag that, will you Rod," she said and continued searching the contents of the handbag. "Two credit cards, one Visa, one American Express, both in the name of Teresa Mayhew, a driving licence in the same name, an address in South West Rocks. Oh, and what's this? A security badge for a company here in Port, Davenport Medical Research. Sounds like it's her own operation. Okay, we'll follow up."

"I'll have the postmortem done by this afternoon," said the doctor. "I doubt it will give any other cause of death, but we'll follow the protocols."

"Thanks, Doc," said the detective and they all left the gazebo into the pleasantly cool air of early morning on the ocean's edge. Trent nodded at the two men standing nearby and they entered the gazebo with a stretcher to remove the body.

* * *

4th April, 2026, Geelong, Victoria

"A heavy blow with a wrench or similar metallic object," said the Medical Examiner, standing by the body on the inspection table in the mortuary. "No other signs of violence, no other cause of death. The victim is Richard Taylor, male, about sixty, well preserved but a few kilos overweight, good quality clothing, a man of some wealth."

"And his home is in a wealthy area, also, according to his driver's licence" said the police inspector standing a few feet away. "It wasn't robbery, his wallet had over two hundred dollars in it."

"Unusual," said the doctor. "You sent somebody to call the home?"

"I did," said the Inspector and looked up at the observation balcony where a young, uniformed police officer had just appeared. "Tony, what have you got?"

"There was nobody at the house," said the officer. "But the next-door neighbour came out when they saw the patrol car. Richard Taylor is divorced, lives alone, retired. He was the owner of a chain of pharmacy stores in every state, sold out to a pharmacy manufacturing company last year."

"Thanks, Tony," said the Inspector. "This is weird," he continued. "No motive, nothing. But we've had a circular, all-stations, advise the Feds, particularly a Chief Inspector Carter, God knows why. And there's a secondary thing. Apparently, we may get a phone call through the computer, electronically disguised, boasting about being the killer. If we do, we have to record the voice and send that to this Carter bloke."

"Beats me," said the doctor. "Okay, I'll write up the report and send it to you."

"Thanks," said the detective. He signalled up to the officer in the observation balcony and left the morgue.

* * *

8th April, 2026, Vaucluse, NSW, Australia

The heat was growing as the four children ran onto the beach.

"This is the best time," shouted the young girl. She was about twelve, like the other three. "Last one into the water is a silly sausage!"

All of them dropped their towels onto the sand and raced towards the water's edge. But they got no further than knee-deep when they stopped, frightened by the sight before them.

The woman's body barely floated in the shallow water, her arms and legs dragging in the sand. Slowly, the four children backed away, returned to the dry beach and stood silently again. Then the girl who had led the group found her bag, extracted her mobile phone and made a call.

* * *

"It's a different voice," said Melanie. They had been loaned a private house for this conference call, the home of the friend of Melanie's boss in a suburb of Canberra. Melanie had not felt they were secure in her office, even with the pc disconnected from the internet and power source.

"What have you found?" asked Jack.

"The call to the Port Macquarie cops was by a man in his early thirties," said Melanie. "He's local, in that region between Coffs Harbour and Newcastle and not much inland. Educated probably to high school graduation level but not widely read. He was nervous when he called the police station, not much boasting or any reasons given for killing, he cut it short."

"And the Geelong killing?" asked Jack.

"Similar profile," replied Melanie. "But not a local. The voice analyst thought he – and it was a he again, was actually from Perth, quite young, probably late twenties, not all that well educated. But he was boastful, obviously wanted to take credit for the war against the pharma companies. The station let him ramble on, so we got a good-length recording."

"And the last?"

"No call about the woman in Vaucluse. We've identified her, Marylin Chambers, aged thirty-five, married, no children. Worked as a marketing manager, successfully so, with a pharmacy company in Sydney, the Australian branch of Consellors, the international firm with its HQ in Toronto. That's the second victim of Consellors, the first one being Felix Honneger who was killed in Byron Bay some time ago."

"And not the same voices as heard in the UK," said Jack. "So we can safely conclude that there's a war against the entire pharmaceutical industry, it's being run by individual groups in Australia, the UK and the USA, though there is almost certainly a leader. Any further developments with the Americans?"

"Six killings reported so far," said Melanie. "All people associated with the industry, one way or another. Three different killers identified by region so far, but nothing strong enough to point to any specific individuals."

"And it's being done cleverly," said Jack. "None of the crime sites have provided any clue, so the killers have learned or been instructed in the use of clothing and techniques to hide all indicators."

"It's a problem," agreed Melanie. "And we're getting abused in the media, though we've tried to keep the details quiet. So it's obvious that the bloke who called me is doing what he promised, telling the media all about this. It's not helping us."

"Of course," said Jack. "But we've been here before. Remember the prime rule of detecting; most crimes are solved because the criminal makes a mistake. Keep investigating, we'll get a breakthrough eventually."

"I know," said Melanie. "But it terrifies me thinking of how many more people will die before we break this."

"Stay focused," said Jack. "And send me every recording you get."

* * *

April 2026, The Sydney Morning Herald

Australian Doctor killed in Zimbabwe

News has been received of the brutal slaying of Doctor Ramesh Sengupta in Zimbabwe. Doctor Sengupta who arrived in Australia with his family as a schoolboy and graduated from Sydney University as a medical doctor. The doctor had dedicated his life to working in third-world countries, treating the poor and under-privileged. He was found dead outside his surgery early one morning, killed by several severe blows with what appeared to be a machete. No motive for the senseless killing has been identified.

The headline leapt out at Melanie as she sipped at her morning coffee. The shock spilt a few drops on the desk, and she put the mug down carefully.

"Oh god, could I have saved him?" she said aloud. "Should I have warned the Zimbabwe authorities of his history with the pharmacy companies?"

A few minutes later, she had calmed down enough to call Jack to tell him of the tragedy.

"Nothing you could have done," said Jack. "For a start, the Zimbabwe authorities would have found out about those events as part of their background checks. And second, you could never have tied in the pharma mob, there would have been no direct link between them and the killers. They'd have just hired local thugs without telling them why they wanted the doctor dead. It's just another episode in this horrible story."

"I'm not sure that helps, but I know you're right," said Melanie. "It just makes me more determined to nail these bastards."

"Keep that thought," said Jack.

With standard farewells, the conversation was terminated. It took Melanie another hour before she could get herself back to work.

Chapter 31

15ᵗʰ April, Zoom Call between Manchester, Toronto, New York and Berlin

"The war is heating up and the body count is climbing." The distress in Tom Fisher's voice was evident.

"It's terrible," said Sarah Jensen. She too displayed huge stress in her voice.

"Are you all aware of the same killings that I've heard of?" asked Jerry Copeland.

"What have you learned?" asked Sarah.

"Three killings," said Copeland. "Ten days ago, Mary Louise James in Dallas. She was the State marketing director for my company, aged forty-two. Eight days ago, Eduardo Arias in Los Angeles. He was thirty, a researcher in the laboratories of an independent research company. Yesterday, Steven Young, aged fifty, the financial officer for a small pharma company called Holbrook Pharmaceuticals. They specialised in copying drugs as they came off the patent protection and immediately producing copies. All were found early in the morning, all killed by a heavy blow to the head, most likely with a baseball bat, The local police stations received identical calls in the electronic voices we have grown to hate, scoffing at police failures to find the killers.

"And we got news that Australia is suffering the same epidemic," said Sarah. "For some reason, Australia is getting serious attention from their killers, apparently there is a woman detective in their Federal Police who is getting particular attention, a Detective Chief Inspector called Melanie Carter."

"I know something of that," broke in Konrad Richter in Berlin. "But before we go into that, I have some positive news."

"Some good news at last?" said Fisher.

"I believe so," said Richter. "The technical wizards at the Military Intelligence operations have broken the code for the electronic distortion and the voice has been analysed. It is a male, aged between thirty and fifty, university education, lived mostly in Buffalo, New York, but probably had some time in the Navy."

"I suppose that's a help," said Sarah. "But too big a population to identify a specific man and he may not live in the Buffalo area anyway."

"But I can help a lot more," said a new voice from the computers of the group.

"Holy shit, Allen Miller?" Fisher was almost laughing, whether from shock or delight was unclear. "How long have you been listening in?"

"A while," said Miller. "I wanted to talk to all of you because I have critical information. You took the computer from that Mumbles character and plugged it into the police system in Manchester, which was most thoughtful of you. I found it and got into it, looking for connections to Wilson. I must admit, the blocks to the dark web were not easy, but suddenly I recognised a procedure I had developed myself years ago and then

I was able to work it out from there. Eventually I identified who was the contact for Mumbles and two others who have also taken part in this war."

"My god, you know they are?" Copeland had stood up, so great was his surprise.

"I do," said Miller. "I couldn't pin down the precise location, as in an address, but close enough to you to take it further. Take these details down. The coordinator in the UK is a Victor Hill, somewhere in the Fallowfield area of Greater Manchester. One of the killers is Barrie Metcalf, in Swindon, the second is Donald Cartland in Solihull, near Birmingham. You can find them fairly easily, I imagine."

Sarah was already on the telephone to her friend, the Superintendent.

Once again, a van filled with six fully-armed Fire-Arms Officers stopped near a house in the Greater Manchester region and the officers, all in black clothing, bullet-proof jackets and helmets and carrying automatic rifles exited and advanced on the house. Two went round the back and the others repeated the standard operation of first banging on the door and when no response was heard, broke in. Sarah and her colleague followed.

The search didn't take long.

"Sir," called one of the officers. "In the back living room."

Sarah entered the room, feeling much trepidation. At first, she saw nothing until she reached the large, luxurious couch, and the sight made her gasp. A man lay stretched out, one arm across his chest, the other dangling to the floor. The bullet hole in his forehead was a perfect red hole.

One of the officers removed his glove and touched the dead man's body.

"Still some warmth," he said. "Dead within the hour, I suspect."

* * *

The police van filled with six Fire-Arms Officers stopped beside the patrol car outside the house on the outskirts of Swindon and the armed men leaped out. Two ran to the back, four followed the Police Inspector and Sergeant from the patrol car and then left them by the front gate and moved to the front door. A few loud bangs on the door and it was then smashed down under the heavy blows of the ram.

Just a few second later, they stared down at the corpse lying on his back on the kitchen floor. The bullet hole in his forehead was a perfect red circle.

The police Inspector touched the dead man's neck.

"Still some warmth," he said. "Dead within the hour, I'd say. Call the team in Manchester, will you, Harry?"

* * *

In an expensive, detached house in the wealthy area of Solihull, north of Birmingham, a crowd of curious onlookers stared from a safe distance when the black-clad AFOs forced their way into the house.

In the lounge room at the rear of the building, the team of police stared down at the body in the armchair. A perfect red hole was in the dead centre of the forehead. The television was still on, showing a police drama with Inspector Frost talking to a medical examiner over the covered corpse on the examination table.

The police Inspector who had followed the AFOs into the house touched the dead man's neck.

"Still some warmth," he said. "Dead within a couple of hours, I suspect. Call the team in Manchester, will you, Sergeant? And somebody turn that television off."

* * *

Manchester, England

The postal delivery came as usual, on the dot of ten in the morning. The postman dropped off the large bag of envelopes, waved at the young man in the office and walked out. Jerry Greene began sorting through the pile. Most were the standard envelopes containing invoices. He put those together to hand to the Accounts Payable clerk. There were fewer and fewer of those each month as suppliers sent the invoices through the computer, but it still kept a clerk working all morning, each day. There was some advertising material, Jerry put those to one side. One envelope was unusual, a large, brown container with several sheets inside. It was addressed to the Chief Executive Officer. Jerry used a knife to open up the sealed side and extracted the documents. The first one made him gasp in dismay.

The full sheet was a colour print of a man sitting on a chair, bound at his chest by thin rope, his legs also bound to the chair legs. His arms were free, holding a newspaper. Jerry saw it was a copy of the Guardian, the headline he recognised as from two days ago. The man's face showed serious terror. The worst part was that he knew the man. It was the company's Chief Executive Officer, Floyd Morris. Jerry had met the top executive of the American firm of Fremont Sims when he had arrived the previous week to conduct a public relations tour of the British subsidiary.

The next sheet was a message, made up of words cut from a newspaper. It read:

"We have him. We will be in touch. The fee for his release will be twenty million pounds. If you go to the police, we will know, and he will be dead immediately."

His hands shaking, Jerry picked up the phone.

* * *

"Seems like your recruits don't always obey you, doesn't it?" said Melanie before the caller on her pc could speak. Already, she felt a crawling disgust at knowing that she had spent a wild night of sex with this man. She hoped she could keep her voice calm and unemotional.

"What the hell are you talking about?" Even with the electronic distortion, Melanie could hear the irritation in the caller's voice.

"I very much doubt you killed Neal Butcher because he obeyed you by executing Mr Sully in the way you ordered him to. Out of interest, did you kill him yourself or did you have another of your recruits do it?"

"You think I'd tell you that? Do you think I'm stupid?"

"Well now, that's a leading question," said Melanie with a laugh. She could sense the growing anger in the man and resolved to keep up the pressure. In her extensive experience of interrogating suspects, she had found that they made mistakes when angry. She was well along that path now and was taking extra pleasure in doing damage to this man.

"Let's have a look," she continued. "Your recruit, Neal Butcher is so keen to play with his toy that he had upgraded for the purpose, that he adds the nine-millimetre automatic to the heavy-lifter drone, fits a device to pull the trigger and uses that to kill Sully. That was clearly stupid because a couple of kids saw the shooting..."

She heard the indrawn breath from the distorted voice. "You didn't realise that we identified Neal as the drone pilot? Did you not realise that we would search his home when he went missing? So it's obvious why you had him killed. You've been pretty good about preventing clues being left at the scene of crime, all the protective clothing, gloves, masks, shoe coverings, but Neal's ego has fucked that up, well and truly, eh?" Melanie let out a deliberate laugh.

There was only silence from her pc monitor.

"And now I see you've branched out into new activities," Melanie continued.

"What the hell are you talking about?"

"Kidnapping now, I see. Your first one in Manchester was quite well done, almost professional. Actually, more professional than I would have expected of you."

"What? I told you before, we've got nothing to do with any kidnappings."

Interesting, thought Melanie. *Does he not know about this?*

"So was that not your operation? You may have a problem if somebody else is starting to play your game. So, Daryll, how do you plan to proceed?"

"What the hell? My name's not Daryll." The anger in the voice was undeniable now.

"No, I know it's not, but it's the name you used on a credit card when we met in Perth. We know that, we know what you look like. How long before we get you, do you think? And what about the new players in the game? What do you plan to do about them? They could really mess up your operation."

There was only silence from the pc.

"This call hasn't gone like you intended, has it Daryll?" said Melanie. "There you were, planning on boasting about another unsolvable killing, and it's all gone sour, hasn't it?"

"You'd better watch your mouth, woman," said the ugly voice. "You won't get me, and I have a lot more people to kill. I'm going to speed up the program, so get used to the idea that you've caused the early death of quite a few people. I'm winning this war, and the drug companies have a lot to pay."

The connection was cut, leaving Melanie with mixed emotions. Taunting the killer would pay off, she knew, but his closing words were all too horribly true. But if he wasn't responsible for the kidnapping of the executive in England, who was?

* * *

Windsor, NSW, Australia

Irene Keogh and her supervisor, Jane Harper worked late that day in the research laboratories. It was past nine and quite dark when they walked out of the building to the parking lot at the back. The lighting was not good, something that had been a cause for employee complaints over the years, but little had been done. Not even the capture and murder of William Goddard had persuaded management to upgrade the security systems.

"I'm always a bit frightened when we work late," said Irene. "I hate this walk into the parking lot."

"Try not to worry," replied Jane. "I doubt the bastards who did that would do it again. Anyway, think about what we achieved this evening. I think we cracked it." They approached their cars near the far end of the area. "Tomorrow we can report that we're ready for clinical trials. Hey, slow down a bit Irene, this old lady is hobbling a bit."

"Sorry, I'm just nervous," replied Irene. "How are you managing with that walking stick?"

"It takes practice," said Jane. "This damned hip sure makes walking a bit painful, but the stick helps. Getting old is a real bummer, Irene."

Four dark shapes leaped out from behind the van parked next to Jane's car. They seized the two women, held rags over their faces as they forced them into the van and slammed the door. Moments later, the van moved off, the two women barely conscious as they left the parking lot and joined the light traffic by the pharmaceutical plant.

Irene woke to full awareness first and lay still on the camp bed on which she found herself. But as the memories of being captured returned to her, she sat up and looked at Jane on a similar camp bed. She was just starting to show movement and opened her eyes.

"Jane, do you feel okay?" asked Irene.

The other woman took a few moments to gain full control of herself, then sat up also.

"More or less," she said. "Chloroform, eh? Who still uses chloroform?"

"Oh god, we've been taken just like William was," Irene muttered, a catch in her voice.

"Looks like it," replied Jane. "But I can't imagine why, unless they want the secret of our new drug. We're not the only people working on it. And we're not going to fetch all that much if they want a ransom."

Irene rummaged in the pockets of her coat. "Oh god, they've taken my phone. Have you got yours?" Tears were choking her voice.

Jane shook her head. "That would be the first thing they'd have done." Suddenly, she smiled, to Irene's astonishment. Mouthing the words very carefully, she indicated "Don't speak." She pointed at her ears and then around the room. Irene immediately understood that Jane thought they were being overheard through hidden microphones, and she nodded. The smile puzzled her, but she knew Jane well and she had obviously thought of something.

The door opened and a man walked in. His face was hidden by a full mask, leaving only eyes and mouth visible.

"Good evening, ladies," he said.

"Why have you taken us," demanded Jane. "What do you plan on doing?"

"Please do not panic," said the man. "We have requested a fee for your release, and I am sure that your company will pay it quickly. We know the work you do and how valuable it is."

"You're the same bastards that took William Goddard, aren't you," snapped Jane. "And you killed him. So why the hell should we believe anything different from you?"

Irene felt astonished at her colleague's courage in challenging the man. She felt overwhelmed with fear and knew she could never have done anything like this.

The masked man took a step backward, obviously shocked at Jane's attack.

"Mr Goddard disobeyed the rules, very foolishly. He took himself down that path, leaving us no alternative."

"Bullshit," snapped Jane. "You're nothing but a bunch of killers. You'll be caught eventually, and you'll all spend the rest of your miserable lives in prison."

The man seemed to recover his self-possession. "Please stay quiet, we will bring you food and drinks as required, and as soon as payment has been received, you will be released."

"We need water," said Jane.

"Of course," said the man and stood aside as another man, also wearing a mask entered with a jug of water and two glasses. He placed them on a small table, the only other furniture in the bare room, and walked out.

"There are blankets under your beds, you will be warm enough tonight." The man turned and left the room. There was a click of a lock being set and then silence.

Jane smiled again, raised her wrist and pointed at the watch. Irene understood immediately. Jane had bought that watch only a week ago after having it recommended by her doctor. She indicated to Irene and they stood up, moved close together and Jane brought the watch up to her lips. She pressed a button and waited. A few seconds later, a voice came from the watch. Jane smothered it almost entirely. Irene only caught the last few words, "... have an emergency?" and then Jane spoke.

"Irene, how are you feeling after the chloroform wore off?"

Understanding, Irene replied. "Not bad, Jane, but the ride in the back of the van was a bit bumpy. We've been kidnapped. Any idea where we are?"

"No," replied Jane, "but I don't think we're too far from the Windsor plant."

"Understood," said the voice from the watch.

"Good," said Jane and both women returned to their beds.

"I don't know how long that will take," said Jane. "But that was a great purchase."

In the emergency response at the hospital, the young woman who had answered the call from Jane's watch studied the screen in front of her, then pressed a button connecting her directly to the police unit.

"We have a kidnapping, two women, within the last two hours. The GPS pinpoints an address that is now on your screen. Strongly recommend an armed response."

"Acknowledged," said the voice in her ear and the connection was broken.

"Holy shit," said the young woman. "I've had some heart attacks, a few falls, never a kidnapping. They talked about this possibly happening in our training, but I didn't expect it. I hope the cops get the bastards who did it." She took a deep breath and returned to monitoring the system.

Just over an hour later, eight armed police officers rammed down the front door of the large house and raced in, shouting, "Armed Police" as they checked all the rooms in the two-storey building. In what looked like a dining room, five astonished men obeyed the instructions to lie on the floor and were handcuffed. At the back of the house, one room was locked. One officer banged on the door and shouted, "Is there anyone in there?"

"Just us chickens," replied a female voice. "We're the ones who set off the emergency alarm."

"Stand away from the door," said the officer. He called to his officer. "Sir, need the door-basher." A moment later, the officer carrying the ram gave just one slam at the door before it burst open to reveal two women standing against the far wall.

"What kept you?" said the older one.

The armed officer raised his mask and laughed.

"We stopped off for a coffee break," he said. "Would you ladies like a lift home?"

"Can you take us to our cars?" said Jane. "Where the hell are we, anyway?"

"Not far from where you were taken," replied the armed officer. "Just a few kilometres out of Windsor. We'll have you at your cars in fifteen minutes. But we'll need to talk to you about what happened."

Irene collapsed onto the floor, weeping hysterically. Jane bent down and put her arms round her shoulders.

"I don't think my friend can manage that. I'm going to take her to hospital first, she's suffering from severe shock. We'll come into the police station tomorrow."

The officer nodded. "That's fine. It's the station in Mileham Street. Come when you can. I'll call an ambulance for you."

Back in the dining room, the police Inspector leading the attack had his men haul the prisoners to a seating position.

"Identification?" he ordered.

Not one of the prisoners showed any response. The inspector nodded to his team, and they began a well-organised search of the house. It only took fifteen minutes while the Inspector stood over the captives, his handgun clearly on display.

The other officers returned, carrying documents.

"Passports," said one of them, handing over the haul to the Inspector who leafed through a few of them.

"South Korea?" said the Inspector. "What the hell is a mob of South Koreans doing in Australia kidnapping people from the pharmaceutical industry?"

There was no response from the men seated on the floor.

"There's a computer here too," said one of the searchers.

"That'll certainly be useful," said the Inspector. "Is the other bus here? Okay, get these bastards into it and bring that computer along, too. Let's get Forensics in to see what they can find."

Chapter 32

Somewhere in NSW

Floyd Morris stayed in a curious state of dropping in and out of consciousness for the duration of the ride in the back of the van. During each of the awake states, he checked his watch and when the van stopped, he worked out that he had been travelling for at least an hour, though he had no idea of how long he had been unconscious before he had been able to make the first check. It could have been a lot longer.

He concentrated on remembering what had happened to him. He had been visiting one of the company's largest European distributors in Reading, Berkshire when two men approached him as he opened the door to the rental car he had parked in the underground parking lot. Startled, he had lashed out and remembered that his fist had made contact with the face of one of the men, but not enough to break his hold. Then came the prick against the side of his neck with no memory after that before returning to awareness. He had no recollection of seeing what happened to Jim Burroughs, his security escort.

He was enough of a pharmacologist to ponder on how it had happened.

Probably Thiopentone, he thought. *So I hope they have a doctor with them to make sure I kept breathing while I was out. And I couldn't have got a full dose, or I'd still be out, so maybe that hit on the thug had some effect.*

Then he remembered the brief period of wakefulness, being tied to a chair with one hand free to hold a newspaper while a camera flashed. But he remembered nothing of being untied and returned to unconsciousness.

Must have a doctor with them, if they can control the anaesthetic that tightly, he thought.

He carefully sat up and saw that he was sitting on a simple camp bed, in a room empty of all decoration or comforts. It had bare walls and the only furnishings beside the bed were a chair and a table.

Goddam, I've been kidnapped. I should have listened to my security experts back in Chicago before I left. Don't go anywhere alone, they said. And Sarah, the Director of Security in Manchester, said the same. She'd been a police officer, she said.

He blacked out once more and when he returned to consciousness, another hour had passed. He calculated that over three hours had gone by since he was attacked in Reading. He saw the jug of water on the table and sank most of it before carefully walking to the door and checking it. It was no surprise to find it locked. He returned to the bed and sat on it. Something would happen soon, he knew.

He was correct. The door to his room opened ten minutes later and a man entered. Floyd was unsurprised that the man wore simple clothing, nothing outstanding or memorable, and his face was covered by a mask hiding all the features from forehead to chin. Floyd checked the skin he could see and saw that it was white but had a slight tinge to it. He couldn't identify it. The hair was jet black and stood up straight, like a brush. It reminded him of something, but he couldn't identify what.

"How are you feeling, Mr Morris?"

To Floyd's American ears, the voice sounded like a well-educated Englishman, perfectly spoken. He said nothing.

"Still a little unsteady, are you? Well, that is natural. You have been out for a while. Obviously, you want to know what is going on."

Floyd just stared at him. The mask stared back.

"We have sent a demand for twenty million pounds for your release to your company in Chicago. The money is to be paid in bitcoin, which you probably know is not a traceable transaction. As soon as we have received it, you will be released."

"Horse-shit," said Floyd.

The man took the one chair by the table, moved it to a short distance in front of Floyd and sat down.

"By that word, I assume you do not believe me?" he said.

Interesting, thought Floyd. *That's a common enough expression in the States and I doubt an Englishman would have difficulties understanding it. I've heard several say 'Bullshit' so it would be an obvious equivalent. What have we got here?*

"Quite correct," he said. "I don't believe you. And

you're talking crap. Our policy has long been that we wouldn't pay a ransom demand if this happened. Nobody is indispensable, regardless of how high on the corporate ladder they are."

"So you face your own death, Mr Morris? That is remarkable. However, I doubt that is the case. We know your record, we know how much you have increased sales and profits since you joined Fremont. Our ransom is just loose change to them. I am sure they will agree to have you returned."

The English is just too goddammed perfect. I've been here often enough in the last twenty years to know how English accents vary in just short distances and I don't think I have ever heard such perfect speech. It's not the pronunciation of Royalty, I've heard that, it's not the speech of the best British universities, we employ some of those in our Manchester plant. The nearest thing I've heard to this is in Singapore and Hong Kong where so many have learnt their English in top schools or in Britain. Is this a pointer to something?

"I think you'll be disappointed," said Floyd. "But do try. Obviously I'd prefer to stay alive, but I'll take what comes."

The other man said nothing, but left the room. Floyd heard the lock click as he left. He sat back on the bed, well aware of the sick sense of fear in his gut.

* * *

Chicago, Illinois

"We pay it," said the Chairman.

"Connor, that's totally against corporate policy." The Chief Financial Officer spoke calmly.

"I don't give a flying fuck about corporate policy." Connor Gates was almost spitting with fury. "Floyd has served us superbly over the years, massively increased sales and profits and you think we'll let him die because of corporate policy? He's been a great friend to all of us, he has a wife and three kids in Wilmette, you think we'll allow such a tragedy for a measly twenty or thirty million bucks? Shit, we could find that in loose change in the back of the furniture in the executive lounge."

There was silence round the conference table. Few people could face Connor Gates in this mood.

"Simon, see to it," said Gates. "At once."

The Chief Financial Officer nodded, and Gates rose to his feet and strode out.

"Thank God for that," said one of the board members.

There were murmurs of agreement as the rest of them left the room.

NSW, Australia

Floyd Morris barely slept for the next three days. Anxiety ate at his gut, wondering of these were the last few days of his life. He had alternative bouts of some confidence that surely the company would pay the ransom. Hadn't he done enough for Fremont over the years? The ransom was a fraction of the increased revenues he had generated. But he knew that the Chairman, Connor Gates was a stickler for rules and regulations and when he thought of that, Floyd's heart sank, not seeing anything flexible in the man. They had held a cool, distant relationship over the years, never friends, but there was mutual respect. He had no idea how much Gates thought of him, whether it was enough to save his life.

He thought of his beloved wife, Carol and three kids, two little boys and a girl, none over ten, in their home in Wilmette, a pretty suburb north of Chicago. Was he never going to take the kids to see the Chicago Cubs play at the stadium so near to their home? Would he never again take them flying in the Cherokee that he kept at the local airfield? They'd loved that, the eldest boy inheriting his father's passion for aviation, talking about joining the US Air Force when he was old enough.

The three days had been a nightmare. He could do nothing but lie on the camp bed. He was served three meals a day by a young man, also fully masked, nothing exotic, several times just fast food from a commercial outlet and weak tea. He was given no newspapers, nothing to read. He was allowed a toilet break when he banged on the door, but that told him nothing. The washroom was just a few yards down a corridor with three other doors. Floyd decided he was in a small house. The only sounds he heard were of jet aircraft. He listened to those intently, recalling his own dreams of one day flying a fighter jet. It hadn't happened, but he'd made do with a private pilot's licence and the delights of his own light aircraft. But the passion for aviation remained.

The door was unlocked and Floyd felt a tremor of fear. Was this it, the execution following Fremont's refusal to pay the ransom? He almost threw up and struggled for self-control, standing up to face his executioner like a man, showing no fear.

"Good news, Mr Morris," said the same man who had first spoken to him. "Your pessimism was unfounded. The ransom has been paid."

"What?" Floyd felt a wash of relief and he sat down on the hard wooden chair.

"We are going to take you back to where we first captured you. You will be blindfolded, we do not want you to know where you have been."

The young man who had brought in his meals entered and carefully tied a heavy blindfold across Floyd's eyes. Floyd managed to get a glimpse of his watch before his vision was cut off and then he was led out of the building, placed in a car and driven off. As he left, he heard the sounds of jet engines again.

When he was let out of the car, he checked. The ride had taken one hour and ten minutes, but he had no way of knowing if the drive had been direct or if a circuitous route had been taken to confuse him. But as his eyes recovered, he looked around. As promised, he was standing by the entrance to the distribution company he had visited before his capture. He walked in and to the reception desk.

The young man behind the desk gasped in shock.

"Mr Morris, thank god you're here. What happened? You look terrible. Can we help?"

"Would you call the police? What happened to Jim, my security guard? And is my car still here?"

"Jim is back in Manchester. Somebody found him lying by the car and called an ambulance. They kept him in hospital overnight, they said he'd been injected with an anaesthetic used for operations and was perfectly okay the next day. And the rental company came for the car when we called them about it."

Floyd nodded and took a seat in the reception area. At one point, he couldn't stop tears running down his face. The receptionist politely ignored him.

"About an hour's drive of here, maybe a little more," said Floyd. "But I have no idea of whether they took a direct route, so it could be much shorter."

"Is there anything about the building you can remember?" Detective Sergeant John Willis was clearly excited about being part of the team investigating the kidnapping.

"Not much," said Floyd. "I'd say it was a house, not a big one and not well furnished or decorated. I'd say

The Pharmacy Murders

it was unoccupied and maybe just rented out for a short term."

"Any sounds or indications you heard? Traffic going by, callers to the house? Telephones?"

Floyd smiled. "Yes, I have some really good stuff for you there."

Willis showed greater excitement.

"We were close to an airfield. It wasn't a conventional field because the only sounds were jet fighters, no light aircraft, no commercial airlines, nothing but jet fighters."

"How can you be sure of this, Mr Morris?"

"I've been an aviation freak since childhood, Sergeant. I spent hours as a kid, at the USAF site near my home. I've had a private licence since I was nineteen and I still spend hours when I can, watching fighters. So what I can tell you is that there were three different aircraft and their behaviour was distinct."

"Distinct? In what way?'

"If this was a military base of the Royal Air Force, there would be a series of take-offs by the same model plane, followed by silence, or one or two or perhaps a series of landings. Or there would have been several planes taking off and landing together in formation. What I heard was the sound of three different aircraft doing touch and go many times."

"Touch and go?"

"What you call circuits and bumps. Take off, fly round the circuit following all the procedures and

236

landing checks including communications with air traffic control, land, run along the runway for a bit, then open up the throttle and repeat. Do that several times. That's what trainee pilots do a lot, it's the best exercise for tightening up techniques. Lord knows, I've done enough of them."

"What does that tell you?"

"It could be a military flight school, but that would more likely be several planes of the same type doing constant circuits and bumps. This was only three models of different types. So either a very advanced fighter school with few pilots being trained, or..."

"Or what, Mr Morris?"

"An experimental site. Which means I know where it is."

Willis laughed. "Farnborough," he said. "I used to go there a lot as a kid, same as you, I loved watching aircraft."

"Farnborough," agreed Floyd. "Now, can you find me a hotel so I can clean up?"

Willis nodded and picked up the phone. "But first, let's find that house. Believe me, an empty house in that region is rare. I'll get our people to contact the estate agents and I'll bet we'll identify the house quickly."

"And call my company in Manchester."

Willis smiled. "Done, sir. They knew the money was being paid, but they hadn't heard what happened next. They're most relieved."

Several hours later, some sleep caught up, a shower and a change with a fresh shirt and underwear that the hotel management had been pleased to get him, and Floyd got a call.

"Detective Sergeant Willis, sir. We found the house, but absolutely no signs of who had occupied it. No fingerprints, no DNA, no accidently left possessions. They'd done a really professional job of cleaning up after themselves. That's a dead end, I'm afraid."

"To be expected, Sergeant. Thanks for the effort."

"We'll keep on the case."

* * *

Somewhere in Australia

The pc monitor flickered into life on the man's desk. The image shocked the man. It was a full-face mask, covering all the features from forehead to chin.

"Who the hell are you?" blurted out the man, deeply shaken. "And how the hell did you get this address?"

"Do you think you are the only people with advanced computer skills?" said the mask. The voice was slightly modified, quite human but the listener could not tell whether it was male or female.

"What?" Shock was joined by fear.

"We really must congratulate you and your team," said the mask. "Killing off all those nasty people in the pharmaceutical industry? What a splendid operation."

The man said nothing, but he felt the hair rise on the back of his neck and along his arms. *Who the hell could know about me? Only that woman cop knows that it's an operation run by a team, but she can't access this computer. Who the hell is this?*

"You have gone silent? Well, I am not surprised, it must be a shock to find somebody else is playing in your sand pit. So let me tell you, we are actually a great supporter of what you are doing. But we have been doing rather a better job than you. Instead of killing these terrible people, we just catch them and demand a large sum of money for their release. We have made millions in the last few weeks."

Finally, the man understood. "You're the people that have been kidnapping pharma staff?"

"Oh, well done, you are quite correct. And we have a lot more money to make. My list of targets is quite extensive."

Calming down a little, the man started to think. The speech pattern of the caller was perfect English, no accent of any kind that he could detect, but it sounded a little stilted.

"Why have you called me?" he asked.

The mask chuckled.

"To be honest, it was to tell you what a terrible job you have done so far. You have hardly started, and we have made millions in less time than you have been playing around. Mind you, we did have to kill a couple of people, but that was because one of them got too arrogant and started saying things he should not have. But while the news media are talking about your minor efforts, they will soon be talking a lot more about our achievements. And we are causing those companies a lot more pain than you have."

The voice was starting to irritate the man. Not only was the boasting about their success and criticism of his own operation, but that stilted, pretentious speech was like a mosquito whine.

"So what do you want?" he asked.

"Oh, nothing really. I just called to tell you that you are behaving like amateurs, and we are the professionals. You really do need to step up your performance."

The man tried to swallow his irritation.

"And just how are we supposed to do that?" he said.

"Good lord, my friend, do you really need to be told? It is your project, after all."

The man said nothing.

"Well then, how about sharply increasing the number of killings? And how about extending the number of companies you are attacking? So far, many of them have no idea about what you are doing. How can they realise they are being punished for their crimes if they are not being affected?"

"It's not that easy," said the man.

"Of course not," said the mask. "All businesses have the problem of insufficient manpower and resources. Let me think about how we might help."

The screen went dark.

The man opened his locked drawer, extracted the notebook and followed the instructions for accessing a particular address on his computer.

"Yes," said a soft voice.

"We've got a problem."

"Explain."

When he had finished detailing the recent conversation, he stopped and waited. It was a few seconds before the voice responded.

"I'll see to it," it said. "Leave your computer on, I'll download a routine to tell me when that caller comes on again and then I'll be able to track it."

The connection was terminated.

* * *

Three days later, the man's pc buzzed. As before, a masked face appeared on the monitor. The man's heart sank.

"You do not seem to have worked hard at your project," said the mask.

"No?" he replied. *Keep them speaking,* his instruction had been. *Maybe our expert will be able to track this bastard down.*

"No," said the mask. "All you have managed to kill are a few mid-level scientists and executives. The companies will hardly miss them."

"And what have you achieved? I suppose you have taken fifty million dollars in ransom?"

"Not a bad guess," said the mask. "Just a little more than that, actually."

That posh accent is giving me the shits. It's too bloody perfect. I've never heard any Pommie talk like that. "I doubt it, you're showing off."

"You think so? Let me tell you, that is just here and in Britain. In America, we are doing even better than that."

Here? Not Britain, not America? They've just made a serious mistake. The bastards are here in Australia. I hope the techie genius tracks them down. I'll take a lot of pleasure in wiping them out. "I think you're talking through your arse," he said. "We'd have heard a hell of a lot more about it if that was true."

"Talking through... oh, I see. No, that is the truth. And we have a lot more pain to inflict. You people are just amateurs."

Interesting again. That's a common enough expression but he didn't understand it at first. He's not a Pom, he's not Australian. What the hell is going on? "We're happy with how things are going," he said. "And I think you're lying."

The screen went dark.

An hour later, the pc buzzed again. This time, the screen stayed dark.

"I found what you needed to know," said the soft voice. "Two captives are being held in a property in Kempsey. Here is the address."

Two lines of data appeared on the screen.

"Do whatever seems appropriate," said the voice and the connection was terminated.

The man picked up the phone and made three calls.

* * *

The Toyota truck moved slowly along the stock track some ten kilometres out of the country town of Kempsey.

"There," said the man in the passenger seat, pointing at a lengthy driveway leading off to the left. The driver stopped and all four occupants stared up at the large house just visible over a hundred metres away.

"Let me check the plates," said the man in the passenger seat. He got out and examined the front and back licence plates before returning to his seat. He nodded. "Okay, all muddied up still. Good idea, just in case there are cameras up there."

The truck turned onto the driveway and made its way along the badly churned up route. A normal car would not have made it past the deep trenches and mud patches. At the top, they all got out, each man carrying a rifle with a pistol in a holster on his belt. A man appeared from within the house and stood on the deck, staring at the arrivals. He also carried a rifle.

"Holy shit, he's Chinese," said the driver. "That explains a lot." He shot the bolt on his rifle and raised it to point at the man on the deck. "I believe you called me."

A look of deep horror appeared on the face of the man. He began to move the rifle into a firing position, but a bullet took him in the chest, and he went down, the legs trembling for a few second before the body went still.

The four armed men rushed into the house. A door opened and a young man appeared, looking frightened. A bullet hit him in the face, exploding out of the back of his head and he collapsed, blood spurting over the door and wall.

Advancing further, the team encountered a heavy door with a solid lock on it. The leader nodded and a blast from a shotgun carried by one of the team removed the lock and a large part of the door, which swung open to reveal two men standing against the far wall, fear showing in every line of their bodies.

"What do we do with these?" asked one of the men of the leader. "They've seen our faces."

The leader closed the door and the group moved away. "We've got to kill them," he said.

"Oh, shit, no," said one of the men. "Hey, we've seen their faces, too. It was alright when we killed some unknown person in the dark, we didn't know who they were. But this? Man, I don't like this. They've probably got a wife and kids. So do I. It's personal now."

"So what the fuck do we do?" said another one. "Let them go? They've seen our faces, they could describe us to the cops. And they probably heard the truck arrive, so they'll know we're somewhere in the region. It's too risky."

"I'm with Harry," said the last of the group.

The leader swore. "No fucking names, alright? We agreed before we left, no names get spoken."

The other three said nothing, but there was confusion in their faces.

"And what about those two we killed?" said one. "They're fucking Chinese! Who the hell knew? And what the hell are Chinese crims doing here?"

"Actually, I don't think they were Chinese," said one. His accent was educated. "I've been around Southeast Asia quite a bit. My guess is they were Korean."

"Makes no difference," said the leader. "They're dead."

"Sure," said the other man. "And so, now what about those buggers in that room?"

"They're part of the pharma industry," replied the leader. "It's obvious what we do, just like we've done with all the others." He pointed at one of the team. "Handgun," he said, and the delegated executioner moved to the doorway. The other three began walking back to the front of the house. On the way, two shots rang out.

"Home," said the leader and climbed back into the driver's seat.

Chapter 33

AFP HQ, Canberra

"I've had a report from Allen Miller," said Melanie. "He's changed the rules of engagement a bit because he's been giving some help to the group of security officers from pharma companies."

Having been advised by Allen that he had downloaded his personal security system to Melanie's computer, they felt safe from the killer group hacking into Melanie's computer and overhearing the discussion.

"Interesting," said Jack. "Did he say why he's doing that?" Alex sat against the wall of the office, listening attentively.

"He said he was impressed by their inside knowledge. One of them is a German, previously with Military Intelligence and somehow, they had Allen's contact number on the Dark Web. This Konrad Richter actually called Allen to ask for help. The German MI techies were able to decode the distorted voices of the British killers and one of the security group people recognised one of them. Apparently, she had been a detective some years before and had actually arrested this man."

"Damn, that's a hell of a lucky break," said Alex.

"And even luckier, she had been in a close relationship with a colleague who is now a Superintendent who was all too willing to help. The police found this man and arrested him, somebody known as "Mumbles" Wilson."

"As you say, that's a massive break-through," said Jack. "What did they get from this man?"

"He told them he got his orders from somebody through Dark Web connections. Even more critical, the cops found his computer and took it to their office for their experts to work on. And when they hooked it up into the network, that's when Allen got to work."

"He found the source of the orders?" Alex sat up in his seat, excitement showing in his face and body.

"He did. And that's when this story got a lot more complicated. Allen said it took far more effort than before, the firewalls in the computer and the protections of the Dark Web were a lot more stringent that Allen had met before, but eventually he made it. He found the general location of the killer, but also the locations of two other killers who had worked for him. The cops located all three, but when they got to their homes, all three were killed by a single bullet to the head."

There was silence in the room for a few moments.

"That does indeed make it far more complex," said Jack. "This war is being run by somebody a lot more powerful than we had thought. And the implications are even worse."

"There's a mole somewhere in the system," said Alex.

"Exactly," said Melanie. "I think it's time we applied a little science to locating the killer."

"What are you thinking?" asked Jack.

"Several lines of attack," replied Melanie. "First, I want you to contact your old lady-friend, Professor Ruth Blackston, who helped us identify the voices in the last case we handled together.[3] She's a genius with voice identification and I bet she could place the background of the bloke who keeps calling me. And after all, I know his face after our unfortunate meeting in Perth." She looked away in embarrassment. That meeting had been a night of sex in the man's hotel in one of her regular but infrequent jaunts away from work to ease her tensions.

Neither Jack nor Alex showed any reaction to her difficulty.

"Let's do it," said Jack and reached for his telephone.

* * *

"Come on in," said Ruth Blackston. "Hello, Jack you old bastard! Good to see you again. Melanie, Alex, welcome to my slum of an office."

Friendly greetings completed all round, she led the three into a room that looked more like a laboratory than any form of living space. It had no windows, and several tables were filled with electronic equipment.

---

[3] See The Internet Murders by Michael Davies

"I had this specially built," said Ruth. "Thick walls, totally soundproofed so that no extraneous noises could corrupt what I listen to, solid floor to avoid similar interference from heavy traffic outside. So, you have the recordings of this murderous bastard, do you?"

Melanie handed over the flash memory on which she had recorded the calls from the killer. All of them had been subjected to the corrective software to restore the original voice. Ruth plugged the drive into one of the devices on the nearest table and moved a chair up to sit before it. She gave a general wave to the others to find seats and they each took one of the wooden chairs in the room.

Ruth donned a solid-looking headset and began to listen to the recordings. On three different video screens on the table, graphs began appearing and Ruth studied them intently. The silence in the room lasted nearly twenty minutes before Ruth sat back and removed the headset.

"Relatively easy," she said with a smile. "Neither well-travelled nor well-educated, probably no more than high school graduate. The accent is almost unmixed, though there is a tiny trace of Melbourne in his vowels. Apart from that, he's almost pure mid-north coast of New South Wales. See those tiny blips on that graph?" She pointed at one of the screens that showed a line almost like a mountain with small interruptions in what was otherwise a smooth curve.

"That compares almost perfectly with similar recordings I have taken around that region and it suggests almost all his life in the Port Macquarie region. The Melbourne influence in that line," she pointed at another graph on a second screen. "Just little blips that indicate southern Victoria, again almost identical with recordings I've taken around the state."

"That's incredible what you can detect," said Melanie. "I would never have thought it possible."

"It's taken some years of research," said Ruth. "What astounded me when I got into this in depth is how even a short time spent in a region can leave a trace in the accent. I've taken thousands of recordings of speech patterns from thousands of people around the world and subjected them to intense analysis from clever devices. Modern technology has helped a great deal and made my job a lot easier."

"And she's the acknowledged expert in the field," said Jack. "You'd be amazed at how many cops around the world have enlisted Ruth's help in identifying criminals."

"It's been the most satisfying career," said Ruth with a warm smile. "Helping you in your last case was a particular pleasure."

"This has been amazing," said Melanie. "It puts us a big step nearer getting this bloke and maybe ending this awful story. Now I think I know what to do next."

"Perth?" asked Jack. "Maybe finding a security camera that got our man?"

"Perhaps," said Melanie.

* * *

Melanie handed her credit card to the cab-driver and waited until the transaction was complete before opening the door and sliding out of the taxi. She had booked herself into the same hotel she had used on her previous trip, having decided the rooms were fine, the breakfast restaurant was excellent, and the rates suited her budget.

"Good morning, Miss Carter," said the uniformed man advancing toward her.

"Good grief, it was months ago when I was here last," she said, quite astonished. "You remember me?"

"Indeed," replied the man with a friendly smile. "I'm quite sure I'd remember you anyway, but I must admit to having a little help." He tapped his right ear and Melanie saw the tiny plug of a hearing aid or wireless.

Aware of the compliment but suddenly interested in possibilities, Melanie let the porter take her bag and followed him into the reception area. The same happened at the desk, as the young girl taking her details also addressed her by name.

"Could I see the manager?" Melanie asked.

"I'll just check," said the girl and picked up the phone. A moment later, she smiled again. "Mr Kwong will be right out," she said.

251

Almost immediately, a tall young man came out of the door behind the reception desk. Melanie thought he looked like a teenager with his smooth complexion and bright, oriental eyes, but knew that was unlikely.

"Miss Carter, welcome to the Waverly Hotel," he said. "Please come into my office."

His accent was pure British aristocracy, thought Melanie and followed him into the large, spacious and artfully arranged room. Pictures hung on the wall, the desk was pure white with just a computer monitor on one corner, a beautiful, life-sized statue of a Chinese woman in traditional dress, holding a baby in her arms stood in one corner. There were three seats around a circular table in the middle of the room. Kwong waved her to one and waited until she was seated before taking another.

"How may I help you?" he asked.

Melanie was fascinated by the perfection of his speech. "Can you tell me how your staff recognized me as soon as I got out of the taxi?" she asked. "I do have a reason for asking, beyond just curiosity."

Kwong laughed. "It's proved to be a real winner," he said. "Let me explain. My parents moved here ten years ago from Singapore. My father has worked in hotels all his life and the last few years in Singapore he was a manager at Raffles Hotel. I'm sure you have heard of it?"

"Who hasn't?" said Melanie with a laugh. "Perhaps the most famous hotel in the world with an amazing history. I've always dreamed of staying in the Writers' Courtyard and having a Singapore Sling in the Long Bar, but I've never managed to accomplish that dream."

"So many have the same aspiration," said Kwong. "One thing they implemented many years ago was facial recognition software. Every single person who enters the reception area is photographed and the face stored in the computer. When anybody enters, their face is checked against the file of stored images and if a match is found, the details are immediately transmitted to the front officer so that they can be greeted by name."

"Now I understand," said Melanie. "It's very impressive."

"When we came to Australia, my father bought this hotel and immediately implemented the same system."

Melanie sensed the excitement run through her.

"Do you know the Hotel Leicester?"

"I should," said Kwong. "I own it."

Melanie had to laugh, even as the excitement rose further.

"And before you ask, yes, it has the same system," said Kwong. "Miss Carter, something tells me you are a police officer, and this is not a social call. You are here on business."

"You are very perceptive, Mr Kwong. Yes, I am Detective Chief Inspector Melanie Carter, and I am indeed looking for somebody and I know that he stayed there at least two nights a few months ago. His name was given as Daryll Hoskins."

"Not his real name, I assume?"

"Correct."

"Miss Carter, may I now assure you that we will treat you with the utmost discretion?"

"Again, Mr Kwong, you are most perceptive, thank you. But while that is necessary, can I assure you that my search for this man involves some very serious crimes, not involving my personal experiences."

"I don't believe I have given you any information that might be considered confidential, Miss Carter, so I don't need to ask if you have a warrant for your search. However, the situation with the Hotel Leicester is different, so can I assume you have a warrant for there?"

"Indeed I do, Mr Kwong." Melanie extracted an envelope from her briefcase and handed it to the manager.

Kwong opened it and studied the document carefully. Then he nodded and touched a button on the side of his desk. "Angela, call up the limousine. Miss Carter is to be taken to the Hotel Leicester." He returned the warrant to Melanie. "As you head there, I'll instruct the hotel staff to check on the booking by this Hoskins person. They will be ready for you."

Melanie stood up.

"Mr Kwong, I am overwhelmed by this hotel, your courtesy and your assistance. I cannot thank you enough."

Kwong laughed. "We aim to please and live to serve," he said.

Melanie echoed the laugh. "And you do both superbly well," she said. "Now I must become Detective Chief Inspector Carter and perform my crime-hunting duty."

* * *

"We have both of you on the computer," said the young woman who had met the limousine when it stopped outside the Hotel Leicester and introduced herself as Leanne Vaughn, the hotel manager. She was dressed in an immaculate suit and exuded style and competence. Now seated in her office, she indicated no judgmental attitude, though she obviously knew about the night of sex Melanie had experienced with the man called Hoskins. "As Mr Kwong told you, we photograph everybody who enters the hotel, whether as a guest or not."

She turned the pc monitor so that both could see the images.

"That's you and Hoskins when you both came here, but I realise that's not what you are looking for." She touched a key on the computer. "This is Hoskins when he checked in."

The image became a clear, large image of the man Melanie recognized. She felt a small shiver of disgust, but at the same time, a feeling of triumph. She had him!

"That's perfect," she said. "Can I get a copy of that?"

"Already done," said Leanne, reached into a drawer and slid a colour picture of the man across her desk.

"Fantastic!" said Melanie as Leanne also pushed an envelope across to her.

"Something else you should see," said Leanne and a new image filled the screen. It was Hoskins again, this time accompanied by a tall, well-endowed young woman with red hair, a very short skirt and an impressive display of cleavage. "This was taken the day after your visit. Looks like he was busy."

"Oh yuck," said Melanie. "I feel scrofulous, just one of his many conquests."

Leanne smiled. "Melanie, from what I know of you and what I have seen of you, even this short visit, I suspect he might have been your conquest, not the other way round."

Melanie couldn't help laughing. "Thank you," she said. "That makes me feel a whole lot better. Can I get a copy of that one, also?"

Twenty minutes later, the limousine had returned her to her hotel. That night, she stayed in, had room service for dinner and breakfast the next morning, before flying back to Canberra, delighted and well satisfied by the trip.

*   *   *

"Let's get that picture to all the cop shops between Coffs Harbour and Forster-Tuncurry," said Melanie. "If Ruth was right, he's probably still in Port Macquarie, but he may have found somewhere else to live in that general mid-North Coast region. Let's see if anyone recognises him and if the security cameras in the region get a trigger from face recognition systems. I suspect we have a decent chance of identifying this bastard."

Jack seemed lost in thought and didn't make any comment on what Melanie had just initiated.

"Jack?" she said. "Are you off with the fairies or thinking about the latest grandson?"

Jack looked up, almost as if waking from sleep.

"Neither," he said. "I've been wearing my profiler's hat again. I'm supposed to be good at that, you may recall."

"Ooh, snarky," said Melanie, not managing to suppress a chuckle. "And what does your profiler hat tell you?"

"It tells me that this Hoskins character, or whatever his name turns out to be, is not the king pin of this operation."

"Go on."

"It must be that we have the same situation here as the team in Britain found. This is at least, a nation-wide operation, probably involving Australia as well as Britain. It also seems to have some cooperation with the US, maybe others we don't know about yet. And while we suspect the kidnapping operations are separate from the revenge killings, they may also be part of it. Either way, our suspect is simply not up to managing the whole thing. Just a high school education, some mistakes he has already made, the way he speaks, I don't think he's even up to managing the Australian segment, never mind initiating it or funding it."

"But he's certainly involved," said Melanie, totally hooked on what Jack was saying.

"Oh, he's involved alright. He's running a good-sized part of it, probably coordinating several killers in Australia. But he's a captain, not the general. Somebody on a much higher paygrade has started this and is running the whole operation in several countries, with a captain like Hoskins in each."

"But would somebody so big have started this just because they lost somebody dear to them? That seems a huge over-reaction, killing people around the world because of the loss of a loved one."

"I agree entirely," said Jack. "Whoever is behind this has lost a hell of a lot more than just somebody close to them. Their loss has been catastrophic, completely life-changing. We're looking for a much bigger fish than Hoskins. He's just a minnow."

"Maybe when we catch the minnow, we might have a lead to the General," said Melanie.

"What a bloody awful mixed metaphor," said Jack, laughing. "Let's go to the pub. I need a drink."

Chapter 34

21st March, 2026, AFP HQ, Canberra

Melanie's day usually started by eight-thirty when she took a mug of coffee to her desk and spent a few minutes thinking deeply about the state of the cases she was working on, and preparing herself for any shocks that could occur. She rarely got ten minutes before the phone rang or her pc warbled with an incoming call, and today was no exception. This time, it was the pc. With a pang of worry, she pressed the key, thinking it would be Hoskins calling up to tell her about another coming murder, but it wasn't.

"Detective Chief Inspector Carter?"

The face was of a remarkably good-looking man. For a few seconds, Melanie studied it, almost missing the standard reaction she observed when a man first saw her, the startled blink, the eyes widening and the brief but intense study. With an amused reaction, she realised that she had done just that herself when she first saw the caller. She looked at the identification on the screen.

"Yes," she said. "Detective Superintendent Douglas Seaton, good morning."

"Good morning," he said. "I'm in the Port Macquarie office. I'm glad I got you first thing, I have some good news for you."

"I'm always glad to hear good news."

Seaton smiled. "Indeed. We don't get much of it in this job. But we've got your man."

Melanie sat up straight. "Hoskins? Good grief, that was quick! What happened?"

"Security cameras picked him up in the Settlement City shopping mall and their facial recognition system erupted like Vesuvius. They called us immediately and kept tracking him to the parking area and noted the car registration. We had a patrol car in the region, they spotted him leaving the parking area, followed him home and arrested him there. He's in our cells now."

With the excitement of that news and the slight disturbance she was feeling at the handsome face in her screen, Melanie forced herself to maintain formal procedures.

"That's wonderful, sir," she said. "How do you plan to proceed?"

"For now, we've charged him with using a false credit card in Perth. We're tracking down the phone call he made to Niel Butcher before Butcher was killed and then we can add uttering threats. However, we've run an analysis of his voice compared to the recordings you have made of his calls and confirmed it's one and the same man, so that will hold him. How would you like to come up here? Your boss says you're a lethal interrogator, you might break him quicker than anyone else."

"I would really appreciate that," she said. "It's a long drive, maybe seven, eight hours. Can we do it starting tomorrow morning?"

"Not a problem. We can hold him that long and we

may be able to get additional nasties to charge him with during the day. I'll look forward to seeing you here in the morning."

The call was disconnected.

"So will I," she muttered to herself and picked up the phone. "Jack, pack a bag," she said. "We have a date tomorrow morning with the captain."

* * *

23rd March, 2026, A House in Port Macquarie

The police sergeant stood by the front door as a constable opened it with the keys taken from the owner now in the cells. "Okay, Rick," she said to the constable. "We've got the warrant, let's get on with our job and tear this place apart."

She waved at the other two officers waiting a few steps away, and they began the expert, well-trained, detailed search of the house and it wasn't long before some key findings were made.

"Interesting," said the sergeant, carefully wrapping up the baseball bat in a large evidence bag. "I reckon that's blood and something else on there. The lab will find that most interesting."

"What about the computer, Sarge?" asked the constable.

"Bag the whole thing. Let the techies get into that."

An hour later, the team was back in the police station and the items from the house were handed over to experts.

* * *

The Police Station, Port Macquarie

"I have to make a terribly embarrassing confession to you, first," said Melanie. Douglas Seaton's office had nothing in the way of creature comforts, no pictures on the wall, a simple desk and a small coffee table with four plain chairs around it. A coffee pot had been brought in by a constable who looked barely out of school, and he had nearly spilt it when he first looked at Melanie. She gave him a pleasant smile and he retreated with a confused look on his face.

Seaton smiled as he poured coffee into mugs that looked like souvenirs of some festival. "He's very young," he said.

"And she does have that effect," added Jack, somehow breaking the last vestige of first meeting tension.

"You were saying, Melanie?" said Seaton.

Melanie took a deep breath.

"Hoskins, or whatever his name is, and I have met before in circumstances that I really don't want to tell you, but I must."

Seaton looked calmly at her. "His name is Donald Hayes. We all know that some pretty bloody awful things happen, often out of our control. If Hayes has done what it appears he has, then anything you have to tell me is critical to the case, but otherwise makes no difference. I have no doubts you will be unharmed by the embarrassment."

263

Melanie didn't relax. "I met Hayes at a club in Perth some months ago. It was a conventional pick-up, I was open to it and it led to my staying the night with him. I left the next morning, and it was only when Allen Miller told me he had identified Hayes as the man who had been calling me to boast about the killings of people in the pharma industry, that I realised the pick-up was specifically arranged and I was targeted. I really don't know why he did that, it seems to me a major breach of his security, but it may just have been some of that macho stuff."

Seaton picked up his coffee mug and took a sip.

"I can see why you're stressed about that. Do you think he'll try and use it when you interrogate him?"

"I have no doubt."

"The problem that gives us is that the public defender will be in the meeting, and she will of course learn about this. In any future trial, it's likely to come out as part of the defence, so you're going to be embarrassed. But you're a single woman, meeting a man in a club and having a sexual liaison is not exactly earthshaking immorality. It won't affect the scale of the crime Hayes has committed and won't last long in the public memory."

Melanie relaxed a little.

Jack nodded. "I agree with that. Even within the law enforcement world, it's hardly worth noting. You may get a few snarky comments, but that's about it."

Seaton took another sip from the souvenir mug.

"Let's finish our coffee, then go and see Hayes. Jack, you can watch on the tv in the next room, and we'll value your professional comments on the man's mental state. But first, Melanie, tell me about that amazing car you have."

* * *

Melanie followed Seaton into the interview room, deliberately walking behind the officer's large frame so as not to be noticed immediately. The first person she saw was a middle-aged woman, she assumed to be the public defender, sitting in one seat at the table. Then, as Seaton took a seat across from her, she saw the man she had encountered in Perth that she now knew to be called Donald Hayes. At the same moment, he saw her, and the reaction was electric.

"Melanie!" he exclaimed and shot to his feet, alarm in every part of his face and body.

Melanie ignored him and sat down next to Seaton, across from Hayes and then stared directly at him. She exerted every atom of the dominant personality she had, willing it to attack the man and it seemed to work. He sat down again, not looking at her, staring down at his lap.

"You two already know each other?" The lawyer seemed puzzled.

"That will become clearer in due course, Ms Chalmers," said Seaton. "For now, we will concentrate on the communications that Mr Hayes has directed at Chief Inspector Carter."

The woman said nothing, but made a note on her pad. Seaton pressed a button on a controller.

"This interview is now being recorded," he said. "The date is the 26th June, 2026 at nine fifteen in the morning and we are in the police station on Hay Street in Port Macquarie. Present are Detective Superintendent Douglas Seaton, Detective Chief Inspector Melanie Carter, Public Defender Annette Chalmers and Mr Donald Hayes." He nodded at Melanie. She looked again at Hayes with her most intimidating glare.

"Donald, you were arrested yesterday and charged with the use of a false credit card. Is that correct?"

Hayes looked confused and said nothing.

"My client accepts that," said the lawyer. "That is a minor charge and I demand that he be released under caution immediately."

"However," said Melanie, ignoring her completely, "we are now introducing fresh charges, that on a number of dates which will be detailed with the documented charges, you called a police officer in the Australian Federal Police, namely Detective Chief Inspector Melanie Carter, that is myself, and boasted about a number of unlawful killings which you had conducted, and forecast several others, all of which have since taken place. Do you have any comment to make on these charges?"

"That's bloody nonsense," said Hayes, his tones loud with anger. "I've never called you in my life.

You've got no proof." He stood up and pointed a finger at Melanie. "That woman's a slut, a prostitute," he shouted. "She approached me in the club in Perth, offered her services for cash and asked to come back to my hotel. I told her to fuck off, but she was persistent. This is just her way of getting back at me, telling lies like this."

"Well, let's see about that," said Melanie. "Superintendent?"

Next to Melanie, Seaton pressed the controller again. An image appeared on the screen. Melanie had taken those from the hotel in Perth, anticipating this line of attack and this one showed her and Hayes at the front desk.

"First lie," said Melanie. "That's us at the reception desk of your hotel. It looks like your claim of moral certitude in ordering me away is not exactly correct."

"Ms Carter, this is disgraceful," called the lawyer. "You went with my client to engage in sex? How will any court treat your testimony with any credit now?"

"You are quite correct, Ms Chalmers, I certainly did engage in sex with your client. I am not proud of that, but it is hardly illegal, especially as he had presented himself as somebody else, with a false persona. And as for credit, how about this?"

Another image appeared, this time that of Hayes with the second woman. Her very short dress and expansive cleavage were well displayed.

"That was the night after," said Melanie. "Not a good pointer to your client's reputation, is it?"

Chalmers seemed to subside. "I will submit these details in court," she said.

"I have no doubt," said Melanie. "But Donald, let us return to your claim that you never called me anonymously after that time. Superintendent?"

Once more, Seaton touched the controller. The sound of Hayes' distorted voice came from an unseen loudspeaker. It was part of the conversation from when he had first called Melanie.

Caller: "Maybe you don't know it, Chief Inspector Carter, but the pharmaceutical industry is probably the most hated industry in the world."

Melanie: "Oh, I see. And you and your funny little friends are going to punish them all over the world, are you?"

Caller: "That's exactly what we are going to do. They've committed fraud, failure to maintain safe manufacturing processes, they've lied about clinical trials and they've committed murder."

Melanie: "And this is world-wide, eh? If it's such a global crime, why are you calling a detective in Canberra? What can I do about it? And while we're on that subject, just why have you called me?"

Caller: "We're starting operations in several countries. We'll expand as we get more agents. And I know you very well. I heard about you some years ago when you tracked down a group of killers who *were committing murders as stories for their books. They were quite mad, of course, but so was the woman influencing them."*

Hayes laughed loudly. "That's not me speaking. You're nuts, Melanie, anyone can tell that's some distorted voice."

Next to him, the lawyer spoke.

"My client is correct, Mr Seaton. There's no way that distorted voice can be attributed to my client. Come on, Donald, I think it's time we left, these people have had their twenty-four hours to hold you."

"Please stay where you are, Ms Chalmers." Seaton didn't raise his voice but the authority in it made the lawyer sit down sharply.

"Clearly you are not aware that the distortion software also has a key that will restore the voice to normal. That key is not available to the general public but can be supplied to law enforcement operations. We applied that key to this and every one of the calls made to Ms Carter. You will be able to verify the process with the software manufacturers. Here is the restored extract of what you just heard."

Once again, the brief sentences were played, this time with standard voices, and it was quite clear that Hayes was the speaker.

"That voice was analysed by experts and concluded to be that of Mr Hayes," said Seaton. "Again, Ms Chalmers, signed statements by those experts and proof of their expertise will be available to you."

The lawyer looked stunned and said nothing.

Melanie took charge again.

"So, Donald, do you still deny that you called me on several occasions to claim responsibility for killing people involved in the pharmaceutical industry?"

Hayes looked defeated and stared down at the table.

"So here's where we are, Donald," continued Melanie. "When we present what we have to the Office of the Director of Public Prosecutions, they will decide what charges to bring against you. I have no doubt that at the very least, conspiracy to commit murder will apply and that's for several murders. Or they may decide that there's enough circumstantial evidence for actual murder. Either way, you won't see daylight outside the prison again."

"Don't threaten my client," burst out the lawyer. "I must request a break so that I can confer with him."

Before Melanie or Seaton could reply, there was a knock on the door. Seaton stood up and opened it to see a uniformed sergeant holding a sheet of paper, which he handed to Seaton.

Back at his seat, the Superintendent read the paper and handed it to Melanie. She studied it, then placed it on the table.

"An update, Donald and you're not going to like it. We conducted a legal search of your house when you were arrested, and guess what we found."

Hayes almost shrank into his seat.

"A baseball bat, Donald. A baseball bat with traces of blood and human bone on it. You won't know this, but the postmortems of several of the killings your operation conducted concluded that the weapon used was a baseball bat to the head. The lab will now conduct tests of the materials on the bat and compare them to several killings. I think the main interest will be on the body of Neal Butcher, the man who killed Mr Sully with a handgun carried by a large drone. That will provide conclusive evidence of your guilt. Of course, there may be traces of other victims on the bat, so you may find yourself charged with a series of murders. Any comment, Donald?"

There was no response.

"I demand a break," said the lawyer. "My client has been subjected to too much stress, already."

"Not quite," said Melanie. She could see that the lawyer was completely dominated now, remaining silent without looking at Melanie. She turned back to Hayes.

"So now, Donald," she said. "Let's turn to something else. My team, which includes a world-class psychologist and police profiler is quite certain that this entire war of yours is way above your paygrade. In fact, we have called you the Captain and somewhere above you is the General. Who's been driving you, Donald?"

Hayes seemed to tremble with fear. "Nobody's been driving me."

"That seems dubious, Donald. And another thing. The whole schedule of deaths caused by your team is too extensive for just you to have done them all. You've had help. Who are your little helpers?"

"Nobody," mumbled Hayes. His voice was almost inaudible.

"And what about your great leader? Who is that? Who hates the pharma industry so much that they have to kill large numbers of people in their sick little world?"

"Nobody," repeated Hayes.

"Remember when you called me once to boast about how brilliant you were and would never be found out, and I said you had already made mistakes? You got really shitty about that, Donald, but I didn't tell you what mistakes you had made. Well, you learned about one of those just a few minutes ago, You didn't know that we could restore a distorted voice and hear the real voice. But now you know, and it's truly buggered you up, hasn't it?"

Hayes remained silent but he seemed to be shrinking even further into a foetal position in his chair.

"So here's another critical failing, Donald. All this time, you've assumed that somebody in your team has the world's best computer hacking skills. You used that skill to break into my computer and listen in to my conversations, but then suddenly you couldn't do it anymore. Did you ever think why?"

Hayes looked up. "All that happened was that when I tried, there was no sound. You'd obviously just found somewhere else to meet."

"That was true for the first couple of meetings, but after that, we were there, Donald, I assure you. The silence was what you were supposed to hear."

"Bullshit. He said he was the world's best, nobody could beat him."

"Oh? Who was that? So there really is somebody who's been driving you. Once more, Donald, who is it?"

Seeming to realise his mistake, Hayes said nothing.

"And that's your other screw-up, Donald. We know you've been using the Dark Web to communicate with your network of killers and to get your instructions from the General and we know it's seriously difficult to break into, but we've got a weapon you don't know about."

Melanie paused and checked the faces of the lawyer and the other police officer. Both seemed completely fixated on what she was saying.

"Have you ever heard of a man called Allen Miller?" asked Melanie.

Hayes said nothing and the lawyer shook her head.

"Miller?" said Seaton. "Holy shit, you've got Allen Miller working with you?"

"We have. So, Donny, Ms Chalmers, did you see the astonishment that Detective Superintendent

Seaton expressed at that name? That's because Allen Miller is considered the greatest computer hacker in the world. He's wanted in many countries for stealing millions from governments and corporations, but he's retired from that life now and he's become a pretty good friend of mine, helping my team find a few nasty people. And do you wonder why your British operation has gone silent in recent weeks? That's because your equivalent person is dead. Allan Miller helped the team in England identify one of the killers, they found him, took his computer and it took Allen just a few days to break the Dark Web and locate who has been running things. Funnily enough, when they went to get him, they found him dead. What's more, they found the other killers dead, also. That's what terrifies you, doesn't it? If your General gets identified, he'll kill all of you, won't he?"

Hayes took a deep breath in shock, or fear, Melanie couldn't be sure.

"So here's the thing, Donald. When the cops arrested you yesterday, it isn't just the baseball bat they got. They found your computer as well. Allen will have it in a day or two." She nodded at Seaton. "Let's have that break now. The poor man has had enough."

Seaton switched off the sound system and stood up. A uniformed officer came in and escorted Hayes out of the room. Chalmers walked out behind Hayes.

"I need to keep the computer here, it's critical evidence," said Seaton. "What do you suggest?"

"Not a problem. Can you attach it to your network? Allen can do the rest."

"For sure. Let's go and have a coffee in the canteen."

"Delighted," said Melanie, really meaning it.

*   *   *

The following afternoon, Mel drove back to Canberra in a warm glow, trying to keep it from Jack in the passenger seat.

"A nice evening with the Superintendent, Melanie?" Jack spoke after a lengthy silence while Melanie seemed to be concentrating on her driving.

"Damn, I thought you didn't know about it," she said.

"You can't hide much from me, young lady," said Jack with a smile. "You were positively radiating a loud smirk."

"It was nice," she agreed. "He's charming, has that rugged athleticism that churns my insides, and you have to admit, he's easy on the eye."

"I suppose," said Jack.

"But no, before you ask, we didn't end up in the sack, we just had a splendid dinner at a French restaurant, finished with a brief snog at the hotel front and he went home."

"Seeing him again?"

"Not likely. Call it a pleasant interlude after the nastiness of interrogating Hayes with all the baggage that it entailed and that was just what I needed."

"Sounds good. That Hayes really is a piece of dirt. I hope we find out who's directing him soon."

"That's what Allen said he was trying to find. I have every faith in him."

Jack merely grunted and closed his eyes. Melanie returned to the intense enjoyment she experienced in driving her Gordon-Keeble and the effortless long legs it had on the freeway.

After dropping Jack at his hotel, she headed back to the apartment she had rented in the suburb of Curtin. A flash of headlights in her rearview mirror caused her a brief moment of irritation, but the beams dropped. A few moments later, the high beam flashed her again briefly, and she realised it was the same vehicle that had done it before.

"Am I being followed?" she muttered. "Now just who would be interested in doing that? Let's see if this is genuine."

She dropped a gear, accelerated sharply for a kilometre, slammed on the brake at a junction and flung the powerful car into a left-hand turn, accelerated again and repeated the manoeuvre at another junction. Resuming normal speed, she watched carefully in the mirror, but no headlights appeared.

"Hah," she said aloud. "Nobody on this good green planet can keep up with Melanie Carter in a Gordon Keeble." At a more leisurely pace, she reached her apartment building, put the car in the underground parking area and took the elevator up to the second-floor apartment she had rented for her assignment in Canberra. Feeling fatigued but satisfied with the trip to Port Macquarie, the results of the interrogation of Hayes and the relaxed pleasure of the evening with Seaton, she poured herself a glass of red wine and sat down before the television to catch up on the day's news.

Only a few moments later, she detected a small metallic sound from her front door. Her well-tuned sense of danger brought her to full alertness. She stood up and moved softly to the bookshelf by the wall. One of her treasured souvenirs of a trip to Uluru, the massive rock in the middle of the country and the few days she had spent touring the outback, was a large, beautifully decorated boomerang. But this was no ordinary souvenir, like so many small ones the tourists bought and spent fruitless hours trying to make return from a throw. This was a kangaroo-killer, a metre long with sharp edges along the front. It was designed to fly just above the ground and strike a kangaroo in the legs, crippling it and allowing the hunter to make an easy kill. It was not intended to return.

Melanie picked the weapon by the long arm and concentrated on listening to any sound. She stood silently, hearing a door opened gently in the corridor and tensed up, knowing the door to her lounge was the next one. She watched the handle of the door moved slowly and silently, then the door was inched open, and a man's shape moved into view. The first part that appeared was a hand holding a gun. Melanie identified it as a Heckler & Koch nine millimetre automatic and it was fitted with a suppressor. She didn't panic, she had always been capable of controlling herself in moments of tension, she just waited.

When the intruder appeared fully in the doorway, the hand holding the gun was well ahead and Melanie acted. She flung the boomerang hard at the man's arm. It turned three times and struck the forearm of the hand holding the gun. The man shouted in pain, dropped the gun and turned, charged out of the apartment and Melanie heard the doors to the stairs open.

She moved to the doorway and picked up the gun, carefully walked to the front door and closed it, applying all three deadlocks with which it was fitted. She had no interest in pursuing her attacker. She had seen no glove on the hand she had damaged, so there would be fingerprints on the pistol. She put on a pair of opera gloves, the only light ones she had and examined the weapon.

"Suppressors are not that easy to get," she said aloud. "They require some special contacts. If there are fingerprints, there's a good chance we'll be able to identify this one, but it suggests gang membership or a contract killer."

Carefully, she removed the cartridge and cleared the chamber of the bullet in place, ready to be fired.

Examining the bullet, it was clearly self-made, not a commercial grade. "An expert," she muttered. "Makes his own, loaded for subsonic speed to go with the suppressor, so no supersonic bang. A real professional, this one."

She thought for a while about reporting the episode to her boss, Chief Superintendent Harvey, checked the time and saw it was after eleven and decided against it. The next morning would do just as well.

* * *

"Good set of prints," said the technician the following morning, "but none on record. This man has a real secret existence, we have no idea who he is."

"And having a suppressor is an indicator," said Chief Superintendent Harvey. "You can't just walk into a gun store and buy one. This bastard is a contract killer, for sure."

"And a weapons expert," said Melanie. "He makes his own bullets, just enough power to be lethal, but low velocity to match the suppressor. Regular shells would still make a bang and destroy the suppressor, possibly causing injury to the shooter."

"That suggests that whoever hired this man is scared," said Harvey. "And it won't stop with this attempt. Melanie, I want you to be armed from now on. You and Welland, draw weapons from the armoury, I'll authorise it."

"I hate the idea," said Melanie. "But yes sir, I agree. We've got somebody quite upset, which means we're closing in."

"Correct. Be bloody careful, Melanie."

Melanie nodded and returned to her office.

Chapter 35

25th March, 2026, AFP HQ, Canberra

Melanie's office had become a familiar scene as she, Jack and Alex gathered for a meeting. Miller had appeared on the pc monitor almost immediately the others had sat down.

"The security systems on Hayes' computer were even better than on the British system," said Allen Miller. "I'd say that whoever is their technical expert did some upgrading after they realised I'd cracked the system there. It took me longer to break in, quite a bit longer, actually."

"You sound embarrassed," said Melanie with a laugh.

"Admitted," said Miller. "But I did get through eventually and got much the sort of interesting stuff as before. I've got names, general location, and some addresses, but as in England, finding the people should be easy. So here goes. There are two people with whom Hayes communicated and those communications closely match the dates of the murders in Australia."

A stir of interest ran round the office.

"The first one is called Nigel Catlin. He's in the Newcastle area. The second surprised me, but it's a woman called Helen Agnew, somewhere around Albury. I found their addresses from their credit card records, council rates and wotnot, and those are coming out on your printer now. Women are rarely serial killers, but then, I imagine this one has some serious bitch with the pharma industry and was pleased to have an opportunity. I've dug deeply with those two, tracked their travel records, hotel stays and so on, and I can show you a tight correlation with their movements and the killings they carried out. If you can grab them, you'll have water-tight cases."

Melanie nodded at Alex who stood up, removed the sheet of paper from the printer and left.

"You've sent Alex to brief the local cops about those two?" said Allen.

"Naturally," replied Melanie.

"Okay, so let's wait until he gets back before I give you any more. I don't want him to miss anything, because there's some critical information coming, and he'll probably be the one researching the next step."

"Agreed," said Melanie, went to the coffee pot and refilled both her mug and Jack's. The two of them sat quietly with their own thoughts for five minutes until Alex returned. He gave a simple nod to Melanie and sat down back in his original chair.

"Let's go on," said Allen. "The next three names are really interesting, because I'm certain that one of them is your General. Jack, I took the profile you had suggested, significantly rich people who had suffered a severe loss of one kind or another at the hands of the pharmaceutical industry."

"Interesting," said Jack. "I really hope it helped."

"Oh yes, Jack, invaluable as always. Now, here are

what I consider your most likely suspects. The first is a man called Agung Harsono. He's an Indonesian, came to Australia in 1965, a pharmacologist, worked for a few years for a research laboratory that did most of its work for the Canadian firm Consellors. Then he left, formed his own research operation, and made a lot of money creating and licencing new drugs to the major firms. Then he hit the big time, created a drug to combat acid reflux, it was massively successful, left all the rest for dead because it usually healed the cause of the reflux within two to three months. He was deluged with offers to licence it at very generous royalty terms that would have made him a billionaire, but Consellors threw an enormous legal action, claiming the drug was theirs and somehow won. They took it, and while Harsono remained wealthy, he didn't get his real rewards. He retreated from the world, lives somewhere up near Cairns."

"That company keeps appearing in the list of very ugly criminals," said Alex.

"Trouble is, it's a bloody great big long list," said Jack.

"Want me to do some serious damage to them?" asked Allen. "I could, easily, as you know."

"No, Allen," said Melanie quickly. "Our job is law enforcement, not revenge terrorism. That's exactly what we're trying to stop."

"I suppose. Okay, likely suspect number two," continued Allen. "Kenneth Marlow, another pharmaceutical genius, started in the usual way, working as a scientist with a major firm, in this case, Fremont Sims in their Chicago operation. Very successful, showed real flair, then another one who struck out on his own. Created a company called Marlow Pharma in Buffalo, New York but decided to transfer operations to the western suburbs of Sydney, Australia after the New York bombing of the World Trade Centre in 2001. He said at the time that he didn't feel safe in the USA anymore and things would get seriously dangerous over the next few years."

"Clever man," said Jack. "He's been dead right."

"So it seems. Anyway, what happened to him was that Fremont Sims developed a massive campaign against Marlow, spread some alarming tales about drug failings and adverse reactions and the share price collapsed. Fremont snapped up the majority shares at fire sale prices and Marlow lost his company. There are some rumours that the whole thing was facilitated by Marlow's financial accountants, but that was never proved."

"God, what a dirty business," muttered Alex. "Jeez, we see enough ugly shit in this job, the terrible things people do to each other, but the business world really takes the cake for evil crap."

Melanie gave him a sympathetic smile, then turned back to the pc monitor. "Allen, your third candidate?"

"A fairly common tale. Ben Conroy ran a small, successful pharma company in Sydney's western suburbs, three times produced a new drug that was highly effective against lung disease, shepherded approval through the Therapeutic Goods Administration and was set to dominate the global market. Then he had the ground whipped from under him when Blackwood Harding in New York made a copy of it with just enough difference in the compound to avoid the patent and sold their version at half the price, together with a massive marketing campaign. When Conroy's firm collapsed as a result, the price went to nearly twice what he had charged and Blackwoods made a killing."

The office was silent for a few moments.

"Enough criminal activity in those examples to last a police force a decade," said Melanie. "Allen, what next?"

"That's in your court," said Miller. "Find those three, see if you can determine if they're behind your pharma war."

The pc screen went blank as Miller departed without further social pleasantries.

* * *

Newcastle, NSW, Australia

The Firearms Officers and their automatic rifles stayed in the black van, while the Detective Sergeant and Constable, wearing flak jackets advanced on the front door and banged hard on it. There was no need for the ram to be summoned to smash the door down, it was slowly opened by a young woman who peered out through the small gap she left.

"Police. Sergeant Graham Holloway," said the senior officer, flourishing his warrant card. The door was opened fully and then the sergeant saw that the woman's face was a flood of tears, topped by red eyes.

"We're looking for Nigel Catlin," he said. "This is his home?"

The woman nodded and stood aside, pointing at the room at the back of the house. The two officers advanced cautiously, but stopped when they reached the doorway. The body was lying in an armchair, legs astride over the raised footrest, both arms falling down the side. The face was composed but spoiled by the neat red hole in the centre of the forehead. Behind his head, a large patch of blood covered the back of the chair.

"My brother," said the young woman behind the officers. "I just got here from school. I'm a teacher. We were going to take our other sister out to dinner for her birthday." Tears ran down her face and she made no effort to dry them.

The constable didn't need a prompt. He walked back to the front door then called on his radio for a medical examiner and an ambulance.

Albury, NSW

One armed officer ran to the back of the house, two banged on the door. The rest remained in the black van parked just behind the wall that separated the front garden from the side road on which the house stood.

Within only a few moments, the door opened, and a young woman stood there. She stared for a few moments at the two men in black combat gear, carrying automatic rifles but seemed quite unfazed.

"Good timing," she said.

"Is this the home of Helen Agnew?" asked the first officer.

"It is."

"Are you Helen?"

"I am."

"Then I require you to come with us," said the officer. "I am arresting you for the murders of between six to eight people whose names will be supplied. You have the right to remain silent…" He continued the standard reading of rights and the woman stood quietly and unaffected by it.

"You'd better come in," she said. "There's something you need to see."

A little puzzled by her reaction, the officers followed her down the corridor to a room on the right. Even before they reached the open doorway, the officer leading them could see the body sprawled on the floor.

"Who the hell is that?" he said, startled out of his professional composure.

"Fucked if I know," replied Helen Agnew. "I was sitting here, minding my own business, when there's a crash as my back door is burst open and this wanker comes running in, waving an automatic pistol."

Her demeanour and speech almost had the armed officer grinning, but he controlled himself. "So what happened next?" he asked.

"What do you expect when some amateur wanker tries pointing a gun at somebody who was in the Special Air Services?" she said. "I took his little toy off him and broke his fucking neck, of course."

"You were SAS?" the officer took a tighter hold on his rifle and shifted away from her.

"Left last year," she replied. "Wonky knee, got invalided out." She held her hands out. "I suppose you'd better put the cuffs on, but I won't misbehave, I promise."

Cuffs on, the group left the house and one of the officers called in to base for an ambulance and medical examiner.

"So why," asked the officer as he sat in the back seat of the patrol car with the prisoner. "Why the killings?"

"My baby brother," she replied. "Fifteen years old, got a liver infection. The doctor gave him this pill, he got worse, died after three months. Then I heard the pill had been withdrawn. One of our medics told me about the bastardry involved. When I met these people on the chatboard, I followed up. I saw no problems in killing the sort of people involved in that dumbfuckery."

"You're a mass murderer," said the officer. "But off the record, this is the first time I feel some regrets about arresting somebody."

The woman shrugged and didn't speak again on the ride.

* * *

"Same model Heckler & Koch, as was used in Chief Inspector Carter's place," said the technician back at AFP HQ. "Same model suppressor, same fingerprints, so the same contract killer. We still have no idea who he was, so we've sent his picture and prints to Interpol. They may know him."

"This is a bigger operation than we thought," said Melanie. "There's big money and big organisation behind this."

"But they're panicking," said Jack. "They may collapse soon, or they may step up the warfare a few more notches."

"We'd better be ready for either," said Melanie.

Chapter 36

27th March, 2026, AFP HQ, Canberra

Melanie's pc warbled, signalling an incoming call. Automatically, she checked the screen and saw nothing. Irritated, she knew this could not be the killer she knew as Darryl calling her, he was already in police custody. She pressed the key to accept the call and started recording.

"Okay, fuckwit, who is it this time?" she said before the caller could speak. "Are you a substitute for Donald Hayes? Are you going to boast about how you sent somebody with a gun to kill me? Maybe you haven't realised it yet, but I beat the crap out of your little helper, broke his hand and took his toy from him. And do you know that we have Hayes in a prison cell? Where do you find these amateurs?"

But the voice was unexpected. While it was still modified, it was not the unearthly, distorted tones to which she had become accustomed, but a gender-neutral voice of almost normal tones. Melanie could not identify whether it was male or female.

"You can have Hayes," said the voice. "He was well past his use-by date and had lost all value to us. And I congratulate you on defeating the intrusion to your home. That was unexpected. It probably won't be the last, your life is limited, but I want to tell you about the next step in silencing you."

Melanie felt a surge of worry. There was something hugely menacing in the unidentifiable voice, but she refused to be intimidated.

"Do tell," she said, as sarcastically as she could make the words.

"Talking of little helpers, you need to look out for your Detective Constable Welland. His usefulness to you is at an end."

Melanie went cold and shivered. Had she put Alex under threat of death by these maniacs? She barely noticed the call being disconnected. Just seconds later, her intercom buzzed.

"Detective Chief Inspector Carter, get to my office immediately," said her boss. "We have a major problem."

Feeling a heavy load of sour anticipation, Melanie made her way to Harvey's office, forcing herself not to run. The door was closed, unusual in itself, and she knocked. Receiving a call to enter, she opened the door and stopped. The scene was also unusual. Harvey was at his desk, instead of sitting at the small conference table where he usually greeted visitors, having a conviction that his desk was too formal and reflected some insecurity, indicating that he needed the symbol of authority to protect him. In a chair before him, Alex sat, seated against the wall. He looked tense. In the centre of the front of the desk was a man Melanie did not recognise. He did not stand when Melanie entered.

"Carson Lundgren," he said. "Office of the Director of Public Prosecutions."

The voice was louder than necessary for a relatively small room and a little harsh. Melanie wondered if this was the normal tone or if this man was feeling some tension himself.

"Yes, Mr Lundgren," she replied. "And why is the ODPP here today?"

"You may not know it, Chief Inspector, the body of a man was found in Queanbeyan two days ago. He was Charles Frasier, a retired executive with the Australian branch of a European drug company."

"Yes, we had heard of it, but because it was in New South Wales, we were waiting to hear from the State Police what the details were." Melanie's disturbance was growing.

"This morning, my office received a phone call telling us that the likely perpetrator was this man here, Senior Constable Alex Welland."

"What utter nonsense." Melanie almost exploded with anger. "Did that anonymous caller, and I am assuming it was anonymous, provide any evidence for that accusation?"

"Actually, Chief Inspector the caller did. Now I must say, the caller was speaking with an electronically modified voice, leaving us unable to identify whether it was male or female, but the details provided are quite conclusive."

Melanie let out a gasp of shock. "A modified gender-neutral voice? I received a call from the same voice just a few minutes before I came here, telling me that Alex was in trouble. I am quite certain that this is a set up from an organisation engaged in a massive program of serial killings."

"I doubt it. Here is what we were given. And by the way, we know about the program you are investigating, and we are concerned at the lack of progress. This development goes a long way to explain it."

"You have to clarify that, Mr Lundgren." Melanie was having trouble keeping her anger in check.

"Of course. The first thing we were told is that Alex Welland's wife lost a relative a few years ago to what appeared to be a defective drug supplied by a pharmaceutical company. The two women were very close since childhood and the death caused serious grief. Did you know about that?"

"Yes, I did. Senior Constable Welland told me about that early in the investigation."

"And did he tell you he had joined into a chatboard of many other victims of this alleged criminal behaviour, relating this episode."

Melanie looked at Alex. He shook his head.

"I never posted any such material," he said.

"We did intensive research," said Lungren. "We found that post, signed as coming from someone using the name, "Aussiecop" and we checked with the managers of the chat board. They confirmed it was from an account set up in the name of Alex Welland."

"And I have never set up any such account," said Alex. "Now I admit, I joined several chat boards to research the background to this program of revenge killings we're investigating, as I told my superior, but the name I registered was just "Alex" and I provided my full details as was required, but I never made a single post. I only read the posts made by other people."

"The evidence and the witness suggest otherwise," said Lundgren. "Now, Chief Superintendent Harvey, the ODPP recommends that you charge Welland with the murder of Charles Frasier and arrest him while we complete the full investigation."

"I will do no such thing, Mr Lundgren," said Harvey. "The evidence you claim to merit such a charge is weak as piss. The most I will do while you continue your work is to suspend Alex on full pay while we do our own investigation of how this occurred."

"That is quite unsatisfactory," said Lundgren. "There is quite enough evidence to merit arrest and holding without bail until trial."

Melanie heard a note of discomfort in the man's voice. It was no longer the domineering tone of earlier. She decided to see if she could increase his distress.

"When you discovered this account under the name of "Aussiecop," did you note the date on which it was set up? Or was that too difficult for you?"

Melanie saw with satisfaction as Lundgren's fists clenched in anger.

"No, we didn't," he said. Melanie heard the tension in his voice and knew she had scored a point.

"In that case, I will support Chief Superintendent Harvey's decision to suspend Alex on full pay while we get to the bottom of this and I strongly recommend that you, Mr Lungren, get back to your office and review correct procedures for investigations based on unsubstantiated witnesses with electronically distorted voices."

Lundgren seemed to fade. He stood up. "I will report this failure to the Director," he said. "It will go higher, believe me."

"Send it into bloody orbit if you want," said Harvey, astonishing and delighting Melanie.

Lundgren said no more and walked out of the room, anger radiating from his entire body.

"Thank you, Sir," said Melanie.

"No worries," said Harvey. "That fat bastard needed cutting down a bit, demanding Alex's arrest. The evidence was nonsense. We already know how some experts can manipulate computer files. Talking of which, do you think your mate Miller could help in this?"

"I'll call him," said Melanie. "Sir, I have to ask. It sounds like there was some stress between you two?"

"You're right," said Harvey with a grimace. "I've worked with the ODPP for over twenty years and have always had a huge admiration for their professionalism and competence. That Lundgren character joined them a couple of years ago and he was a pain in the arse. He recommended arrests when there was not the evidence for a prosecution and complained to the Director when I refused. The Director said he had to give him time to learn the trade and asked me for patience. It's been difficult, and this last episode was typical."

"I see," said Melanie. "I must admit, I found it difficult to stay civilised with him."

"You did it well," said Harvey with an unexpected chuckle. "Meanwhile, Alex, we must show some reaction to this. There is enough there to justify suspicion, even if we know it's crap. So you must consider yourself suspended until this gets cleared up. Stay home, you can't come in here, but I doubt that will limit you."

"I have all the computer power I need at home," said Alex. "Thank you for the support, Sir."

"It was essential," said Harvey. "I have no tolerance for arrogant bastards like that telling me how to run my department. Now push off, the pair of you and do some work."

With smiles on both their faces, Melanie and Alex left the office.

"Half an hour with Allen, if we can get him," said Melanie. "And then go home."

"I'd better call first," said Alex. "My unexpected early arrival would be a shock."

* * *

"Allen, we've had a strange development," said Melanie a few minutes later. Briefly, she described the events of earlier. "Can you help?"

"Probably," said Miller. "But it indicates some pretty good hacking skills as I've already discovered. But we can assume who's behind this. I'll get back to you."

"Thanks, Allen." Melanie disconnected the call. "Alex, call home and then go. Keep your computer on, keep working and we'll talk as necessary."

Alex nodded and left.

* * *

AFP HQ Four Days Later

"Alex, you there?" Miller's face appeared on Melanie's screen and a few seconds later, Alex also appeared, the two faces taking two corners of the screen.

"Yes, sir," said Alex.

"Good," said Miller. "Almost all good news, at least as far as clearing Alex's good name. I found the chat board you had been shown to have posted and I found your registration. It was made only two weeks ago, and not by you, though I couldn't identify who did make it. However, the post you had supposedly made, complaining about the loss your wife suffered,

297

although that was dated two years ago, it showed as actually having only been last week. I found the operating system record and that was clear."

"That's a relief," said Alex, displaying a wide smile.

"Indeed," said Miller. "Now the bad news. I could not reconstruct the voice that spoke to Melanie and to that Lundgren bloke. That's a personally created system done by somebody very clever indeed and I can't so far find the key. I doubt if anyone at the ODPP could do it, either. Nor could I trace the origin. Again, somebody knows what they're doing, the call went back to Madrid and then got lost."

"But Alex is in the clear, it seems. Thanks Allen, you've earned your keep." Melanie felt a huge weight drop from her shoulders.

"My pleasure, Melanie, Alex. Pass the news to Harvey, I'm sure he'll enjoy shoving it up Lundgren's capacious arse."

"Damn right," said Melanie. "I'll do that right away. I look forward to watching his reaction."

"Enjoy," said Miller.

Harvey's face was not as relieved as Melanie had expected when she passed on Miller's news.

"I have no doubt Miller is correct and Alex has nothing to do with this," he said. "But I don't think it will satisfy Lundgren."

"It won't?" Melanie was astonished. "Why not? Surely that's conclusive?"

"To us, it may be. But Lundgren called me yesterday and he's still rabid. He said he doesn't care what we think will show Alex to be innocent, he's convinced Alex killed Fraser and he's going to press charges."

"So what are you going to do?"

"I have to play along. Alex remains on suspension and if he's arrested, we'll apply for bail. That's not often granted for murder charges, so he may be facing some time in a cell, a dangerous position for a cop."

"I have an idea," said Melanie and returned to her office.

Sydney Morning Herald

Prosecutor found to have child pornography on his computer.

A senior prosecutor with the Capital Territories Office of the Director of Public Prosecutions has been removed from office and charged with having child pornography on his computer. The material was found when a secretary had to look up material on the prosecutor's computer and found the file of pictures which had not been safeguarded by a security lock. The Director made a statement to the media that such behaviour was inexcusable and could not be tolerated. The prosecutor would be charged, but the Director did not reveal the name and would not do so until the case has come to court.

"Your doing, of course," said Melanie.

"Of course," said Allen Miller. "It was too easy and well deserved."

"But we're destroying a man's career," said Melanie. "I know he's destroying Alex, but is this merited?"

"It will get Alex out of the horrible situation," said Miller. "But in a few days, I'll email the Director and admit that I placed the material on Lundgren's system. That will save him. But I will also explain why I did it and I do know that he's aware of my reputation, so he'll believe me."

"But won't that just enable Lundgren to attack Alex again?"

"Not when I've emailed Lundgren to tell him what I did and how easy it would be to damage him again any time I want to. Lundgren will be fired anyway for his attack on Alex, And his record already has him under observation, but he'll be able to find decent work elsewhere and Alex will be in the clear."

"Sounds like a good solution," said Melanie.

Chapter 37

AFP HQ, Canberra

"Nigel Catlin's computer gave me nothing," said Allen Miller. His face in the pc monitor revealed no emotions. "He had wiped it clean just hours before he got shot, so he must have been aware that the entire operation was winding down. And he hadn't just deleted everything, he'd reformatted every sector. There's no way I could recover anything at all."

"And Helen Agnew?" asked Jack. "That's one dangerous woman, if ever I met one. She hasn't said a word since being booked. Her public defender was as frustrated as the cop trying to interrogate her."

"She'll get her just desserts," said Melanie. "The search of her house was intensive, but hidden in the loft, they found a baseball bat with enough tissue traces for a DNA comparison with her victims. There was no computer, so it's likely she's hidden that elsewhere. We may or may not find it one day."

"What about the dead man they found in Agnew's house?" asked Allen.

"Not a thing," said Melanie. "The bullet that killed him certainly came from his gun, and it was the same gun as killed Catlin in Newcastle and the same model of Heckler & Koch as I got at my place. But obviously a different set of prints as on the gun I got. The medical examiner's reports on Catlin and the unknown killer at Agnew's house showed that he could have driven from Newcastle to Albury in the time. But his car hasn't been identified yet, so we have absolutely no idea of who he was. It is thought that he could be a contract killer, otherwise unconnected with this saga, just hired by whoever is running this to clean up the scene."

"No fingerprints?" asked Allen.

"Nothing on record," said Melanie. "So he's had no dealings with Australian police in the past. His face has stirred no reaction with Immigration, so we don't know if he came from somewhere else. He's a total mystery. We've sent picture and prints of both bodies to Interpol, but we may never know who they were."

"And Donald Hayes in Port Macquarie? Any more from him?"

"Not a peep," said Melanie. "Total silence since we saw him."

"Probably terrified that whoever is running this will have him killed, just as with Catlin and was attempted with Agnew," said Jack. "And probably justified."

"Which brings us to the three possible Generals that Allen identified," said Melanie. "Alex, bring us up to date."

Alex wore an air of smug satisfaction. He held no notes.

"I've been busy, Ma'am," he said. "I found all three of the possible Generals."

"Good work," said Melanie. "Let's have it, then."

"The first is easy," said Alex. "Agung Harsono, the Indonesian returned to his family home in Jakarta twelve years ago, suffering from bowel cancer. He died eight years ago, no dependents, no family. His two sons had both died in their teen years. I think we can write him off our list of suspects and there's nobody who could have been doing all this in revenge for Agung."

"Seems an obvious conclusion," said Jack.

"The second is Ben Conroy," continued Alex. "You may remember from Allen's briefing that he ran a small, successful pharma company, produced a new drug that was highly effective against lung disease, shepherded approval through the Therapeutic Goods Administration and was set to dominate the global market. If I may use Allen's own words, he said it so precisely. Blackwood Harding in New York made a copy of it and sold their version at half the price, together with a massive marketing campaign. Apparently, that's Blackwoods' major business model, they take an approved drug, take it apart in a well-equipped medical lab and then make a copy that is just enough different to avoid the patent, but just as effective. When Conroy's firm collapsed as a result, the price went to nearly twice what he had charged and Blackwoods cleaned up."

"Definitely a good motive for revenge," said Jack. "Serial killers have done their thing for far less motive than that. Where is he now?"

"I have an address in a small, high-class village in the Southern Highlands, a place called Burradoo. I've already called the local police, they know all about you, of course, and they are happy to let you come and interview this man. They only ask that one of their Criminal Investigation officers be present. Of course, if an arrest is made, it's theirs."

"That's protocol," said Melanie. "Of course that will happen. It's pretty good of them to let us come and interview the man. And the last, Alex?"

"The last is Kenneth Marlow. He was the one destroyed by Fremont Sims, lost his company after some criminal work by Fremont that shattered Marlow's share price, at which point they bought the company and his products. He retired, though still a very wealthy man, I have an address in Queensland, at Surfers Paradise. I did the same, called the local police, they know all about this case, of course, they're more than happy to have you go to interview. I've already submitted the required paperwork for an AFP visit to Queensland."

"Excellent work, Alex," said Jack. "Melanie, isn't it time Alex took his sergeant's exams?"

"Any time he wants to, I'll endorse it," said Melanie. "And I have no doubt he'll pass, but he needs a couple of years extra seniority before he can get the stripes. Anyway, then I'll have to look for a replacement and I don't want to face that yet."

Alex smiled. "Moving right along..." he said.

The other two laughed.

"Let's organise the visits," said Melanie. "Alex, liaise with the local cops, we'll call at the homes, any arrests would be premature."

"On it," said Alex and left the room.

* * *

3rd April, 2026, Southern Highlands, NSW, Australia

"I thought you might turn up one day," said Ben Conroy. He showed no surprise when Melanie, Jack and a Detective Inspector Julie Moorcroft appeared at his front door.

"Why's that?" asked Melanie.

Conroy studied her carefully. Melanie was used to that, and it didn't disturb her. She thought the local Inspector was a worthwhile study also, a tall, elegant woman in her forties and was grateful that she had displayed no hostile reaction to Melanie's appearance. A brief discussion on meeting at the local police station had cleared the air and Moorcroft was quite happy to let Melanie lead the questioning.

"This whole war on the pharma industry is making waves around the world," said Conroy. "But let's not stand out here, come through." He closed the door after them and led them to the back garden, a large expanse of carefully maintained lawn with flowering bushes around it. The smell of jasmine permeated the air. He waved them to white-painted metal chairs on the concrete surface outside the back door but stayed standing. He was a tall, lean man, looking very fit and the facial skin belied the sixty-six years that they knew about.

"As I was saying, this is causing havoc round my old industry," continued Conroy. "And I must admit, I could have some sympathy, but killing people is an appalling way to show one's anger."

"Why sympathy?" asked Melanie.

"I'm sure you've done your research," said Conroy. "There are pages of trials where nearly all the pharma companies have bent the law more than a little and faced heavy fines."

"And yours?" asked Jack. "Were you had up for anything?"

Conroy looked hard at him.

"No, my company was never charged with any crime, felony or misdemeanour."

"But you said you could have sympathy for whoever is doing this," said Inspector Moorcroft. "Let's get this straight out. Are you behind this wave of murders?"

Conroy's expression didn't change.

"As you obviously know, I have very good reasons for hatred of the organisation that stole my company and many millions from me. But as has been said, the best revenge is to live well, and I certainly do live well. In your research, did you find that I have a guest lectureship at the Australian National University in

Canberra? It pays very well. And with that, goes free use of a well-equipped laboratory with the freedom to work on anything I want. In the last few years, I have created three new drugs which the University has steered through the approval process and then licenced to pharma companies. They have made a great deal of money out of that and given me a most satisfactory commission, far more than I need to live as comfortably as I do. I have this delightful house in one of the most attractive parts of the world, my life is totally stress free, which is certainly not the case for most people who work for a living. So, Inspector, why the hell would I want to engage in a stressful, horrible, high-risk operation hurting people who have done me no harm? Hurting the company's reputation and share price is not a real revenge, it just hurts a lot of people's savings. If I wanted revenge against the people who did actually damage to me, I would concentrate on the executives at Blackwood, not innocent people working at living their lives. Believe me, if I wanted that path, I would have succeeded."

Melanie had no trouble believing him. From the expression on Inspector Moorcroft's face, it was clear that she felt the same. But it wasn't over yet.

"You were not at all surprised to see us when we arrived," said Melanie. "Did you not wonder why we had selected you for a visit?"

"I assumed it was because you had somehow found the story of my company's collapse," said Conroy. "It would have seemed like a reasonable indicator of somebody wanting revenge."

"Indeed it would," said Melanie. "But there have been far more people with dreadful tales of relatives and loved ones killed by the pharma industry. I heard from one doctor of a deliberate change of product name to continue distributing one lethal product in third-world countries. So why have we picked on you?"

This time, Conroy's expression was less friendly when he stared at her. He folded his arms in a gesture of defiance.

"Bardacom?" he said. "Yes, I knew of that. And the others."

"They didn't bother you?"

Conroy looked annoyed. "Of course they bothered me. But what was I supposed to do about them?"

"Report a crime, maybe," said Melanie. "Perhaps we should tell you why you are the object of this meeting. In our investigations of this wave of murders, we have been able to review some communications on the dark web from some of the established killers. These were conducted in intense secrecy, which you will understand if you know what the dark web is. You were one of those contacts. Now, is there anything else you can tell us?"

Conroy unfolded his arms, put his hands in his pockets and turned to stare at his garden. Finally, he turned back.

"I have to admit, I haven't been totally honest with you," he said.

Melanie sensed the other two become tense. She said nothing.

"A couple of years ago, I was called on my computer by a voice that was electronically distorted. It said that it knew about the loss of my company and said it knew all about some of the criminal behaviours of major pharma companies. It suggested I might like to join in a war against the industry in general and get some satisfaction by damaging some of them."

"And your response?" asked Melanie.

"I told whoever it was to go fuck himself, what do you think?"

"You didn't think about going to the police?" asked Moorcroft.

"No, I didn't. Why would I get involved and probably suspected in the whole thing? Anyway, I assumed it was just some fuckwit causing trouble."

"Did you record that conversation?" Melanie asked.

Conroy shook his head. "No. Like I said, I assumed it was some fuckwit causing trouble. I didn't take it seriously."

"And did that caller ever call again?"

"No. I think he saw that I was not at all interested. Now, let me ask you a question. How many are there like me that you've identified on the dark web?"

"Can't tell you that," said Melanie and stood up. "We'll head home, Mr Conroy. If we find a reason to talk to you again, we'll be in touch."

"Then can I suggest that if you haven't identified them as suspects, you might want to talk to Agung Harsono and Kenneth Marlow?"

Silence hung in the air for a few seconds.

"Why those two?" asked Melanie, forcing herself to hide her astonishment.

"Because they have almost identical histories to me," replied Conroy.

"We have investigated Agun Harsono, but he died some years ago and left no dependents," said Melanie.

"Sorry to hear that. We talked a lot about our experiences, but I know that Agun was a strict Buddhist. He would not take action against his tormentors. But that means you've pinpointed Kenneth Marlow. Have you grilled him yet?"

"No comment," said Melanie and stood up.

Conroy nodded and stood silently as the three visitors found their way to the front door and out.

"Thank you, Julie," said Melanie as they stood by her car and the Inspector's more modest Honda. "I'm sorry we couldn't have had a more dramatic meeting, but I really appreciate your support in letting us interview him."

"My pleasure, Ma'am," said Julie Moorcroft. "It was a privilege to meet you both. I've heard about your previous cases. We study them in our orientation classes when we join the unit."

They shook hands and climbed into their respective vehicles.

"Home, Jack and be prepared to leave tomorrow," said Melanie. "It's about an eleven-hour drive. I'll call the local cops, arrange to visit this Marlow bloke the day after."

* * *

5th April, 2026, Surfers Paradise, Queensland

"Impressive," said Detective Inspector James Rankin. The door in front of him was a full two metres or more in height and nearly two metres wide, built out of red cedar and framed in steel strips horizontally and vertically. The button he had pressed had not resulted in any audible consequence. The door matched the rest of the house that they had seen on the half-kilometre driveway from the road, where wide gates had opened as they arrived, without any communication. Rankin had pointed to the camera built into the brick gate posts.

"Definitely not one we can break down with any shoulder charge like they use in tv cop shows," agreed Melanie. "Not even if you did it."

Rankin was built like a large rugby player, neither as tall nor as wide as the door, but definitely on an impressive scale. His brown suit hung a little loose on the large body, as if he had lost weight recently. He had met Melanie and Jack at the police station that morning and the three had become immediate friends. He had demonstrated detailed knowledge of the war on the pharmacy industry and had shown no difficulty in letting Melanie take the lead in the interview to come at the home of Kenneth Marlow.

Without a sound, the huge door swung inward, and a woman stood in front of them. Melanie estimated early fifties, she looked quite healthy, no obvious excess weight and she was dressed well, in a green and white dress.

"I am Detective Chief Inspector Melanie Carter, Australian Federal Police," said Melanie, displaying her warrant card. "This is Detective Inspector James Rankin, Queensland police and this is Professor Jack Savage. Is Mr Kenneth Marlow at home?"

Without speaking, the woman stood aside and the three entered to see a large hall, black and white tiles on the floor, two storeys high with a balcony running round the middle. Several ferns stood in white pots at intervals round the walls.

"And you are?" asked Melanie, looking at the woman.

"Gabrielle Harper, his daughter," she replied. "Come this way."

She led them to the far end of the hall, past several closed doors, to one that stood open. She stopped by that one and indicated they should enter. Immediately, the heat in the room hit them. It was much warmer than was comfortable and Melanie felt sweat rising on her neck. She could see that the two men in their formal suits were experiencing similar discomfort.

The room was large, windows in two of the walls, looking out onto extensive gardens, the other two walls covered by portraits of men and women from what looked like the Victorian era. Six armchairs were arranged in a circle in one corner, a space where one chair would be.

Seated by one window was a man in a wheelchair, looking calmly at them. A heavy rug was draped round his shoulders, with just a glimpse of a white silk shirt showing at his neck, and from the waist down, over his legs to his feet, he had a blanket.

"I am Kenneth Marlow," said the man. "Why do you want to see me?"

Melanie introduced themselves again. "This is in regard to a number of murders of people involved in the pharmaceutical industry over the last two years. We have some questions for you."

"How interesting," said Marlow. "Please take seats." He waved them to the circle of armchairs and used a control lever on one arm of the wheelchair to place himself in the space in the circle.

"Naturally, I am well aware of this crisis in the industry," he said. "And it's obvious that you might think that I have a major motive for conducting it. I must congratulate you on your detection and identification of me as a likely perpetrator."

"Fremont Sims certainly caused you massive harm," said Melanie. "Were you not tempted to get some sort of revenge?"

"You don't know the full story," said Marlow. "Yes, they stole my company and its world-beating product from me, costing me some millions."

"And you have said that you think the financial people managing the share market had a hand in that?"

Marlow frowned. "Yes, they did. I reported them to the financial authorities but both they and Fremont had a lot of power in the business world, and nothing was done."

"But you said that's not the whole story," said Rankin, the first words he had spoken since entering the house.

"Correct," said Marlow. "You may or may not know that one of the most successful and profitable drugs that Fremont has sold for the last few years is Trimecal. It is considered a very effective remedy for bone density loss."

"I know it," said Jack.

Marlow looked briefly at him. "What you won't know is that my company created Trimecal fifteen years ago," he continued. "We completed all the trials and steered it through the major process of getting it cleared by the Food and Drug Administration in the USA. That's when Fremont started their campaign of attacking my company, spreading some severe lies and crashing my share price, at which point, they took over the company. I decided to let it go, I was already very wealthy and was starting to suffer some medical issues that left me too tired to want to fight a war."

"Let me guess, bone density decline?" asked Jack.

"Correct," said Marlow. "Naturally, I was able to get a supply of Trimecal, even before it was approved here in Australia. I'd created it, I'd seen the clinical trials, I expected strong results. Instead, my condition deteriorated and now here I am, as you see. It became so bad, that I cannot keep my body warm, hence this heat, and I'm sorry for that. But any cooler and I'd be unable to function."

He paused and re-arranged the blanket on his lap.

"This was not what should have happened," he continued. "I'm enough of a pharmacologist to suspect a problem and I still have the essential equipment to take the drug apart and see where the problem lay, and I found it at once. The prescription had been altered, the critical element had been replaced by a much cheaper one and now the drug had no effect on bone density, quite the reverse."

"What happened?" asked Melanie. "Surely the same happened with other cases?"

"Not many," said Marlow. "I heard from several colleagues in the USA that this had happened with one batch of the revised drug, but it was hushed up by spreading a shit-load of money and using some powerful political allies. The original recipe was restored."

"But a lot of people have been damaged," said Melanie.

"And that's when I began thinking," said Marlow. "I'd been in the industry long enough to know the extent of criminal behaviour, not just with Fremont, but all of them. They've falsified clinical trials, they've applied pressures on distributors and doctors, they've defrauded insurance organisations, most of them seemed to be just Mafia-style operations. I decided I'd make them pay."

The room was deadly silent.

"What?" said Melanie, not really believing what she had just heard.

"I decided to make them pay," repeated Marlow. "Yes, I'm the man you're looking for, I began this war of retribution and I'm only sorry I haven't taken it further. But I consider it one of the best things I have ever done."

"Have you considered that it's not just the pharma companies that have paid for their crimes?" asked Jack. "A lot of people have died who have had nothing to do with those deeds. And the collapse of share prices around the world has caused a lot of elderly retirees and others to lose massive parts of their savings. Does that not bother you?"

Marlow laughed. "Who gives a shit? If they were part of this massive crime wave, they deserve everything they got. And no, I don't care about all those poor retirees. If they couldn't set themselves up better, I have no sympathy for them."

Melanie stood up, quickly followed by the other two.

"Detective Inspector James Rankin, it's your responsibility to make the arrest. While you do that, Jack and I will see if we can find Gabrielle. I'll also get medical advice on how to handle the arrest and treatment of Marlow while in your care."

Marlow said nothing but wheeled himself out of the circle and back to his position by the window. There was a small table there with a coffee pot and cups. He lifted the pot and poured himself a cup. Melanie led the way out of the sweltering hot room with relief and began to walk along the black and white tiled floor, but almost immediately saw Marlow's daughter, Gabrielle walking into another room. She followed and stopped at the doorway.

The room was a technical laboratory. Several banks of computer equipment filled most of the space. Gabrielle sat at a desk, headphones over her ears and a microphone at her lips. Behind Melanie, Jack and the Inspector followed. Gabrielle took no notice but concentrated on her monitor.

"Look at this," said Jack, pointing to a framed document on the wall by the doorway. Melanie followed his gaze.

"A Ph.D. in computer science," she said. "That's interesting."

"I'll bet she's the computer whizzkid that's almost as good as Allan Miller and facilitated her father's operation," said Jack.

Melanie nodded and moved to Gabrielle who removed her earphones and looked up at her without expression.

"You managed all the communications?" asked Melanie.

Gabrielle said nothing.

"And you despatched the various killers to murder the victims?"

Gabrielle didn't respond.

"Then if that is so, you are guilty of involvement in a series of murders in several countries. I will ask you now to come with me to your father's room where Detective Inspector James Rankin has just formally arrested your father and he will do the same to you."

Melanie stood while Gabrielle rose, still saying nothing, and walked with her and Jack back to the other room. The scene was unexpected.

The situation at the far end was clear. Marlow was dead. His head had fallen to one side, both arms were draped down the side of the wheelchair. A coffee cup lay on the floor under one hand, the stain of the spilled coffee contrasting with the perfect carpet.

"He poured himself a coffee when he got back to the window," said Rankin, no expression in his face or voice. "He had a pot by the side. I didn't see him add anything to it, but as I read him his rights, the cup fell to the floor, he collapsed, and he was dead."

"He had four months to live," said Gabrielle. She had tears running down her cheeks. "He decided not to bother now that you'd been here. He's a pharmacologist, he knew exactly how to end it without pain."

Behind them, the sound of vehicles echoed down the hall as the search specialists arrived to begin working through the building.

"Let's go," said Melanie.

* * *

The captive North Koreans sat silently in the large cell where they had been locked before being individually interrogated. The police had sent for an interpreter, though the indications so far were that all of them spoke excellent English.

One of them finally spoke in Korean.

"We have failed," he said. "We were sent by our great leader to perform a critical task that would hurt the evil western nations and we did not succeed. We have embarrassed our great leader. We will never get home again."

The others did not look at him. Two of them were weeping.

"We know what we must do," the leader continued. "Let us do it now."

The Inspector walked from his office to the cell block, accompanied by the Korean interpreter and stopped short.

"What the hell?" he said.

All the prisoners were sprawled on the floor of the cell.

"They're dead?" swore the officer, anger exceeding the initial shock.

"Without a doubt," said the interpreter, showing no emotion. "All of them would have been fitted with a false tooth filled with arsenic. They knew they would never get home again, and even if they did in some sort of prisoner exchange, they would have been executed for their failure."

"Fuck," said the officer.

* * *

Inspector Rankin switched on the recorder in the interview room and waited until the beep had faded.

"The date is the 16th of April, 2026 at the police station at 23 Orchard Avenue, Surfers Paradise, Queensland," he said. "Present are Phillip Surtees, Attorney acting for Gabrielle Harper, Gabrielle Harper, Detective Chief Inspector Melanie Carter of the Australian Federal Police and Detective Inspector James Rankin of the New South Wales Police. I will now hand over the interview to Detective Chief Inspector Carter."

"Thank you, Detective Inspector Rankin," said Melanie, following the standard protocols of such events. "Gabrielle Harper, do you understand why you are here?"

"Go fuck yourself," said Gabrielle.

The response surprised Melanie, but she tried not to show it.

"Mr Surtees, does your client understand why she is here and what the objectives of this interview are?"

The lawyer had opened his eyes wide at Gabrielle's response and he had shot a quick glance at her, but he spoke calmly.

"Yes, Chief Inspector, my client understands."

"Good," said Melanie and looked back at the woman. "Gabrielle, you were arrested after being found in a room with highly sophisticated computer equipment and communications facilities in the home of Kenneth Marlow, your father. Mr Marlow had earlier confessed to having been the instigator and driver of a global project to punish the pharmaceutical companies for their alleged crimes in the industry. Can you tell us what your involvement in that project was?"

Gabrielle laughed. "What the hell do you think it was, you silly bitch?"

Melanie ignored the comment and continued.

"When our expert examined the computer found in your room, he found messages between that computer and a number of people who have been found guilty of murdering many people in the pharmaceutical industry in Australia, Britain and the

USA. Were you responsible for sending and receiving those messages?"

The sneer on Gabrielle's face became more intense.

"Your expert? That fucking amateur Allan Miller? He's a nothing compared to me."

Melanie was sensing some discomfort in herself and couldn't identify the reason. She tried to ignore it and pressed on. The interview was not going as she had expected. Over the years as a detective, she had become accustomed to the objects of her interrogation offering little resistance beyond initial defiance. During her first case with Jack Savage, he had told her that she possessed a dominant personality that invariably defeated the interview subject. Only once had she met serious resistance and that was when interrogating a woman who had herself demonstrated a superior dominant personality and had influenced a number of submissive, damaged personalities to committing murder. But the defiance had eventually folded after a monstrous clash of wills.[4]

"It was Mr Miller, yes," said Melanie. "And his inspection of the computer revealed some very sophisticated security features. Did you develop those?"

"Oh, let's give Miller a little credit," said Gabrielle. "I got the basic ideas at one of his seminars on the Dark Web while I was doing my doctorate. But even then, I

---

[4] "The Ninth of the Month Murders" by Michael Davies

could see how to improve on them massively. Which I did."

"So it was you that developed those features?" asked Melanie. "Then let me ask you again, were you responsible for sending and receiving those messages?"

"You think that was my entire job?" Gabrielle's contempt was obvious.

She's boasting, thought Melanie. *That's a sign of some desperation, she's trying to demonstrate her superiority. The collapse may not be far ahead. But why am I feeling this discomfort?* "Was it not?" she asked.

"You saw my father," said Gabrielle, the smile of contempt still on her face. "He was a weakling, barely able to move and he'd been that way for years. Do you seriously think he could run a global operation like that?"

"So who ran it?" Melanie shifted in her seat. *She's confessing to everything,* she thought. *But I still feel like she's the teacher lecturing a dim pupil. I can feel her personality radiating out. Is she even more dominant than I am?*

"I did, you fool," snapped Gabrielle. "I saw these crooks running their companies like mobsters, losing millions of dollars. And when they destroyed my father's company, that took millions from my inheritance. Do you think I'd let them get away with it?"

Melanie was feeling as she was forcing her way against a powerful psychic wind. The force of the woman's personality was diminishing her own strength and Melanie could sense she was getting less and less confident with every second.

I'm losing it, she thought. *This woman has a personal power that is breaking me. I have to draw on every atom of strength that I have, and I don't know how long I can hold on.*

"And what did you do?" asked Melanie.

"What the hell do you think I did? I got into the files of these crooked mobs, found the people who had been killed by false medical trials or wrongly approved drugs, identified their relatives and sent them emails from the secure systems I developed. Eventually, I identified a few like Hayes here in Australia who could be used to recruit more like themselves and send them out to kill off people I nominated for them. It was easy."

"That appears to be a full confession," said Melanie, her throat dry from the internal struggle she was making. "I will leave it to Detective Inspector Rankin to arrest you on these extra charges."

"And where do you think the evidence is?" said Gabrielle. "On that computer?"

"Of course," said Melanie, feeling herself shrinking in power with every second.

"You think I'm as stupid as you?" retorted Gabrielle. "I'd installed a neat little routine in the system, and I set it running through my phone when your cops arrived at the house. Everything on the computer has been deleted, every disk wiped clean. There's absolutely nothing there to say I'm guilty."

"And I must endorse Ms Harper's claim," said the Lawyer, Surtees. "That confession you have recorded will be denied as having been made under pressure. Ms Harper, I believe we can leave now."

"Not just yet," said Rankin. "The original charges still stand and until we can verify Gabrielle's claim, will continue to stand. Mr Surtees, you can stay here with your client to discuss her situation, after which, Gabrielle, you will be escorted back to your cell."

Melanie and Rankin walked out of the interview room and to Rankin's office.

"I can't believe it," exploded Melanie. "Can she really get away with this? Will it remain as Marlow's crime and she's innocent because the evidence has gone?"

"It may be," said Rankin. Anger was evident in his face. "We've both seen crooks get away on technicalities, but never for such a monster crime as this."

"And you won't this time, either," said a voice from the computer on Rankin's desk.

"What?" exclaimed Rankin.

"It's Miller," said Melanie, laughter bubbling out of her and overwhelming the depression she was feeling. Allen's arrival lifted the black cloud hanging over her and released the pressure on her soul. "Allen, how did you find us?"

"Not a problem," said Miller, as the other two moved to Rankin's desk so that they could look at the monitor screen. "I knew where you would be, breaking into this office system was no great deal."

"So what did you mean, we won't this time?" asked Melanie.

"Gabrielle may have a point, that she's possibly a better computer expert than I am, but I'm not totally past it yet," said Miller. "And she didn't set her system running when the cops arrived, it was over an hour later, and that gave me time to break into it. The first thing I did when I accessed her system was to look for exactly the sort of safety routine she said she'd developed, the one that wiped the system clean. I would have implemented exactly the same feature in her situation."

"And you killed it?" said Melanie, hope rising inside here.

"Of course I killed it," said Miller. "The system is just as she left it, minus that little routine."

Rankin laughed. "Can I be the one to tell her?" he said.

"I think you deserve that," replied Melanie. "Allen, thank you once again for saving the day."

"My pleasure," said Miller and the screen went blank.

Chapter 38

8th April, 2026, AFP HQ, Canberra

"This goes well above all our pay grades," said Chief Superintendent Blake Harvey. "The crims are from another country, we have to be guided by what the politicians say."

The Federal Police group were all seated in a smaller conference room, not the secured room they had used before to prevent anybody hacking into the proceedings. Melanie had requested this of her boss to his intense curiosity, but he had agreed after Melanie had told him he would see the reasons quite soon.

"But your team seems to have cracked it," continued the Chief Superintendent. "At least we've stopped the killings of pharmacy people, so we must congratulate all of you. But the people in ASIO are still baffled why South Korea would do this kidnapping stunt. It makes no sense, they're a constant ally of the West."

At that moment, a knock on the door sounded and another agent appeared. It was not the junior officer or secretary that might usually deliver messages, but a more senior man that Melanie didn't recognise.

"Inspector Markham?" said Harvey. "Is something wrong?"

"News, sir," said the newcomer. "Definitely not for anyone without a proper level security clearance, so I've brought it. It came from ASIO a few moments ago."

He handed a paper to Harvey, watched with great curiosity by the rest of the room's occupants. Harvey read the paper quickly and put it down.

"Guess what," he said. "They're not South Koreans, they're from the north. The government in Seoul says the passports are first-class forgeries, they appear to be genuine, which indicates somebody in the department that issues them is suspect. But the individuals are definitely not citizens of South Korea."

"What do they want us to do with them?" asked one of the agents.

Markham cleared his throat. "Our ASIO contact said he got the impression that the Koreans would like us to drop them down a deep black pit. Or we could subject them to Australian justice, whatever that would do. But if we returned them to Seoul, they'd be shot soon after arrival."

"Attractive as that would seem," said Harvey, "I think we have a rule here that we will not return criminals to any system that applies the death penalty."

"But what about the American operation?" asked the agent, Inspector Spencer who had worked with Melanie when she first joined the Federal Police. "Can we identify those people?"

"And that's where I come in."

The PC monitor that Melanie had requested be brought in and connected to the internet flickered into life and a man's face appeared.

"Allen Miller at your service."

"Miller?" Harvey almost shouted, so great was his shock. An outbreak of astonished conversation erupted round the room. None of them had seen Miller's face before and his reputation was well known around the world.

Melanie burst out laughing. "That's why I asked you," she said. "Allen has some useful information for us all."

Slowly, the hubbub subsided, and Allen remained calmly waiting.

"As Melanie said, I have some useful information for you," said Miller. "You know that the cops that raided the Windsor kidnapper site took away the computer found there. Melanie asked them to hook it into their internet so that I could have a look at it, which I did. I found a lot of useful stuff. First of all, I found the contacts for the British and US kidnappers and passed them to the local authorities. They were very grateful."

"So that whole kidnapping operation is over and done with?" said Harvey.

"It certainly is. Actually, the leaders of the British crew were already dead. And the Americans are very keen to charge all their prisoners with kidnapping and first-degree murder, which carries the death penalty, so the people in Pyong Yang will be quite happy."

"This is wonderful," said Harvey. "Mr Miller, I must congratulate you, you have done amazing work.

I know you're a criminal wanted all over the world, but on this task, you have been a wonderful asset."

"And that's not all," said Miller. "The next bit might delight you also."

"How?" asked Harvey.

"I found the money they took," said Miller.

Another buzz of interest ran round the room.

"One hundred and eight million dollars in the USA," said Miller. "Fifty-three million pounds sterling in Britain, sixty million Australian dollars. These sums were all in local accounts, about to be transferred overseas."

"And I suppose you took that?" said Harvey, a trace of contempt replacing his admiration.

"Well, yes," said Miller. "I retained a significant portion as my professional fees. But the rest I returned to the companies that had paid it out."

There was silence round the room.

"And the sums you retained?" asked Harvey.

"That took some work," said Miller. "But in the end, I found the identities of all the people killed by the instigator of this horror story, Kenneth Marlow. I set up a bank account in each country and I shared the money between them, proportional to the number of murders. It will hit the accounts some time tomorrow and I have inserted articles in the major newspapers asking that the money be given to the nearest relatives of the victims."

Before anyone could comment further, there was another knock on the door.

"Now what?" said Harvey. "Have the North Koreans asked for a prisoner swap, or something?"

The door opened and Inspector Markham entered again.

"This must be critical," said Harvey.

"You might say that," said Markham. "We just got a call from the police that raided the kidnap site. All the kidnappers are dead. Suicide, they all had arsenic-filled false teeth and they bit down on them, all at the same time. The Korean interpreter who was there said the same can be expected from all the agents everywhere else. Failure is not tolerated by that government."

There was dead silence in the room.

"Then I think this case is closed," said Harvey. "Just the reports to write."

The meeting broke up with numerous muted conversations between the agents.

Chapter 39

"This has been the toughest one we've had," said Melanie, sipping at her coffee. "And yet again, we've done the lion's share of the work but didn't get to make any arrests."

"I don't think that's a problem," said Jack. "What we did has been recognised by everybody who matters and it sure as hell looks good on your record. When do you head back to the New South Wales State cops?"

"When I get back from leave, which starts right now."

"What will you do?" asked Jack.

"Jack, you know very well what I'll do. And I'm sure I'll feel a hell of a lot better when I get back."

Jack laughed and Alex tried to look at the far wall and not show any reaction.

"Any idea where?"

"Not yet. I'll decide tonight. But there's still one problem remaining. We came to the conclusion that there was a mole in the AFP, but we've never got any idea of who that might be."

"Agreed," said Jack. "But with the entire organisation wiped out, all the killers located, and the top man identified and removed, there's nothing more the mole could do. He or she just has no tools to work with."

"And yet again, the world's greatest hacker comes in to save the day."

"Allen!" said Melanie as the familiar face appeared on her monitor. "What else have you got?"

"Recall that you left Marlow's daughter's computer system when you were there? In all the excitement, you didn't even switch it off. I've had a wonderful time playing with that, and like I told you after you had interrogated her, that's when I found her routine to wipe the system clean."

"You're right, you did tell me," said Melanie. "I assumed the local blokes have since taken that."

"They did, eventually. But it took some organisation and lots of skilled help. I had plenty of time to get into it and it was a lot easier than with Hayes' computer, because now I had the system she had used. It's been invaluable, because the woman had developed some extraordinary security systems that I've adopted, as well as some hacking enhancements. They were good to see, because they were based on my own systems, but she had improved on them. I owe her a great deal."

"So what new stuff have you got?" asked Melanie.

"The new stuff you were talking about when I came in."

"The mole? You have the mole?" Melanie stood up in her excitement.

"As I went through Gabrielle's computer file, I found one number that kept appearing, both as calls in and calls out, far more frequent even than the calls from Hayes. It was disguised, but eventually I tracked it to a PC in Canberra. That linked to the AFP system and then it was easy to see who it belonged to. I think you need to go and call on this man."

* * *

"Where is he?" asked Melanie as she and Alex stood by Inspector Spencer's desk.

"No idea," said a policewoman bringing files through the office. "I saw him this morning, but he left quite suddenly about half an hour ago."

"Can you track him on his phone?" Melanie's voice reflected the anxiety she felt.

"Of course," said the policewoman and bent over Spencer's computer. In less than a minute, she stood up. "He's in the parking lot of a company in North Canberra. It's the corporate office of an Australian pharmacy chain, R.A. Callisters."

"Oh shit," said Melanie. "Constable, tell the boss, call for backup, give me the address." She raced out with Alex, ran past her office to call for Jack and they reached her car within seconds. Switching on the siren that had been fitted years ago and never used, she called on the full power of the Gordon-Keeble to cover the short distance to the address in North Canberra she had been given.

The parking lot was nearly full. Melanie parked just inside the entrance and dialled the number for Spencer, putting the phone in its cradle and switching the call to the loudspeaker. She picked up her binoculars and directed them at the building.

Spencer answered almost immediately.

"So you found out?" he said. His voice was clear but without depth in the loudspeaker.

"Howard, what's this about?" Melanie tried to keep her voice calm and without tension.

"You lot are supposed to be detectives," said Spencer. "You never reviewed my file, did you? If you had, you'd have seen that I lost my sister ten years ago when she died of liver disease, when the drug she'd been prescribed didn't work. The company that made it was found guilty of lousy manufacturing processes, fined, but made just a slight change and kept on making it."

"And one day, somebody approached you and suggested you might like to make them pay?" Behind her, Melanie heard the arrival of police vehicles and the careful movement of armed police officers into strategic points with views of the building.

"You're right," said Spencer. "That's after I'd posted on one of those chat boards. Your fuckwitted moron of a detective, that Welland fool never even saw that one."

Beside her, Alex moved the phone from his ear. "There are forty-three people in the building," he said softly. "The snipers have looked into every room that they can and say everybody has been moved into a single room in one corner. Spencer is carrying an AR-15, but they can't get a clear shot as he's moving around and keeping away from windows."

"He'd know exactly how to keep out of range," said Melanie. She redirected the binoculars to the corner room Alex had pointed to. She could see a number of people all close together in one section. The powerful binoculars made her feel she was standing by the window, looking in.

Then she spoke back into the phone. "Howard, it's all over," she said. "There's no point in continuing this war. Marlow is dead, his daughter who's been directing you is in prison awaiting trial, the entire organisation all over the world has been dismantled. Don't waste any more innocent lives."

"Nobody's innocent," said Spencer. "They're still doing what they've been doing for years. They've killed far more people than we have, and everybody we've killed has played some part in this slaughter. None of the people they've killed had committed any crime at all."

"Howard, you won't make it better by killing more people. Please, Howard, let it end now."

"No chance, Melanie. You can tell all those firearms officers you've got hidden round the grounds they won't see me. I'm sure they've been ordered to take the shot when they can, but they won't get the chance. You can go away. If you don't, I'm going to start shooting these people I've got here."

Dimly through the telephone's loudspeaker, Melanie heard a scream of mixed fear and rage and she saw one person detach from the unseen crowd in the room and hurl himself at where Spencer was standing to one side of the window. The two crashed against the window, Spencer was crushed against the glass, his face distorted and highly visible in Melanie's binoculars as if just a metre away. Then the window disintegrated into a bloody mess as a bullet smashed into Spencer's body which erupted into a horror of blood. Deeply shocked, Melanie dropped the binoculars and fought a wave of nausea. Screams were loud and people could be seen milling around.

"Go!" The officer commanding the armed squad snapped out the order and a line of men raced to the building door, entered and a few moments later could be seen at the windows.

"Ma'am, you'd better get up here," said the officer's voice in her earphones. Sensing that what she would find would be horrible, Melanie began walking to the building, Alex just a step behind her.

She was right. The scene was horrible. Spencer was lying dead by the wall under the smashed window, his torso a bloody mess from where the heavy calibre bullet had gone right through him. The automatic rifle lay an arm's length away. Alongside Spencer was a man, also dead, his head almost blown away by the bullet that had killed Spencer and then hit him where he had grabbed hold of the hostage taker.

All the hostages were in obvious distress. Many of them were weeping, others just sat on chairs, their heads in their hands, some with their shoulders shaking from the force of their grief and shock.

"His name was Richard Green," said a woman standing nearest to Melanie. "He was our boss." Her voice was barely audible through the sobs.

"These people will need a lot of counselling and support," said Jack. Melanie hadn't seen him enter the room. "There's an ambulance coming for the bodies, and a bus for the hostages. We'll take everybody to the hospital for a medical examination and maybe sedatives. God, what a mess."

Melanie couldn't speak. She was struggling with trying to grasp how the amazing bravery of Richard Green had saved them from a far worse slaughter and couldn't help but wonder how many of the people here would be able to return to working for this company in the future.

She nodded at Jack, tears coming to her eyes and walked out of the room.

* * *

"I think I'm getting past it," said Melanie. Depression was enveloping her like a storm cloud.

"Come off it, girl, you're not even at your prime," replied Jack. "What's brought this on?"

"Several things. What we talked about before, the arrests we haven't made. Then seeing the murder of Dr Sengupta in Zimbabwe. Somehow, I should have been able to warn their authorities it could happen. I took the easy way out and did nothing."

"Melanie, we talked about this before. The Zimbabwe people would have known about his conflict with the pharma companies, and they would have known about the war of attrition we've just stopped. Nothing you could have done would have made them protect him more than they did. So what's the next thing?"

"Jack, you told me a long time ago that I had a dominant personality. I knew it, that's why I almost always break down a suspect when I interrogate them, that's why I even cracked Nona who was so dominant, she made several people commit murders."

"Yes, so what's made you think otherwise?"

"That Gabrielle woman, the daughter of Kenneth Marlow. She beat me down, I could feel myself getting smaller as she laughed at me, I could feel her personality overwhelming me. I met my match there."

"She's a psychopath, Melanie. Such people are often very powerful personalities, because they cannot allow any thought to enter their mind that anybody else might be better than them. That's not a dominant personality, it's a severely damaged psyche."

"You can tell me that, Jack, but all I can see now is that I've failed. I'm past my use-by date."

"Let's have a look at this 'failure' as you call it. Have you any idea of the positive effect you've had on the world?"

"Can't say I have. What effects are you talking about?"

"Let's start with Alex Welland. You found him as a patrol car officer in the Traffic Division, you recognised his brilliance as an analyst and researcher and moved him to a path that offers far greater promotion opportunities. And he's grown into it and maturing at an astonishing rate. He'll be a sergeant in two years and I reckon he'll be a Superintendent, possibly higher by the time he retires. You did that."

"I suppose so."

"And then the absence of arrests. Okay, you didn't get put in the book as the arresting officer on all our cases, but those cases made policing history that are in all the casebooks studied by cops moving to detective. Remember what that fine young woman, Detective Inspector Julie Moorcroft said when we visited Ben Conroy in the Southern Highlands. She had studied your cases in her training programs. So has every other detective. Your cases are master classes, and every detective in the last few years has benefitted from them."

"Okay, that's helping, Jack."

"And so to the last point, then I'll go and have a drink. So you're not the most powerful personality in the world. Close to, but there could well be people with more dominant personalities who are still sane. Hell, everybody has to realise that there's always someone smarter than they are, or richer than they are or better at something. Even the golf or tennis players who rank as number one in the world get beaten sometimes and one day, some kid comes along who is obviously better. It's that thing called life."

"Okay, Jack, that does help."

"The thing to remember, Melanie, is that you've had a massively influential effect on the cops in this country. You've got a lot of years ahead of you and I confidently expect to see you reach the highest ranks in the service. And in the process, you'll solve a lot of nasty murders and help a lot of young detectives grow further than they might have done without you. Okay, so can I go and open that bottle of single malt scotch that is plaintively bleating my name in my lounge?"

Melanie had to laugh. "Sure Jack, go and get rat-arsed but make sure you're sober again when I call you on the next case of serial murders."

She heard the laugh at the other end of the phone line. "Well, thank you Ma'am, I'll do that."

Melanie put down the phone.

* * *

The following morning was spent in a brief review of the previous day's events, then Melanie spent an hour writing up her report. Jack got into his car to head north to his home on the coast and Alex also started two week's leave by getting back to his wife and child.

Melanie looked at the map of Australia, She had been to all the capital cities except Darwin for her exploits in easing her stresses, but this was the wrong season for the Northern Territories. With the events of the last few months still leaving scars on her soul, she knew that she needed more than just a weekend of wild abandon. An idea struck her, and she turned on the computer.

Twenty minutes later, she had found a promising hotel and night club, and she booked her flight to Auckland in New Zealand. She'd never been there, and it looked like excellent hunting territory. More than ever before, she needed the coming activities to help her get over the horrors of the last few days.

She got up from her desk and went to pack. This time, she packed for a week.

www.ingramcontent.com/pod-product-compliance
Lightning Source LLC
Chambersburg PA
CBHW070051120726
47909CB00002B/354